What the critics are saying

On *Kieran The Black*:

"Lizzie and Kieran make a wonderful pair. They sizzle in the bedroom—and anywhere else they feel so inclined." – *Sensual Romance*

"Sizzling passion, medieval intrigue, and an alpha hero to steal your heart...This is my first read of Julia Templeton's work but it won't be my last. She understands the concepts of eroticism and romance and blends the two seamlessly." – *Romance Reviews Today*

On *God Of Fire*:

"Ms. Black has written a wonderful story of a woman aching, needing something her world cannot provide for her. An erotic mating, a sensual adventure that would test her beliefs and her strength, as well as her passions." – *All About Murder*

"Ms. Black does a fine job of bringing you a good story plus a lot of sexual action. [She] can scorch the hell out of you with her sexy stories that just leave a person clamoring for more!" - *Suzanne Coleburn, The Belles and Beaux of Romance*

Discover for yourself why readers can't get enough of the multiple award-winning publisher Ellora's Cave. Whether you prefer e-books or paperbacks, be sure to visit EC on the web at www.ellorascave.com for an erotic reading experience that will leave you breathless.

www.ellorascave.com

Ellora's Cave Publishing, Inc.

PO Box 787

Hudson, OH 44236-0787

ISBN # 1-84360-394-2

Kieran The Black, edited by Allie McKnight.

God Of Fire, edited by Martha Punches.

Cover art by Bryan Keller.

Warning: The following material contains strong sexual content meant for mature readers. *Warrior* has been rated Hard R (Kieran The Black) and Borderline NC-17 (God Of Fire), erotic, by a minimum of three independent reviewers. We strongly suggest storing this book in a place where young readers not meant to view it are unlikely to happen upon it. That said, enjoy…

WARRIOR

In order of appearance:

Kieran The Black

By Julia Templeton

God Of Fire

By Jaid Black

KIERAN THE BLACK

Written by

Julia Templeton

To Allie — the best editor a writer could ask for. Thanks for everything you do!

Prologue

Kieran the Black was a notorious Norman Knight, who, rumor has it, decapitated the heads of three Saxon soldiers with a single swipe of his sword – a sword that measured six and a half feet in size – the very height of the great warrior himself.

Six and a half feet! Lizzie smiled to herself and turned up the volume on the "audio tour" she had rented at the exhibition's front desk.

She, along with a dozen other journalists, had gained entrance into the coveted William the Conqueror exhibition two days before its scheduled opening to the public. Because she was a lover of all things medieval, and a member of the Society for Creative Anachronism (SCA), this assignment had been right up Lizzie's alley, and she'd jumped at the chance to attend.

Now, standing before the relics of the ultimate warrior, Kieran the Black, Lizzie's heart gave a jolt. What would it have been like to be alive in the days of men like Kieran D'Arcy – when men were six and a half feet tall, and built like brick shithouses?

"Born 1036. Died 1067. You were only thirty-one," Lizzie said aloud, resisting the urge to run a finger over the fine gothic carving of the warrior's name on the marble plaque. Something about the Norman knight stirred her soul. Perhaps because at the age of seven he had left his impoverished family to serve as page to a ruthless knight who had physically and verbally abused him. Maybe that abuse had turned Kieran's heart black, earning him the name Kieran the Black. Maybe it had given him a warrior's mentality – kill or be killed.

"Would you like to see it?"

Startled, Lizzie turned to find an old woman with frizzy white hair and enormous blue eyes standing at her side. She took off the earphones. "Sorry?"

"Would you like to see it?" The old woman nodded toward the sword encased in one-inch thick glass. "The Black One's sword."

Lizzie glanced over her shoulder. Seeing no one else about, she turned back to the woman who wore a somber black suit and crisp white blouse — similar to the employee uniforms of the exhibit hall. "Do you work here?"

The woman smiled and pushed on the glass. The side popped open on invisible hinges. Lizzie lifted her brows but remained silent as the tiny woman lifted the battle-scarred sword with little effort and put it into Lizzie's suddenly damp hands.

Lizzie faltered, but held fast. The sword was heavy. So heavy, it nearly brought her to her knees, and she stood five feet, six inches tall. The woman beside her couldn't be five foot even and she had managed the sword with one hand.

Lizzie could not believe her good fortune. She wanted more than anything to have the woman take a picture of her with the treasured piece, but didn't dare ask for fear of someone seeing the flash of the camera. With her luck the exhibit hall would somehow get a hold of the photo and she and her magazine would be banned from the UK.

The woman looked directly at Lizzie, her expression serious. "The Black One was not the bad man they make him out to be."

Lizzie nodded. "I know he wasn't bad. He couldn't help what he became."

"He was a product of his time. A mercenary who lived and died by the sword."

"That's so odd that you say that. I was just thinking the same thing. He was very much a product of his time. Oh, and then to be betrayed by his best friend. Now that is wrong on so many levels." The sword felt warm in Lizzie's hands, and with every passing second grew warmer.

The woman laughed lightly. "You know of The Black One then?"

Lizzie grinned, excited to have found someone who shared her enthusiasm for the knight. "Yeah, he fascinates me. I can't explain it, but—"

"There is a rumor that if you hold the sword in your hands like so," the woman placed her hands over Lizzie's, "and rest the point of the sword on the edge of any version of Kieran's crest—see the ridge that runs right down the middle? Set the point of the sword right there—and you will be able to experience life as you've never known it."

Okay, now she was getting freaked out. Lizzie turned to the woman, who watched her expectantly. She was about to ask if she was on Candid Camera when the woman nudged her. "Go ahead…give it a try."

Lizzie glanced over both shoulders and seeing the way clear, she did as the woman asked. She set the tip of the sword on the crest, right into the ridge.

"And now?" Lizzie asked, brows lifted high, waiting for a camera crew to jump out and shout "surprise".

The woman smiled, took a step back and said, "Have a nice trip."

Chapter One

La, la, la, la — la, la, la, la, la, lah…

The melody rang over and over in Lizzie's mind until she opened her eyes and yelled, "Enough already!"

Silence met her outburst a second before a panel ripped open and a woman stared at her, eyes wide in excitement. "Milady, you are alive!"

Lizzie frowned. She lay in a four-poster bed with heavy drapes pulled all the way around — or had been pulled all the way around until the woman had yanked the drape open and daylight spilled into the room, nearly blinding her.

Dressed in a beautiful kirtle of green with a leather girdle reminiscent of the medieval era, the woman raced for the heavy wood door. "I will give the word!"

"What word?" Lizzie asked, taking in the room with a glance. The stark walls were interrupted by an enormous floral tapestry. Two chairs stood near a hearth where a fire blazed, heating the high-ceilinged room.

The woman stopped just shy of the door and turned. "I will give the word that you are well, milady. You have been abed ever since the attack. I have had to force food and drink down you for weeks now."

Lizzie sat up against the headboard. "The attack?"

The woman frowned, crossed the room and pressed a hand to Lizzie's forehead. "Do you not remember the siege?"

Lizzie shook her head. "Where am I?"

The woman looked pained. "I think that…"

"Does this have to do with Kieran the Black?"

The woman gasped. "You remember then!"

Lizzie's heart skipped a beat. What had the old woman at the exhibition said? *And rest the point of the sword on the crest and you will be able to experience life as you've never known it.*

Life as you've never known it? She gave the room a once over. Could it be she *had* stepped back in time?

With heart pounding in her ears, Lizzie threw her legs over the side of the bed and flew toward the window. She pushed open the shutters and looked out. The manor house sat beside a river. In the distance, Lizzie could see the motte-and-bailey castle in the final stages of being built sitting high on a mound. The keep and numerous outbuildings filled a huge bailey, and around it, a large moat. Upon seizing England, the Normans had thrown up the wood structures to defend their newly acquired lands. In time the wooden fortresses would all become the gorgeous stone castles that still existed in her time.

Lizzie scanned the bailey and manor grounds looking for one man in particular. She had a feeling she would know the warrior at a glance. "Where is Kieran?"

"He is gone hunting, milady."

"Will he be back tonight?"

"Yes, milady. Shall I prepare a bath?"

Lizzie pinched herself. Feeling the tweak of her skin, she smiled. No, she wasn't dreaming. She was in 1066 or 1067, in the body of—

"Who am I?" she asked, wincing when the lady gasped.

"You are Lady Elizabeth of Aedelmaer, wife of the Baron D'Arcy." The woman squeezed Lizzie's hand. "I fear your father and your brother were not as fortunate. They did not live through the Battle of Hastings."

Lizzie's brain raced, trying to recall the history. Lord Aedelmaer and his eldest son had been killed in battle, leaving Elizabeth the only living descendent. Knowing this, Kieran had forced her into marriage. In turn, Elizabeth had taken to bed and willed herself to die.

That was then, this is now.

And Kieran the Black wouldn't know what hit him.

A wisp of blonde hair floated on the breeze and it took Lizzie a second to realize it belonged to her. *Blonde hair?* She had mousy brown hair with streaks of gray running through it—not pale, almost white hair.

Until now. Now she was the young Lady Elizabeth of Aedelmaer, wife of Baron D'Arcy, not thirty-nine year old Lizzie Johnson, ex-wife of Brent Johnson, small-pricked womanizer extraordinaire.

She chanced a glance down at her body and laughed under her breath. God, she had a kick-ass body—firm, full breasts, small waist and womanly hips. "What's your name?" Lizzie asked, looking over her shoulder at the woman.

The maid looked like Lizzie had struck her. "Mary, milady."

"Forgive me, Mary. I am having a hard time remembering."

Lizzie glanced past Mary's shoulder and saw a mirror—or rather a looking glass—that showed a blurred image of a young blonde.

Lizzie held her breath. Seeing her reflection, she let the breath out in a rush. "Yes!"

Elizabeth was eighteen if she was a day, with not a single blemish on her porcelain skin. Her every feature was sheer perfection, right down to the long blonde hair that fell in silky waves all the way to her tight round ass. She smiled to herself imagining what Brent would think if he could see her now.

Lizzie realized that the other occupant of the room might be confused by her reaction. She forced a straight face and turned to Mary. "I had a dream that The Black One had turned me into a middle-aged crone."

Mary looked relieved, and she smiled. "Milady, you are as beautiful as ever."

Life was good! She was young...and she was married to Kieran the Black. A shiver of excitement raced up her spine. She would see the warrior in the flesh. "Will you get my nicest gown for me?" She turned back to the mirror. "Maybe something blue to match my eyes."

There was not a single line on her face. She released a sigh and resisted the urge to dance around the room. Her fellow SCA members would *not* believe this.

* * * * *

Three hours later Lizzie was dressed in a light blue kirtle with gold embroidery and a gold girdle that hung low on her small hips. *Ha!* Small hips…that was a first!

She walked slowly toward the bailey, taking in everything around her. The wooden tower on the hill loomed above her. Men worked tirelessly on the structure, even in the waning light.

The wooden walls of the bailey stood at least ten feet tall and as she crossed the bridge, over the moat, several soldiers stopped at the bailey entrance and watched her, their expressions showing their surprise. Obviously they had not expected Lady Elizabeth to have made such a miraculous recovery after having been in bed for so long. She smiled and their brows lifted in response.

The bailey thrived with activity. The hall was the only building completely finished. Villagers and serfs worked side-by-side on a large stone structure that Mary told her would be the chapel. How strange that the craftsmen used crowbars, chisels, and trowels, just like they used in the future.

The heavenly smells coming from the baker's hut made her gravitate to the doorway.

"No, milady. We are already late," Mary said, pulling her out of the baker's hut.

Having been independent all her life, this having a hovering servant underfoot was something Lizzie would have to get used to.

Mary's hand rested on Lizzie's arm, guiding her out the door. "Milady, dinner has begun. Let us adjourn to the Great Hall."

The Great Hall was a large, two-story structure with enormous wood beams overhead. Impossibly large tapestries hung on the high walls. An enormous hearth with fire blazing sat in the middle of the room, providing warmth to the inhabitants. The room was alive with activity. Pages dressed in russet-colored tunics served dinner on large platters. Boisterous laughter reached out to her, luring her in. Music floated on the evening breeze, the soft melodic sound of a lute made Lizzie smile. She'd attended a medieval reenactment last summer with her fellow SCA members, and this seemed almost the same, except for the subtle difference that this *was* real.

Long tables sat in regimented rows and above them a single table where the lord of the manor sat with his higher-ups.

The lord of the manor sat there now. Lizzie's pulse skittered.

Kieran the Black.

He was magnificent. Broad shouldered, heavily muscled, with black hair, and fierce blue eyes — that were riveted on something across the hall. Ripping her gaze away from the gorgeous warrior, Lizzie turned to find what held his attention. A half-dressed redhead with full breasts covered by a tiny gold top, small waist, and long legs, belly-danced her way on a stage, her hips swaying provocatively to the appreciative audience.

Lizzie's stomach tightened. It seemed that men were all alike, no matter what the century. Had she been the Lizzie of old she would have bowed out gracefully, knowing she couldn't compete with the likes of the belly dancer. But she was the new Lizzie, and by damned she wanted Kieran D'Arcy.

Well, if she was to compete with the belly dancer, she had to get serious. Lizzie put her hand to her stomach and yanked on the material, effectively pulling the gown down so a good deal of cleavage swelled above the bodice.

Man it felt good to have young, firm breasts.

Since dinner had already started, she had two choices: she could easily slip onto one of the benches at the lower table and watch the goings-on, or she could go out of her way to get noticed.

She looked at Kieran...her husband. A more manly man there could never be. He positively screamed rugged masculinity. A shiver of excitement raced through her. As though sensing her perusal he abruptly turned her way. Their gazes locked, and Lizzie sucked in a breath.

And nearly choked on it.

Kieran's hot gaze slid down her body, slow, like a deliberate caress. She lifted her chin and the warrior's lips twitched. He stood, his height shocking her. Geez — he really *was* six and a half feet tall. She smiled despite her effort not to.

Surprise flitted across his face.

"Come. Join us, Lady Elizabeth." His voice was low, sending a shiver down Lizzie's spine. "Come." He beckoned her with outstretched hand.

Gasps filled the hall, the music stopped and all eyes turned to her.

Well, she *had* wanted to be noticed.

"Milady?" Mary said, looking uncomfortable. "Mayhap I will take my place with the others."

"Okay, Mary. I'll see you later." Smiling like an idiot, Lizzie approached the knight who at closer range was even more beautiful than she'd imagined.

His bright blue eyes were in such contrast to his dark hair and skin. Long, thick lashes covered the orbs that — if rumors were right — glowed in battle. His dark tunic clung to his broad chest and narrow waist. The chausses formed to long powerful legs. Her gaze skipped over the blue tunic that covered what was clearly an impressive cock.

Lizzie stopped a few feet from him and folded her trembling hands together.

He reached out, took hold of one hand and brought it his lips. He had nice hands — long-fingered, calloused, huge, masculine. And his lips on her wrist were soft and full.

Lizzie swallowed hard against the lump in her throat. It had been six years since she'd had sex. Six years since her divorce. Standing so close to six and a half feet of raging masculinity made her keenly aware that she longed for sex, and her body was responding to his touch. Her gaze shifted down his powerful body and up again, her nipples tightening, sending a pulsing need straight to her crotch. God had definitely broken the mold after making this bad boy.

When their gazes met, the side of his mouth lifted. *"Aimez-vous ce que vous voyez, petite?"*

It took her a moment to remember the man was French, and that English was a language he had only recently acquired. She had taken two years of French in high school and pulled the words together. *Little one, do you like what you see?*

Her pulse quickened as she went up on her tiptoes and whispered into his ear, "As a matter of fact, I do."

* * * * *

For the first time in his thirty-one years, Kieran was unprepared for a foe, particularly a mere woman. Particularly in the shape of a beautiful eighteen-year-old Saxon lord's daughter who had fought their marriage tooth and nail, then taken to her bed, starving herself, rather than come to his bed willingly. *His wife.*

Yet, this woman, this saucy vixen, bore little resemblance to the cold woman he'd vowed to protect until death. Nay, *this* woman's eyes held a passion that stole the breath from his lungs. She had eyed him, her light blue gaze lingering on his loins before meeting his gaze yet again. No blush, no giggle, just a knowing smile that promised much.

He motioned to the table where his men, ever alert, watched intently. No doubt they were as struck by the change in their lady as he. "Please, have a seat, milady."

Elizabeth stepped past him to the table, taking the seat at his right, which his vassal, Hugh, had just vacated.

He motioned for the musicians to resume their playing. He wanted time with this lovely creature, *his wife*, without others hearing their every word. Kieran took his seat, his gaze straying over her. Elizabeth had always been beautiful, but when she smiled as she did now, it brought her beauty to another level. "I am pleased by your recovery, milady."

She met his steady gaze without blinking. "Thanks. I've never felt better."

In truth, her eyes sparkled, and her skin glowed—very odd in one that had lain near death not so long ago. He must remember to thank his wife's maid for forcing food down her throat. "You speak differently."

She smiled again, displaying small, white teeth. "Do I? Well, I suppose I can say the same for you."

He saw the amusement in her eyes and wondered what she

meant exactly. Obviously she understood French. He had been shocked when she'd responded to his question. She snickered and he laughed under his breath, finding her quick wit refreshing. Had he known this to be his wife's true nature, he would not have left her to languish for so long. But since she had shown no interest in him he had taken his leman to his bed.

"Would you like to break your fast, milady?" he asked, motioning to a page. "'Twould seem you would be weak from lack of nourishment."

She pulled her chair up to the table. "Sure, I could eat a horse."

His eyes widened.

She laughed. "Not literally, Kier—milord, though my stomach has been churning for hours. Mary was nice enough to bring me some bread when I woke, but that will hardly carry me for the rest of the night."

"Aye, especially when you have been without food for so long."

The page sat the trencher before her. "Thanks," she said, winking at the young boy whose cheeks turned bright red. Kieran had talked to many of the villagers since taking Aedelmaer. When he asked them about his wife, the response had always been the same. Elizabeth was a quiet, polite, yet horribly shy girl who seldom left the manor. She loved embroidery and weaving. Upon their first meeting she did not once look him in the eye. Rather, she stared at the brooch on his mantle instead. Yet now Elizabeth sat by his side, winking at pages, smiling at the serfs below them, and looking about the hall as though for the first time. No shy maiden was this. Nay, Elizabeth had a wisdom about her that intrigued him immensely.

Elizabeth sighed and picked at the pigeon meat with delicate fingers and smiled upon tasting. The page, sensing her great appetite, brought her a bowl of steaming pottage. She ate with great aplomb, barely stopping to take a sip of ale. She grimaced, the face she made amusing.

"You do not find the ale to your liking?" Kieran asked.

Elizabeth glanced up at him, her light blue eyes soft and warm. "It's fine. I'm just not used to it."

She held his gaze so intently he shifted in his seat. He had never been accustomed to a woman regarding him so keenly. If a woman wanted him, she merely kept flashing him coquettish glances throughout the evening, yet Elizabeth did not once drop her gaze. She stared at him like this was the first time they'd met and she seemed to like what she saw…and had even said as much. The sides of her mouth lifted and she turned to look across the hall.

"Who is that?" She nodded toward the stage where Gwendolyn, his leman, danced. The auburn-haired beauty watched him beneath her lashes as she rotated her hips back and forth, rolling them in a way that usually made his cock rock hard. He looked back at Elizabeth who watched him intently, waiting for an answer. How could he speak about his leman with his wife?

"She is Saxon," he blurted, disliking the guilt that suddenly assailed him. He had found the woman in a village near Aedelmaer. Her hut, along with the other villagers' homes, had been burned to the ground—along with its fields and crops. He'd hardened his heart long ago to the ways of war, ignoring cries of pain and anguish, which is what garnered him the hated nickname *The Black One*. However, it had been impossible to ignore Gwendolyn. He'd sat upon his horse, watching his knights-in-training destroy the village. The wench had come out of nowhere and clung to his leg, telling him she would do anything if he spared the village.

He had not spared the village, but he had taken her with him. True, he had not known Elizabeth at the time, but after her less than enthusiastic reception, he had kept Gwendolyn in his bed.

"Does she not have a name?" Elizabeth's voice, laced with sarcasm, broke into his thoughts.

His lips twitched. "Gwendolyn."

The page set a bowl of pudding before Elizabeth and she smiled sweetly at the boy. In turn, the page watched her adoringly. She tasted the pudding, winced in disappointment and set the spoon in the bowl.

"Not to your liking?" he asked the obvious.

"I thought it would be sweeter," she said absently, sitting back in the chair, her gaze never leaving Gwendolyn's swaying body.

They sat in silence. Elizabeth watched Gwendolyn, and he in turn watched Elizabeth. She sat ramrod straight, her breasts rising high along the bodice of her gown. She lifted her chin a fraction. She turned, her gaze trapping him. "She's your lover, isn't she?"

Kieran choked.

"That's what I thought." She smiled devilishly and to his shock, his heart skipped a beat. "I can tell by the way she looks at you. She's practically undressing you with her eyes. No woman would be that bold unless she'd actually seen you naked."

He could not believe his ears! No woman would speak thus, yet this woman, this *lady*...nay, *his wife* did so, and without blushing. Her English was different from any he'd heard, yet he found her...fascinating.

She laughed under her breath. "From the furious expression on her face I think it's safe to say she won't be warming your bed tonight. Too bad..."

Kieran could not have heard her correctly. Elizabeth certainly did not imply what he thought she was implying, did she? He didn't know if he should be offended or amused that his wife spoke so bluntly. He soon concluded he was thrilled to have the smiling, laughing Elizabeth, rather than the cold, crying, hysterical girl who had met him on his arrival to Aedelmaer.

Elizabeth kicked off her shoes, crossed her legs and rested her elbow on the arm of the chair, leaning close to him. She smelled of jasmine and something else... "Is that rosewood?" he asked, desperate to change the subject.

She glanced up at him. "Why, yes, it is. Smell." She put her dainty wrist up to his nose.

He looked down at the smooth white skin laid out like a sacrifice before him. He could not help it—he reached out and with gentle fingers brought her wrist to his nose.

"What do you think?" She watched him intently—expectantly. "Nice, huh?"

Who was this witch beside him? This woman who talked of things only men would dare speak of. The woman who asked him to smell her skin, who wore no shoes, who bared her ankles and dainty stockinged feet to not only him but every person sitting below the high dais. His cock hardened, throbbing mercilessly against his belly. He shifted in his seat, hoping to ease the ache.

"It's nice, isn't it?"

He inhaled again, resisting the urge to close his eyes. Others watched him closely—particularly his soldiers. He could feel their gaze on him. It would not be wise to appear besotted with Elizabeth, despite the fact she was his wife.

He dropped her wrist.

"Oh look, here comes your mistress." Elizabeth's voice dripped with sarcasm.

True enough, Gwendolyn walked toward him, her hips swaying provocatively, the bells at her wrists, hips and ankles tinkling with every step. Few seemed to notice her approach, and Kieran was thankful. The woman knew not her place. How dare she confront him in front of his men...and worse still, his wife! Furious, he flashed her a look of warning, but the woman paid no heed. She kept coming.

Elizabeth seemed to be amused as she watched Gwendolyn approach. She sat up straight, a soft smile on her flawless face, and stared at the woman without blinking. "Your mistress doesn't look too happy with you—or me for that matter. Am I sitting in her seat?"

He had no time to reply. Gwendolyn stopped at his side and stood with hands planted firmly on generous hips. "Milord, I will retire for the night." She glanced past him to Elizabeth for a second, her anger apparent. Elizabeth's expression did not change a wit...just a small, knowing smile. Gwendolyn's gaze shifted back to him. "Will you be joining me soon, milord?"

The blood roared in Kieran's ears. He could not believe his leman would humiliate him — and his wife, by blatantly seeking him out in the hall to ask such an intimate question.

Elizabeth abruptly turned her back on him, giving all her attention to the man at her right, Kieran's vassal Hugh de Vesli. Hugh was six years Kieran's junior, and as light in appearance as Kieran was dark. Hugh leaned forward, whispered something in Elizabeth's ear, which made her laugh aloud. No matter where he went, women flocked to Hugh like moths to a flame, and now it was no different as Elizabeth's laughter erupted once again.

It is no different…save for the fact the woman who laughs is your wife.

Kieran lifted his leather tankard and took a long drink of ale. His blood raced in his veins, and not for the woman who stood at his side awaiting his response. Nay, he wanted to toss up his wife's gown and take her until she cried out his name. With a trembling hand, he set the tankard down, nearly overturning it when Elizabeth laughed again.

"I bid you good night, Gwendolyn." The words were curt and cutting. She looked away, her cheeks flaming red, realizing too late her error in confronting him here.

Knowing the willing wench, she would find her way into his chamber tonight anyhow. He had taken over the lord's chamber in the Saxon manor until the tower was complete. The room he now occupied sat just down the hall from Elizabeth's chamber — a room he had avoided since she had fallen ill. On the one occasion he had visited his wife, Kieran found the chamber too stifling and he had avoided it ever since. Yet he wondered if he might visit her now that she was well. Visions of Elizabeth's firm breasts and a thatch of pale curls covering her sex filled his head, causing his cock to jerk and throb.

"I am much relieved that you are well, Elizabeth," Hugh drawled, the side of his mouth lifting in a smile that Kieran thought resembled a smirk. His trusted vassal had ridden at his side for years, and in truth, he thought of him as one would a brother... Yet now Kieran yearned to choke the life from him.

For the next hour, Kieran drank ale and endured the incessant chatter of his vassal to his beautiful Saxon wife who seemed to have enthralled all sitting within hearing distance. They all sat forward in their seats, entranced by her strange accent. She nodded at everything Hugh said, appearing to be captivated by the bouts of courage he boasted of. Once, she rested her hand on Hugh's bicep and Kieran just about came out of his skin with jealousy.

Most of his men knew little English and probably had no idea what she said, but it didn't seem to matter. Everyone laughed when Elizabeth laughed. In truth, her laughter had an infectious quality that made one smile at the very least. Her easy manner contradicted the woman who had wept throughout their short wedding. The woman who had sworn she would rather die than be "a filthy Norman's wife."

It did not make sense — nor did the jealousy that threatened to strangle him.

Hugh leaned closer to Elizabeth, his lips just inches from her ear as he whispered something that Kieran could not hear. Her flaxen hair stirred, the silky tresses floating —

With a curse Kieran stood abruptly. His chair made an awful screech against the dais. All eyes turned to him, including Elizabeth who looked over at him, her light eyes sparkling with good humor and vibrant health. What would she do if he tossed her over his shoulder and stole her away to his bed? A nerve twitched in his jaw. He forced a smile. God's teeth, he actually trembled. "I bid you good night, *wife*."

Elizabeth smiled. "Good night, *husband*." Without another remark, she turned her full attention back to Hugh.

Hugh, oblivious to his own endangerment, nodded to Kieran and then smiled at Elizabeth. Kieran took his leave...when all he wanted to do was take the lady in his arms and carry her off to his bed.

Mayhap it would be best to take his leman to his bed this night and pound her into the mattress. His body yearned for release like never before. In truth, the desire his wife had built within him had reached a fever pitch he'd never known. Even now he could smell the sweet haunting scent of Elizabeth's body, the feel of her soft skin beneath his fingers as he held her dainty wrist.

He shook his head to clear his thoughts. The woman was up to something. She did not go from near-death, cold-hearted lady to smiling vixen in the blink of an eye. What could have caused such a transformation?

Chapter Two

Walking the pathway to the manor house, Lizzie felt the eyes of Hugh de Vesli, Kieran's trusted vassal and right-hand man, on her. The pretty-boy watched her with confidence, his smile beaming as he waved to her. How confident and cocky he was. Traitor! "That's right, stud. You might be smiling now, but I guarantee you won't be for long."

"Did you say something, milady?"

Lizzie had forgotten about Mary, who already stood at the manor's front door, holding the door open for her.

"I was just commenting on Hugh. He's very handsome, isn't he?"

The maid looked flustered. "That is not my place to say, milady."

"You have an opinion, don't you?" Lizzie asked, walking past her into the dark hall where candles flickered in the dark, cold interior. The manor definitely lacked a feminine touch. The huge tapestry that took up one entire wall depicted a hunting scene, complete with blood, guts and gore. Lizzie decided *that* would be the first thing to go. "Well, Mary, you've yet to say anything? What do you think of Hugh?"

"Aye, I think Sir Hugh is handsome, but his lordship is as well."

Lizzie smiled to herself. She was not blind. Every woman in the hall had been practically panting after Kieran, especially the redheaded belly dancer. The bitch. "Do you think so?"

Mary nodded vigorously. "Aye, when he looks at you with those eyes — 'tis like looking into a sapphire."

Lizzie resisted the urge to laugh at the blissful expression on the maid's face. "How right you are, Mary. Tell me, what do you know of his lordship?"

"His lordship is well-liked among his followers. I daresay

he has been quite kind to the Saxon. Indeed, I feel fortunate to have a roof over our heads when so many others do not. If we are loyal to him, and pay him homage, he in turn will protect us."

Elizabeth started up the stairs to the bedchamber. "And what do you know of this Gwendolyn?"

Mary shrugged. "I know nothing of the woman, save she arrived with his lordship—"

"And she's been sharing his bed ever since."

Mary caught the sarcasm. "Does that not please you? You seemed relieved he had taken a leman. You told him that you were engaged to Lord Richard of Langaer. Baron D'Arcy told you that Richard had already been promised a bride, the beautiful widow of a wealthy Norman count."

Lizzie crested the stairs and turned to Mary. "That is why I locked myself away?"

Mary nodded. "At birth you were betrothed to Lord Langaer, and in recent years I believe you loved the young man, though I do not know why."

"What do you mean?

"He is a cruel man, milady. I have heard rumors that he beats his serfs for the slightest misdeed. I think you are better off having married Baron D'Arcy."

"What happened to Richard?"

Mary took a step closer. She glanced over her shoulder, then down the long hallway to Kieran's quarters. "Richard has sworn fealty to King William, yet rumor circulates that he is a part of a Saxon uprising."

"What of his Norman bride?"

"Killed," Mary whispered. "The night of their wedding."

A niggling began in the back of Lizzie's mind. Richard appeared to be evil enough to have something to do with Kieran's death. After the massacre, only a squire had made it back to Aedelmaer alive, and he had told the castle steward that Hugh de Vesli had killed Kieran D'Arcy.

Lizzie put a finger to her lips. "Let's be quiet. I don't want to disturb Kieran."

Lizzie passed straight by her room, but Mary stopped. Lizzie turned and the maid shook her head and mouthed the word "no".

Lizzie motioned her over. The maid's shoulders dropped but she did as Lizzie asked, following behind.

Putting her ear to the door, Lizzie listened. Mary's eyes went wide and her mouth dropped open. The door, at least three inches thick was impenetrable. There was no way to hear what was going-on on the other side—

"Someone comes," Mary said, pulling on Lizzie's arm. They reached the door to her bedchamber right as Kieran's squire took the last stair. "'Tis his lordship's squire."

"Milady," the young man said, nodding. Lizzie felt a wave of compassion for the young man who would lose his life with Kieran in the ambush. In his late teens, he had lived a life similar to Kieran's—raised to serve a stranger, who would in turn mentor him in his quest to be a warrior. The young man with shoulder-length blonde hair, gorgeous green eyes and almost feminine features didn't look like he could hurt a fly. Maternal compassion filled Lizzie and she had to resist the urge to hug him.

"What is your name, squire?" Lizzie asked, keeping her voice authoritative.

"Olivier, milady." His gaze shifted to the wall behind her.

"How long have you been in his lordship's service?" Lizzie asked.

"Eleven years, milady."

Eleven years! He couldn't have been five or six when he began.

A door opened down the hall and Lizzie turned. Kieran stepped out into the dark hallway with nothing but a sheet covering his narrow hips. She smiled appreciatively. His body was spectacular—all hard, corded muscle beneath smooth olive skin. Sure, he had a few scars across his chest, and a nasty one near the groin that fell beneath the sheet, but the silvery marks made him even more...dangerous. A shiver raced down Lizzie's spine, as she fantasized what he looked like without the sheet.

Kieran cleared his throat and Lizzie ripped her gaze back to his. His blue eyes were dark, glowing, and heavy-lidded with passion — much like Brent, her ex-husband's had been early in their marriage — before he'd become an adulterous asshole. And Brent couldn't hold a candle to Kieran. Kieran was all male, a man who lived and died by the sword, where Brent was a man who lived and died by how much money he had in the bank, and what trophy he could find for his arm.

She forced away the awful thought of her ex and focused on the here and now.

"Do you have no other duties to attend to, Olivier, that you must frolic in the hallway with these ladies?" Kieran asked, his voice gruff.

Olivier blushed to the roots of his hair and shook his head. "No, milord. I made toward your cham —"

"Actually, I stopped him," Lizzie said, smiling at Olivier. The boy grinned — until he glanced in Kieran's direction and the smile turned into a somber mask. "We did not mean to *interrupt* you."

Kieran frowned. "What do you mean *interrupt* me?"

Lizzie smirked, and her gaze fell to just below the top of the sheet. She could see his cock had come to life, pressing against the tight confines of the sheet. Her blood warmed, swooping low in her belly and causing a throbbing between her legs. He would be an animal in bed. An image of him thrusting into her came to mind and she squeezed her legs tight. "What do you think I mean?" she asked, lifting a brow.

His mouth opened, but he said nothing. Good, she had shocked him. This Norman knight needed a little shaking up. She was no meek and mild woman. She had lived thirty-nine years, seen her share of heartache and pain, and more importantly, she knew men. She knew they had the ability to kill a woman's spirit, make her feel like she was a nobody, and leave her self-confidence in the dust — while he, in turn, walked away, taking a woman half his age to bed and marrying her before the ink on the divorce decree had even dried.

But no more. She had a fresh start, and by God, she would

live like there was no tomorrow. And she would start by taking this warrior to her bed ASAP.

Kieran cleared his throat. "I sleep alone, Elizabeth."

His confession surprised Lizzie, and by his expression, he must have surprised himself by telling her. Good, maybe she had gotten under his skin—even if just a little bit.

She smiled, hoping the relief she felt at hearing his declaration wasn't too obvious. "Then I won't keep you." Lizzie turned to Mary, who stared unblinking at Kieran's muscular body. "Come, Mary." She pulled the maid into the room and shut the door loudly.

On the other side of the door, Mary turned to Lizzie. "He is not happy with you, milady."

Lizzie shrugged. "I don't care how he feels about me." That was a bold-faced lie, but Mary didn't need to know everything.

"Let me help you from your gown, and then I'll let you get to sleep. I am certain you are exhausted after all the activity." Mary laid a chemise over a chair near the fire, and then proceeded to light several candles around the room.

"That's all right. I'll get ready for bed without your help." Mary looked hurt, and Lizzie smiled reassuringly. "The room is cold and I want to warm my bones before putting on my night—chemise."

Mary stoked the fire, her face impassive. "Milady, you say you remember little of the past."

Lizzie, who had been staring into the flames looked at Mary. "That's true. I remember very little."

The maid worried her bottom lip with her teeth. "You seem so different. So very unlike the girl I have known since birth."

"Different? In what way?"

"In every way. You have smiled more this day than you ever had." Mary grinned. "I am pleased you are back, milady. I am pleased you are so happy."

"I wasn't happy before?"

Lizzie knew the answer even before the maid replied, "Nay, you were not happy. You were miserable."

"That was in the past, Mary. I'm not that Elizabeth

anymore. I choose to be happy. I can't change what has happened to me. I can't bring back my father or my brother. I'm married to Kieran, so I'll embrace my circumstances and make the most of it."

"I am glad." Mary reached for Elizabeth's hand and patted it. "I want you to be happy, milady. I want you to make his lordship happy."

"And I'm committed to do exactly that."

Without another word, the maid dropped her hand and walked over to the bed to turn down the linen sheets. Lizzie knew she had little time to seduce Kieran, convince him he could trust her, and then tell him Hugh was going to kill him.

Not the easiest task.

Her mind shifted to Kieran's rock hard body, and the promise of what lay beneath the sheet he'd had wrapped around his narrow hips. His erection had been huge—far larger than Brent's. She shook her head, regretting she had wasted ten years on a man who had used her as a doormat.

"I will leave you then, milady. I will return in the morning to rouse you."

Lizzie glanced over her shoulder at the maid who had already opened the door. "Not too early, huh? I'd like to sleep in."

Mary's eyes widened. "Of course, milady."

* * * * *

Lizzie woke early to the sun filling the room. Though she'd been exhausted, sleep had been a long time coming, especially knowing Kieran slept on the other side of the wall. All night thoughts of the warrior's half-naked body had invaded her dreams, making her wake in a sweat with the sheets draped around her overly sensitive body. With heart pumping, her fingers had crept between her legs, running over the sensitive flesh she wanted Kieran to touch. With a curse she'd jumped out of bed and gone straight to the window, letting the cool air clear her racy thoughts. She didn't want to have to touch herself. She wanted *Kieran* to touch her...*everywhere*.

By damn, today would be the day.

Now with the dawning of a new day, her intent was clear. She had to save Kieran from certain death, and therefore she must earn his trust. Not an easy thing to do when Elizabeth had sworn she rather die than submit to him. Lizzie shook her head. That Elizabeth had no sense. Did she not have eyes in her head? Kieran D'Arcy put all men to shame. Drop dead gorgeous, tall, built like nobody's business, Lizzie thought the girl should have thanked her lucky stars and danced all the way to the chapel.

Kieran had already sensed a change in her yesterday, but that was just the beginning. Lizzie was about to rock Kieran the Black's world.

With that thought uppermost in mind, Lizzie freshened up by running a wet cloth rinsed in rosewater over her skin. Visions of her Jacuzzi bath flashed through her mind and she felt a moment of homesickness. How sad it would take centuries for the world to experience indoor plumbing.

Dressing in her most formfitting kirtle, Lizzie made her way to the main hall to find it virtually empty, save for a few servants cleaning up. Talk about "you snooze, you lose". Things definitely started early in this time.

Lizzie found Mary in the bailey, starting for the manor. She told Lizzie that Kieran and his men had left to hunt. "Would you like me to walk with you?" Mary asked, but Lizzie shook her head.

"That's alright. I'm just going to clear my head." Truthfully, Lizzie just wanted time to think, to strategize, and get her bearings. She walked about the bailey, watching the builders as they went about their tasks. She smiled, recognizing one familiar face among the strangers. Olivier. She waved and the squire quickly looked away.

Lizzie frowned, and then walked around the bailey, saying hello to everyone she met, noting that Olivier stayed nearby. Most people she spoke to were kind, some stared with mouths open, wide-eyed, obviously stunned at Elizabeth's transformation. She wanted to win these people over. They were her people after all, and winning their trust was part of her ultimate plan. Just like she would win over Kieran.

She left the bailey and started for the village, noticing her shadow following closely behind. Coming upon a few cottages, she increased her pace. She passed by a man with a heavy-laden wagon and slipped behind a thatch-roofed hut.

Sheer panic flashed across Olivier's face as he stood in the middle of the road, looking every which way. Disbelief, then panic came over his handsome features. No doubt he feared having to face the wrath of his liege lord with the news he had let her out of his sight.

His back to her, he removed his hat and ran his fingers through his hair. Lizzie walked up to him and tapped him on the shoulder. "Good morning, Olivier."

He nearly jumped out of his skin. "Milady!" He turned, his face flushing.

"If I didn't know better, I would guess you were following me."

He refused to look at her, so she lifted his chin with her fingers, and he met her unwavering gaze. "I was told to watch you, milady." His voice cracked.

Even though she already knew who told him to watch her, she asked, "Who told you to watch me?"

"Baron D'Arcy."

Kieran. She took Olivier by the hand. "Well, then if you are to watch me, we might as well have a good time of it."

Olivier proved to be a fun, albeit, skittish companion. It seemed no matter where they went he continually looked over his shoulder—as though he expected Kieran to appear and chastise him for actually being a kid for once. Lizzie knew Olivier had experienced a tough life, and she wanted him to have just a taste of what life had to offer. To feel cared for—if only for a while. Plus, she enjoyed his company. He made her feel young. In Olivier's eyes she was a young Saxon princess, not much older than himself. For the first time in a very long time Lizzie actually felt like a kid again.

They spent a good hour in the village talking to the peasants and serfs, and finally ended up by the river, skipping stones. "So, how did you come to serve under Kieran?"

Olivier threw a stone, it skipped further than all the others and he smiled, the gesture making Lizzie's heart constrict. She felt a kinship with this young man—like an aunt would feel for a favorite nephew—or perhaps a mother for her child. She winced, having wanted and tried for a child for years, to no avail. She, like Brent, had been an only child, so nieces and nephews had not been a part of her life. Brent's new wife had given birth just two months after their wedding—a testament to how long the affair had been going on behind Lizzie's back.

"I became his page in Normandy at the age of six. I was the fourth son in my family, and my father believed that Baron D'Arcy could give me a better life than he could, and he has. You know his lordship started as a mercenary?"

Lizzie knew that, but she enjoyed hearing the enthusiasm in his voice and the way his eyes lit up as he talked of his liege lord. "Did he really? Hmmmm."

Olivier nodded. "Aye, milady. D'Arcy is the fiercest knight of all William's men. He is one of the King's most trusted men, and I would follow him to the ends of the earth."

And even into death....

Lizzie shook the unwanted thought aside. She could not imagine the life sucked out of the young man beside her. The very thought made her want to pull him close and protect him. Unable to help herself, she pushed a stray lock of hair out of his eyes. He stiffened but did not pull away. No doubt he had not known the feel of a mother's touch upon his cheek since he was a babe. Lizzie smiled and cupped his jaw. "Then he is most fortunate to have a squire as loyal as you. One day, Olivier, you will be a fierce knight and you will make some lucky woman a wonderful husband."

She dropped her hand and he quickly looked away.

"What does Kieran think of me, I wonder?" she asked, nudging Olivier, hoping to settle his uneasiness.

Olivier glanced at her, his brow furrowed as though she were daft. "He thinks you are most beautiful, milady."

"Did he say as much?"

Olivier nodded. "Aye, he did. He also mentioned that when we first arrived at Aedelmaer you seemed so different."

"Oh? Different...in what way?"

"You said nothing, save that you would rather die than be the baron's wife." He watched her and Lizzie met his gaze. "Not once did you smile, nor laugh—as you did last night in the hall, or as you do today. In truth you do not seem like the same person."

"And what do you think of the new me?"

"The men wonder if you are the same Elizabeth or perhaps someone has taken the old Elizabeth hostage and returned with the lady of our dreams." He looked away, two bright spots of color high on his cheeks. "The men enjoy your laughter. They believe you to be the woman who can make our liege lord happy."

"And what do you think, Olivier?"

He swallowed hard, but kept his gaze level. "I think they are right."

Lizzie could not help herself. She leaned forward and kissed him on the lips.

* * * * *

Kieran could not find Elizabeth anywhere. After searching the manor house, the bailey, the hall, and then the manor again, his agitation and frustration had grown. Mary had no idea where her ladyship was, which left only one person with the answer.

Olivier. He had asked his trusted squire to look after his wife for him, and yet, it seemed the young man had disappeared as well. Where could they be?

A niggling began in the back of his mind, but he refused to believe that any ill had befallen the two. The blacksmith had mentioned seeing the two leave the bailey earlier. Another guard had mentioned seeing them in the village, and a villager said he saw the two walk toward the river.

The villager added how happy Elizabeth appeared—much happier than he, or anyone else, had *ever* seen her. Quite a declaration.

Kieran walked in long strides toward the river, fuming that Olivier would be so careless to leave the sanctuary of the bailey when threat of a Saxon uprising was imminent. How many times had he told the boy to be wary? That Olivier had Elizabeth with him only intensified Kieran's fear. Richard of Langaer, Elizabeth's jilted betrothed had sworn homage to William, yet rumors swirled that Richard favored an uprising. The man had been fortunate enough to retain part of his lands, and rather than be happy with what he'd attained, he would side against William.

Yet it was another disquieting rumor that also played heavy on Kieran's mind: Richard had poisoned his Norman bride and buried her before the death could be contested. Apparently he had nothing to fear for the family had not pushed the point. The man clearly could not be trusted. Though Richard had sworn fealty to King William, he could easily be swayed to take sides with the Saxon. Would the man dare come back to Aedelmaer and lay claim to Elizabeth?

He had heard of other Saxon princesses kidnapped in the dead of night for such a purpose. Images of Elizabeth lying beneath a faceless Saxon lord turned Kieran's blood to ice. He and he alone would be the one to teach his wife the ways of desire. He would be the one to take her beneath him and fuck her until she begged him for more.

Kieran walked the path near the river, his frustration growing with every step when he heard her voice. Then her unmistakable laughter—a tinkling sound, followed by the unmistakable sound of Olivier's laughter.

Kieran sighed with relief. They were safe.

He did not make himself known. Instead, he came up from behind them. The two sat side-by-side on a rock at the river's edge. Olivier sat cross-legged, while Elizabeth's bare feet dangled in the water. Elizabeth with her gown up to her thighs, her long, shapely legs kicking in the water. Kieran devoured the sight. His squire said something, and Elizabeth hit him playfully in the shoulder then leaned against him, her head against his shoulder for a brief moment before tossing a stone. It skipped impressively against the softly rolling water.

For the first time in his life, Kieran envied Olivier. Surely the lady did not prefer the boy to a man? He shook the thought aside. Olivier was but seven and ten, almost ready for knighthood—something that Hugh constantly pointed out. Kieran had looked to Olivier as one would a son. The boy had been in his service for so many years he seemed like family, and he could not care for him more if he were his own flesh and blood.

Yet as he watched Olivier with Elizabeth he wondered what the young man was thinking. The two were of the same age. Mayhap he was smitten, and in turn Elizabeth taken with the young squire.

Kieran almost called out to them when Elizabeth leaned forward and kissed Olivier. It was a brief, chaste kiss that left the young man blinking.

Chaste kiss or not the blood roared in Kieran's ears.

As though sensing they were not alone, Olivier turned. "Milord." He jumped to his feet, his eyes enormous, his expression sheepish. "I..." He clamped his mouth shut and dropped his gaze to the ground between them.

Kieran expected Elizabeth to make haste in covering herself at his approach—or at the very least blush at being caught kissing Olivier. Yet she did neither. Her legs lingered in the crystal clear water while she looked up at him, a sweet smile on her angelic face, as though a moment before she had not been seducing his squire. "Hello, milord," she said, her voice silky soft. "How was your day?"

From his height he could see the tiniest hint of rose-colored nipples above the gown's low neckline. It did not help that she leaned back, arching her back slightly, her beautiful breasts straining the soft material of her gown. His cock twitched and he was grateful he wore a long tunic to cover his arousal.

"Olivier, you may return to the manor and ready my bath." His voice came out clipped and curt.

"Yes, milord."

"Good bye, Olivier. Thanks for being such a great companion," Elizabeth said, looking past Kieran to the young man who walked briskly to the manor. To his credit, Olivier did not turn back or offer a reply.

Silence greeted him, and for the first time in a long while Kieran felt like a smitten boy. He had never had to court a woman. They had always come to him instead. Yet this was no easy woman. This was his wife. How did one "woo" his own wife? He had no idea.

Elizabeth glanced up at him and patted the spot beside her. "Milord, come join me."

At least she was making it easy for him. He looked at the spot his squire had just vacated. He was not a man known for leisure. His gaze scanned the area, and seeing no one about, he removed his boots and rolled his chausses over his calves.

She watched his every move, her gaze not once straying from his body. There was an understanding in her eyes he had not noticed last night. It was as though she could see all the way to his soul. God's breath, she would be the death of him if she did not quit staring in such a way.

He sat down, leaving a hand's breath between their thighs. The material of her gown bunched up around her creamy skin, open to the sun...and so damn close to his fingers. His cock reared against his braies. "You have taken a liking to my squire I see." He brushed the sweat from his brow with the back of his hand.

She grinned, the gesture making her even lovelier. "I adore Olivier. He is so kind, so sweet, and yet so innocent for all the years he has lived amongst warriors."

Kieran frowned. "Warriors?"

She lifted a tawny brow. "That's what you are. Right?"

He shrugged. "I fight for God, King and country. If that is what you call a warrior, then a warrior I am."

He looked down at their legs — his large, muscled and dark, hers white, slender, beautiful. How solemn she seemed, much like last night at dinner and again in the hallway when her eyes had darkened with desire. He knew she had no experience in the ways of men—yet her eyes told a different story. "Do you fear me, Elizabeth?" he asked before he could stop himself.

She frowned. "Why would I fear you?"

"You said you would rather die than feel my touch."

She stiffened at his side, and he wondered if she did so because of fear. She sat up and put a hand on his thigh, just inches away from his cock that reared and jerked at the slight touch. "When you first came to Aedelmaer I had just lost my father and my brother. I had heard of this man called The Black One, and I was terrified of you.

"But I don't fear you now, and I would not prefer death to your touch." The side of her mouth lifted in a saucy smile. "In fact, I think I'd rather like your touch."

He watched her, half-expecting her to laugh and tell him she jested. Instead of laughing at him, she leaned toward him, lifting her chin, her lips parting.

She wanted a kiss!

Blood heated his veins, sweeping low into his belly, filling his cock with a need that surpassed any he had ever known. He bent and kissed her. Her full lips opened and her tongue swept over the seam of his lips, seeking entry. A part of him wanted to rear back in shock by her experienced kiss. Had she gained her experience with Richard, the betrothed she'd so mourned for? He shook the thought away, and pulled her against him. To his delight, her arms wrapped around his neck, and she drew him down next to her. Her tongue parried with his; her hands wove through his hair, stroking his shoulder, moving over his chest where she played with a nipple.

"God's breath, woman," he said against her lips. "I will spend myself if we do not stop."

She pulled away from him and stared into his eyes—the blue depths luminous, full of passion. "Then don't stop."

With a groan, he rolled over her, his knees nudging her thighs apart. He lifted her gown, his fingers tracing paths up her calves, over warm thighs that were spread wide for him…and to the thatch of downy hair that hid the treasure he sought. He stroked the soft folds of her womanhood that were already wet for him. She arched against his hand and moaned low. With heart pounding as loud as a drum, he slipped a finger within her hot, tight sheath, while his thumb stroked the tiny nub.

Reaching down between their bodies, her fingers clamped around his cock, caressing him from root to tip and back again. Either she was a quick study, or she had done this before. The thought was unnerving, yet he could not help but be pleased by her blatant enthusiasm.

Kieran did not hear his vassal's voice. Instead, it had been Elizabeth's reaction that alerted him they were not alone. Her eyes widened. "Sir Hugh," she whispered.

He would kill his vassal and take great pleasure in the man's pain. With an oath, he fell onto his side, pulled Elizabeth's gown over her and adjusted his own clothes just as Hugh crested the hill. "Milord. There is a messenger awaiting you in the Hall. The matter is most urgent."

The words were as effective as a dousing of ice water. An urgent matter? He stood, and held out his hand to help Elizabeth up. She took it, grabbed her stockings and slippers, and followed him up the incline. Hugh looked from Kieran to Elizabeth, then back to Kieran. The side of his mouth lifted in a knowing smile, but he said nothing. Kieran glanced at Elizabeth. She looked out over the countryside as though for the first time. He could see the delight shining in her eyes, and he wondered if he had been the cause. What had he expected from her—remorse? Aye, he had. He still could not wipe out the vision of Elizabeth meeting him two months hence.

Did he dare hope that Elizabeth's heart had changed and that she cared for him, if even a little?

Sensing his perusal, she glanced at him and smiled. No blushing maid this woman. His gaze shifted from hers, over her full breasts, and along her jewel-encrusted girdle, which accentuated her woman's mound where he yearned to bury himself to the hilt. Remembering the feel of her honeyed walls, he brought his hand to his nose and grinned as he inhaled the musky scent of her femininity. Her eyes widened in shock, and she looked away, yet the smile remained.

He laughed and she glanced at him, her teeth biting into her lip as she looked at Hugh who walked two steps ahead of them, apparently unaware of what he had nearly witnessed. In truth, Kieran would have taken Elizabeth right there on the river's edge, and he knew in his heart that she would not have stopped him.

He hated to depart her company, but when he came upon the manor, he turned to her. "Perhaps you desire to rest before we dine this evening."

She nodded. "Yes, I'd like a nap."

He wondered of the afternoon she'd spent in his squire's company. Would she seek out Olivier again? "Elizabeth?"

"Yes?" She lifted a brow in question.

"Why did you kiss Olivier?" he blurted before he could stop himself.

Instead of blush or stammer in embarrassment, she smiled softly, putting his fears to ease with the genuine expression. "Because I adore him, and when we have a son, I hope he's just like Olivier."

When we have a son.

The desire he had kept in check since Hugh's interruption at the river returned, causing a deep ache in his cock. He could not wait until tonight when finally he would consummate his marriage.

Chapter Three

Lizzie slept right through dinner. The previous night had taken its toll, and her "nap" turned into four hours of dreamless sleep. Mary left her a plate of lukewarm stew, and pudding that was not sweet enough for her taste. Olivier had told her earlier today that sugar was a luxury, hard to come by and thereby incredibly expensive. Lizzie managed a few bites of the bland pudding, while she worried about the news Kieran had received.

What if it the herald brought a summons to Langaer?

She *must* talk to Kieran tonight. She changed into a chemise that would do little to keep the cold away. The room still held a chill. That's one of the few things she missed about her time. Central heating. Thank goodness the bed was piled high with furs.

A knock sounded at the door. Figuring Mary had come to tuck her in, Lizzie opened the door and lifted her brows in surprise. Kieran stood before her, his expression intense.

The man definitely filled a room. "Kieran?" Her voice squeaked.

He shut the door with his foot, took the few steps that separated them and lifted her into his arms. Lizzie clung to his broad shoulders while he strode across the room. He tossed her on the bed, his chest heaving as he looked down at her with eyes so hot they smoldered. He pulled off his shirt, his shoes, and his braies. Lizzie's heart pounded so hard, she could hear nothing over it. Her gaze shifted from his, down over his wide chest and the deep scar there, before moving over the rippling six-pack of his abdomen...and lower still.

Her stomach tightened and a hot ache grew between her legs. Her six years of celibacy was about to end. She bit her lower lip and looked down.

Lizzie smiled despite her effort not to.

The man was huge—his thick, long cock reared up against his navel, the head the size of a plum.

"Tell me now if this is what you want, Elizabeth. Your eyes tell me it is so, but I will hear it from your lips."

Hell, yes! Her throat was so dry, she nodded vigorously.

The side of his lip curled slightly in a cocky smirk before he leaned over her, his hands encircling her ankles. His surprisingly gentle hands moved up her calves, over her knees, and to her thighs, drawing the nightgown with it. With a fierce growl he pulled the gown from her and tossed it aside.

He stood back, looking down at her—at *all* of her.

Lizzie lay on the bed, her entire body trembling as his gaze shifted from hers, over her breasts and down to the juncture of her thighs. For an instant she was the Lizzie of old—with the small boobs and out-of-shape body of her past life. She remembered Brent's comments about her fat ass and she nearly brought her hands up to shield her body, but then she saw the heated look to Kieran's eyes and dropped her hands to her sides.

"Magnifique," he whispered, putting all her fears aside with the French word for magnificent.

His hand captured a breast, teasing the nipple with thumb and forefinger, while the other roamed down her stomach. Lizzie could not stop from trembling as he cupped her mound, his thumb grazing her clit before delving into the soft, slick folds.

Lizzie's breath left her in a rush as his fingers expertly circled her clit, lifting it with his fingers, teasing her relentlessly.

It felt so good, so damn right. Her hips lifted from the bed, urging him on, spreading her legs wide as he slipped a long finger into her.

Every nerve ending in her body came alive as he eased another finger inside of her. His long-tapered fingers moved in and out, simulating sex while his thumb stroked her clit.

Lizzie could hear the pounding of her heart in her ears, and a humming that started deep inside her and grew with every minute. Her body tightened, and her breaths came in small, jagged gasps. Kieran's fingers continued their onslaught and then it happened—her insides clenched tight, building within her, welling up, until like waves slamming against the shore, her climax rocked her entire body. She cried out, her hands at her sides, clenching the sheets in her fists as she rode it out.

She lay back on the bed, staring up at the canopy with a silly-ass smile she couldn't wipe off her face to save her life. She had just been ravished by Kieran the Black. *The* Kieran the Black.

He crawled up her, a soft smile on his face, and he kissed her—his lips soft and gentle. Lizzie opened her mouth to him, wanting to taste him, wanting to feel his need. Her tongue slid along his lips, urging him to open. She sensed his surprise at her aggressiveness, but he didn't deny her and instead opened to her. He tasted like sweet wine and she couldn't get enough. Her tongue delved within his hot mouth, taking everything he gave. She pressed her sensitive breasts against his hard chest, reveling in the feel of his hard muscles against her soft body.

"I want you," she whispered against his lips.

With a moan, his lips left hers to travel down her throat. His hot breath fanned a breast, the nipple puckering, lengthening. He took the sensitive nub into his mouth, teasing it with his teeth, sending a rush of arousal through her again. The gentle tug of his teeth sent a jolt to her cleft that grew hotter and wetter by the second.

She lifted her hips and felt his cock, hard and huge against her belly. Instinctively her legs opened wide. She wanted him inside her *now*.

Her hands were in his hair, the full dark silky locks in such contrast to her light skin as she watched him love her. As though sensing her wicked thoughts, he looked up then, his eyes half-mast, sensual. Damn, the man was sexy! And he was hers.

"Ma belle adorée, vous m'avez ensorcelé."

My precious beauty, you have bewitched me. The words thrilled her, bringing her need for him up yet another notch.

Unable to stand the pressure growing inside her, she reached between their bodies and took hold of his glorious cock. Her body tightened with anticipation. He groaned as her hand slid up and down his hard length. She couldn't help herself. Lizzie slid his thick shaft between her slick folds, letting him feel her need for him.

Kieran's entire body shook with need. The woman beneath him was his wife—the same woman who had defied him at every turn when he had arrived to claim Aedelmaer. Already he'd brought her to climax. He'd felt the evidence with the squeezing of her tight sheath against his fingers, her soft whimper as she moaned his name over and over.

Now she lay beneath him, panting for him, her legs spread wide, telling him without words that she desired him as much as he desired her.

He would not second-guess himself anymore. Without another thought he slid inside her, and his heart skipped a beat at feeling the barrier that marked her as virgin.

He went up on his elbows, staring down at her flushed face. Her eyes were closed, her mouth slightly open—a woman in the throes of passion. Abruptly she opened her eyes and stared up at him. The desire he saw in those blue depths took his breath away. She desired him…wanted him…lusted after him, just as he lusted for her.

She smiled softly, pleasure written all over her face. Lifting her head slightly, she kissed him softly at first, then opened wide, her velvety tongue thrusting against his.

And he was beyond redemption.

With a thrust, he broke the barrier that proved he was the first. She gasped in pain against his lips and he stopped, fully imbedded within her tight sheath, letting her adjust to the intrusion. Kissing her softly, his lips traveled to her nose, her forehead, her eyelids, and then made a track back to her sweet lips. He waited for her to push him off…to cry…or whatever virgins did when they lost their maidenhead. Yet Elizabeth did none of those things.

Instead, she smiled against his mouth. "You feel good inside me," she whispered, the words making his cock lengthen and thicken. When she shifted beneath him, arching her hips, he grinned like a fool.

It took every ounce of will to keep from spilling his seed within her. Never had he experienced such red-hot desire. He would not take his pleasure and leave her wanting. Nay, he wanted to savor the feeling, show her this first time how good it could be between them. He wanted to make his mark on her, let her know that he could make her touch the stars.

Slowly he moved in and out of her, trembling with the effort to keep from spending himself. With a satisfied moan she met his rhythm thrust for thrust, while running her hands down his back, up over his shoulders, then back down, over his hips, cupping his buttocks. She squeezed.

Sweet Jes — if she did not stop he would come before she was ready.

He pulled out to where just the head of his cock kissed her opening. She squirmed beneath him, her hips arching, searching, seeking him. He bent over her, took a pebble-hard nipple into his mouth and sucked greedily. With desperate hands, she pulled his hips down, and he thrust himself to the hilt. Within seconds her sheath clamped around his cock.

"Kieran," she whispered, her voice pleading. "Oh yeah…"

Feeling the last of her spasms, he stilled within her and flicked his tongue over her nipple. "What, my sweet?"

"Fuck me."

The words were shocking, yet exciting, bringing him to a fever pitch. With a wicked smile, he drove into her, time and again, pounding against her, his need out of control. Her fingers dug into his back, and she met him thrust for thrust, her breathing harsh. "Oh yeah," she whispered, "that's it."

Keeping his own climax at bay he captured her mouth with his, his tongue thrusting into her, simulating the pounding of his cock into her body. She dug her heels into the bed, arched and moaned into his mouth as her insides clenched around him.

He could not hold off a minute more. With a satisfied groan he followed behind with the most explosive orgasm of his life.

* * * * *

Lizzie smiled up at the canopy of the bed.

Now *that* had been worth six years of celibacy.

Kieran slept beside her, his body spooned against her own. Never had she felt so protected, his large body fitting to hers so perfectly, his heart pounding a steady rhythm against her back. Brent had always rolled off of her immediately after his climax, leaving her in the wet spot while he sawed logs. Not Kieran. He had rolled them to the opposite side of the bed and held her close, his large body spooning her, making her feel small and protected.

He put all men to shame. Not only was he total eye-candy, he was a master in bed, taking her to a pinnacle she had never known possible. She had *never* been fucked so soundly, and damn did it feel good.

She felt a nudge at her back, and realized that a certain part of him was already awake. Instantly horny, she turned over to face him, her fingers caressing his thick erection. She stroked him, loving the feel of silk over steel. Kieran moaned, then one brilliantly blue eye popped open and he smiled. "Witch," he said, pulling her closer.

Pushing him onto his back, she straddled his hips. Her hands splayed against his massive chest, her fingers running over the flat nipples that hardened at her touch. She went lower still, over his rippled stomach, marveling at the strength beneath her fingers.

He watched her, his bright eyes turning dark with passion as she met his gaze. His hands moved to her thighs, splaying, touching her hot cleft. His blue eyes darkened as her hands moved down to his cock and she encircled his girth, stroking him from base to tip. With the other hand she teased his balls, smiling when he moaned low in his throat.

He shifted beneath her, and his hands moved to her breasts.

She arched her back offering herself to him. Lifting her hips, she sank down on his erection, taking him slowly within her. He watched her descent, his throat convulsing as he swallowed hard. She enjoyed the feeling of being in control, liked watching his face from this vantage point.

Fully impaled on his cock, Lizzie moved her hips, rotating in small circles at first, relishing the feel of his huge shaft. She tossed her head back, letting her hair skim his thighs as she rode him furiously, like a woman possessed. She had a lot of unfulfilled years inside of her, and by damn, she was going to make up for them.

Kieran sat up enough to take a nipple into his mouth. She wove her fingers through his hair, anchoring him there, as she moved slowly up and down his hard length.

His hands moved up and down her back, his fingers dipping down to her ass, kneading it, then stroking the crack before moving back up again. One of his hands cupped the back of her head, pulling her mouth toward his. His lips took hers in a kiss that stole the breath right out of her lungs.

Feeling the first flutters of a climax, she pressed hard against him. His hands moved to her hips, increasing the rhythm. "That's it, Elizabeth, let it go."

And she did let go. With a moan that came deep from inside her, she fell on top of him, pressing down hard until her body convulsed with a climax that made her bones feel like butter.

* * * * *

Kieran leaned up on his elbow, watching the woman who had bewitched him.

Who was this woman who stood naked before him? This woman who just hours ago had been a virgin, untouched and untried. Kieran smiled to himself, pleased that his wife enjoyed lovemaking as much as he. In truth, she had behaved with such enthusiasm one would have thought she'd been educated in the best brothels of his homeland. But the proof of her chastity was smeared on the sheets, and between her thighs.

But not for long. She sank into the hot bath, moaning with pleasure as the warm water enveloped her. He smiled, taking pleasure in her enjoyment. Never had he lingered after lovemaking. Never had he been tempted. But he had not been able to pull himself away from her side all night. Now, with the day dawning before them, the light spilling into the room, he cursed the duties that would take him away from her.

Last night he had received news of several Saxon lords banding together to overtake the Norman strongholds near the Welsh border. Kieran's presence, along with other tenant-in-chiefs of the region, had been requested at Langaer, the fief of Richard, Elizabeth's ex-betrothed. Kieran thought it odd that the meeting about a Saxon uprising would be held at one of the few Saxon-held fiefs, but he would not question his King.

Already his body rejected having to leave his wife when they had only just found such joy in each others arms. He would never have dreamed a woman could have such power over him. Never had his thoughts lingered on a woman the way his thoughts lingered on Elizabeth. Everything about her was intriguing. Her beauty, her spirit, the way her eyes said so much about what she was thinking. He had a connection with her that he'd not thought attainable with another human. In truth, a fortnight could pass in this bed, and he would not care or worry about a thing.

Aye, he was truly bewitched.

"Come join me." Her soft words interrupted his thoughts. Needing not to be asked again, he got out of bed and walked toward her. The blood pounded in his ears as her gaze followed his every step, wandering over his body hungrily. The corners of her mouth lifted seeing his full arousal.

Yes, she was a witch to have such power over him.

The wooden tub was not made for two, but he did not care. He would not reject her invitation, and when she scooted forward and looked over her shoulder, he stepped into the tub behind her and she rested back against him. Her head lay back against his chest, the soft strands of her hair tied up away from her face. Never had he known such peace and tranquility. He had not known that *this* could exist between a man and a woman.

Resting his arms against the tub's rim, he savored the feel of the warm water, but more importantly, the touch of Elizabeth's soft skin against him.

They lay content in each other's arms until the water grew tepid. "It's getting late," Elizabeth said, breaking the silence. "We should join the others in the Hall or they will wonder what happened to us."

He frowned. "Who cares what they wonder."

She smiled saucily and his heart jumped, along with his cock. Elizabeth rolled over, laying on him now, her lips on his chest, kissing a path downward.

"Sit on the tub's rim," she whispered, and he did as asked, bracing his arms against the edge.

On her knees, she moved between his legs and took his already rigid shaft into her mouth. His hands moved to her breasts. He pulled at her nipples as she suckled him expertly, taking him deep into her mouth.

He looked down on her pale head, her lips around his cock, sucking, licking, her tongue running along the ridge, and he grew harder, longer, thicker. His heart pounded heavily as her hand played with his sac, caressing him with soft, gentle fingers.

A moan tore from his throat and his fingers wove through her hair, anchoring her as she sucked harder, her tongue masterfully licking the length and encircling the head.

He pushed her at arm's length, and without a word, lifted her onto his lap so she straddled him, legs outside the tub anchoring them. His cock reared between them, and he lifted her, setting her on him. She stared at him as she took him inside her body, her eyes closing, her mouth opening.

She would be the death of him.

"Yes," she whispered, a sensual smile on her lips as her arms wrapped around his neck and she began to ride him, her pace fast and furious, as though she couldn't get enough of him. Before he spilled himself, he put his hands on her hips, stopping the motion, lifting her slowly, up and down, showing her the slower rhythm he needed. She nodded in understanding, and he took a nipple into his mouth, smiling as she arched against him, her fast rhythm returning as fierce need overtook her.

She groaned loudly, her face a picture of sheer bliss as she rocked against him, her tight sheath pulsing around him, bringing his need up a notch. With the fading contractions of her climax pulsing around him, he pulled her down, while he rotated his hips, and filled her with his seed.

* * * * *

A week went by in a blur, and Lizzie had never known such happiness in all her thirty-nine years.

It was awesome to be eighteen again, and in love. In her own time she would never have gone back to that horrible age when she was so uncertain with the world and herself. But being Elizabeth D'Arcy, wife of Kieran the Black was a dream come true, and she wouldn't change places with anyone. Life was perfect. She had thirty-nine years of living under her belt, and a hot, gorgeous husband who lusted after her eighteen-year-old body and whom she lusted after in return. She had never known love could be like this.

To add to her joy, Kieran had encouraged she start tending to the rose garden near the tower they would be moving into soon. Gardening had been a hobby of hers back in her own time, but she had lacked time with working seventy hours a week for the magazine. Now she had more time than she knew what to do with, but she loved it...and it appeared Kieran appreciated her efforts, because he complimented her on the garden's beauty every day, telling her that when they moved into the tower rooms, he would love to look out at the garden because it would always remind him of her.

She smiled at the memory, the soft expression on his face as he had said those sweet words. *Kieran the Black?* What was so black about the man? He did not have a black heart, nor a dark spirit. The history books had it all wrong. His enemies might look at him as The Black One, but everyone around him absolutely adored him, including herself.

Her gaze strayed to where Kieran and his men sparred. The clash of swords in the warm afternoon captured her attention. Olivier stood at the ready, holding sword in hand when Kieran had need of it. He had been attending Kieran more these past few days, and Lizzie sorely missed the squire's companionship.

Mary had taken his place, which was fine, though the maid tended to treat Lizzie more like a child than an adult. She had to continually remind herself that the maid looked at Elizabeth as though she was a child. She had a long way to go before that would change.

"The men leave in two days," Mary said, bending over to cut another rose she then placed in the basket.

Lizzie's stomach clenched. "Where do they go?"

"Langaer."

"Isn't that Richard's fief?"

Mary nodded. "Yes, Lord Faulkner," she replied, reminding Lizzie with a look that she should not use Richard's Christian name. It seemed too familiar, Mary had commented, especially now that she was the Lady D'Arcy. "There is talk of another Saxon uprising. Neighboring barons will meet at Langaer to talk strategy. I believe many question Lord Faulkner's fealty to King William."

Lizzie swallowed past the lump in her throat. "Is Hugh going with Kieran?"

Mary looked at her as though she'd grown another head. "Of course. His lordship would not go into battle without Hugh at his side. Not to say this is battle, milady. Hugh is his lordship's vassal. It is expected."

Lizzie had watched Hugh since her arrival. He had been absolutely charming from day one, and nothing in his demeanor to date made her believe he was anything but a loyal vassal to Kieran…but history had recorded otherwise.

He had taken to her immediately and not given her any reason to be suspicious.

Lizzie's gaze strayed to the soldiers whose bodies glistened with sweat, and came to rest on the man who had wedged his way into her heart. Kieran—

Shoulders broader than anyone else's, stronger than anyone, the Alpha-male incarnate. He was glorious—every hard inch of him. She smiled remembering their oral play of last night, the stroke of his tongue against her cleft, the way he sucked on her clit until she'd shouted his name for everyone to hear.

Lizzie stood, seeing that Kieran's battle partner was Hugh. The smaller man's face was a mask of intensity. Kieran, on the other hand, looked at ease, the corded muscles bunching beneath his skin with each rotation of the sword. The action seemed automatic, effortless, so in control as though the sword was a part of him. Also a turn-on.

Then Kieran caught sight of her. His attention diverted, he smiled — until the edge of Hugh's sword nicked his bicep.

Lizzie's heart skipped a beat. Even from a distance, she could see the red line of blood pour from the wound.

Hugh's face changed, from intense warrior, to what? Satisfaction — or was that horror? Hugh dropped his sword like it had burned his fingers and his face turned white beneath his tan skin. Lizzie saw the flash of Kieran's teeth as he smiled at his vassal, and reassured him with a slap to the back. However, Kieran's lighthearted attempts didn't seem to reassure the knight who ran a hand through his hair.

Lizzie resisted the urge to run to Kieran's side. Fortunately she didn't have to. He was already walking her way. His hand pressed over the wound, blood spreading between his fingers. His face softened when she approached, his eyes turning a dark shade of blue.

Her heart gave a little jolt of excitement, but she quickly pushed her lust aside and focused on his arm. "Are you all right?" she asked, unable to hide the concern in her voice.

"'Tis but a scratch." His voice was silky soft.

She shook her head. "A scratch? I don't think so. Blood is flowing from the 'scratch' and down your arm."

"Think you that I am a child, woman?" His brow furrowed, yet there was a sparkle in his eyes that told her he was amused by her concern. No doubt he had been through far worse on the battlefield.

She smiled softly. "I would never accuse you of being anything but a full-blooded man."

His eyes darkened. "Will you tend me, lady wife?" He

lifted a dark brow, his gaze shifting to her lips.

She had not once felt empowered in her relationship with Brent. He had never allowed it. He had kept her under his thumb at all times and she, thinking his control meant love, allowed it. Yet with Kieran it was different. He allowed her to be the aggressor at times, even seemed excited by it and she loved him for it.

* * * * *

Inside their bedchamber, she washed the wound with warm water. The "scratch" needed stitches. Olivier appeared at the door with needle and thread. Seeing Lizzie, he grinned widely.

"The boy desires you," Kieran whispered under his breath, a hint of jealousy there, which Lizzie found almost comical. Kieran was such a man, and Olivier…though he was the same age as Elizabeth, Lizzie looked on him as a child. Of course Kieran had no idea that she was almost twice Olivier's age in "real life", and what she felt for the young squire bordered on a maternal bond, and had nothing to do with attraction. Now…had she actually been a teenaged girl—that would have been a different story. In Kieran's eyes he saw an eighteen year-old woman and a seventeen year-old man spending a lot of time together. Lizzie would love to see her husband's face if she told him she was actually eight years older than he was. Ha!

Lizzie turned to the squire. "Olivier, come in." She smiled invitingly, and patted the space beside her. She noted Kieran's brow rise, but he said nothing.

She took the needle and thread from Olivier. "Watch and learn," she said, with a wink.

Olivier grinned and obediently did her bidding. Kieran's expression was impossible to read, but he watched her closely. Lizzie hid a smile, perversely enjoying the Norman's jealousy toward his squire—a young man who thought his liege lord walked on water. He deserved it after flaunting his leman in front of his men for so long. Granted, that had been before Lizzie had arrived, but still…

Trying to forget about the redheaded Gwendolyn who made herself scarce these days, Lizzie worked quickly, chatting away her nervousness. She had gotten a D in sewing class, and Kieran's jagged skin was much tougher than any material she'd ever worked on. She was glad Olivier was contributing to the conversation because Kieran remained silent. She looked up at her husband once to find him watching her, his eyes soft, the side of his mouth curved in a soft smile.

Her heart gave a little tug, and warmth flooded her. Oh, but she loved this man already. God help her if she were to be ripped out of his life unexpectedly...or he out of hers. True, she did miss some of the creature comforts of her own time — mostly phones, computers, the Internet, and her beloved sugar. But this time suited her better in all ways. Especially the men of this time. She grinned up at Kieran and her heart gave a little leap at the desire she saw clearly shining in his eyes. Licking her lips, she hid a smile upon hearing his quick intake of breath.

He could not travel to Langaer. She had to find a way to keep him home.

She tied a knot in the thread. Bending over, she cut it with her teeth, then pressed her lips against the wound. "All done, milord." She took a step back and studied her handiwork.

Kieran smiled at her, then glanced at Olivier — at the door, then back to Olivier, the meaning clear.

Olivier's cheeks flamed and he stood abruptly. "Milord...milady," he said, and with a nod, left the room.

"I think you make the boy uncomfortable," Kieran said, his voice silky.

Lizzie glanced between his thighs where his erection strained against his braies. "I think it is you who makes him uncomfortable. Can you blame him? Is that a lance in your pocket, or are you just glad to see me?"

He chuckled. "Come here, witch."

She walked over and straightened the tapestry on the wall.

"What do you think of Hugh?" she blurted.

His frown deepened. "What do you mean?"

She shrugged innocently. "I mean what do you think of

him?"

"He is my vassal. We have fought side by side through many a battle."

Lizzie knew she treaded on dangerous ground. How did she go about telling him that his right-hand man, and so-called best friend, was out to get to him killed.

"Why do you have to leave tomorrow?" she blurted.

He looked surprised she knew of his plans to leave. "We are a country in turmoil, Elizabeth. Your Saxons are angry and we must set them at ease." He walked toward her and made to pull her into his arms but she stepped away.

"I fear for your life," she said, failing to keep the fear from her voice.

He seemed amused, the sides of his mouth curving softly. "I have gone into battle many times, Elizabeth, and come out unscathed. This is but a meeting between the other tenant-in-chiefs and myself. All will be fine." He backed her up against the wall, pressing his hard shaft against her. Red-hot desire flooded her and she grabbed his ass with both hands and pulled him tighter.

"Lusty wench," he said, pressing his lips against her forehead.

Man, did he feel good. Lizzie tried to keep her focus on him leaving, but it was tough when his hard cock pressed against her belly. Lizzie squeezed her eyes closed, listening to the pounding of his heart against her ear. That heart would cease to beat if she kept silent.

Taking a deep breath she put him at arm's length and took a deep breath. "Kieran, listen to me. What if…what if I told you that your trusted vassal will kill you before you set foot at Langaer?"

His eyes turned cold. "You speak of treason, lady wife."

Swallowing hard, she met his gaze without blinking. "I speak the truth."

"You will stop this madness at once, woman!"

"Hugh is going to kill you. You can't go to Langaer. You will be killed as sure as I'm standing before you right now."

The look he gave her was incredulous and though she wanted to shrink from it, she stood her ground and watched when he walked in long strides toward the window where the clash of swords could still be heard. Lizzie didn't move. She knew who he searched for. His back was tense, the muscles clenching beneath his dark skin. She wanted to go to him, to feel his heart beat against her ear, just as she had a minute before — before she'd opened her big mouth.

She had to save him, so that she could have those moments in the future. Because she could not lose him now, not when she had already fallen in love with him.

He ran a hand through his hair, and then turned to her, his face a solemn mask. "Why would you accuse Hugh of such treachery?"

"Because it's the truth."

The nerve in his jaw twitched. "How do you know?" His voice was clipped, curt.

"I just do."

He crossed the room to her, but stopped just short of her. "You will tell me now."

Lizzie closed her eyes. She always knew it would not be easy to tell him. She had expected him to deny what she said, but the anger she saw in his blue eyes made her take a step back.

She took a deep breath and blurted, "I know because I can see into the future."

He shook his head, as though he hadn't heard her.

"I swear to you, Kieran. You will be killed at the hands of Hugh de Vesli. I have seen the future and I know it as fact."

Kieran stared at her without blinking, his features harsh. "Nay, Hugh has pledged his homage and fealty to me. He is my comrade, my vassal, my friend. He would not betray me. He is loyal, more loyal than any man — or *woman* I've known."

She did not miss the slight and it stung. "Why would I lie to you, Kieran? What would I gain from it?"

He walked toward the door. "You are Saxon."

I'm American, actually — an American who doesn't want you to die. She wanted to shout the words but she couldn't for fear he'd have her declared mad and thrown into the dungeon. "I'm telling you because I care for you. You are my husband and I want you to live."

"You speak madness."

At the door, he turned to her, hands on narrow hips, looking better than anyone had a right to. She didn't want to fight with him...she just wanted him to listen. "I'm not crazy. Think about it, Kieran. Think back over the years. Has Hugh ever shown jealousy toward you? Has Hugh ever wanted to best you in any way, shape, or form?" Lizzie released a frustrated sigh. "Please don't go to Langaer. Stay here with me...where it's safe."

* * * * *

Stay here with me, where it's safe.

The words rang over and over in Kieran's ears. Sitting on the dais with Hugh at his side, he listened to the conversation around him with half an ear. Elizabeth remained in their bedchamber rather than come down to dine with him. She had told Mary to tell him she had no appetite. He did not like what she had said about Hugh and it bothered him. He did not want to believe Elizabeth. Hugh had been his vassal for six years now. They had fought in every battle together. Hugh was a worthy knight, and Kieran had never questioned his honor.

Yet now, Elizabeth's fear made him question his most trusted vassal's loyalty, and he hated it. Was Hugh as loyal as Kieran thought him to be? He rubbed the wound he'd received just that afternoon.

Kieran glanced over at Hugh, who was looking down at the servant's table. There, looking back at the young knight was Gwendolyn, her lips raised in a saucy smile. It did not bother Kieran one wit that his ex-leman wanted Hugh. All the better that she took up with someone else and leave him be. In truth, he was relieved she had not caused a scene in front of Elizabeth. Since kicking her out of bed on the night Elizabeth had appeared from her deathbed, he and Gwendolyn had not crossed paths, and he wished it to remain that way.

He took a drink of ale, his fingers tightening around the goblet as Elizabeth's accusation vibrated in his ears. Dinner continued, and Kieran watched, eating little, drinking less, and thinking far too much. Memories of the determination on Hugh's face whenever they sparred together, or arched, or even hunted. Kieran had not given it much thought, but perhaps the man did think ill of him in some way.

Many of the peasants filed out of the hall, and then his soldiers, most preparing to bed down for the night. Only a small party would leave tomorrow morning, the rest of the soldiers would stay to protect Aedelmaer.

A short while later Hugh wished him goodnight, and Kieran sat back in the chair, watching the younger man leave the hall.

Kieran followed, stopping to talk to Olivier for a moment.

He found Hugh behind the armory...and he had company. Gwendolyn was on her knees, Hugh's hands in her hair, pulling her closer to his cock. Gwendolyn sucked greedily, her hands on the young soldier's thighs, her head moving at a frantic rhythm. Hugh's head fell back on his shoulders, and he groaned low in his throat.

Was Hugh ever jealous of you, or what you had?

Kieran left the two alone. As he walked out of the bailey toward the manor, his gaze shifted to his bedchamber window, hoping to catch a glimpse of his wife. She had been furious with him. Her words and her strength surprised him. Most women of her age were unsure of themselves, but there was a maturity to Elizabeth most women her age lacked. She always held his gaze steadfast, never relenting, not even in the throes of passion. She watched him, as though she sensed his thoughts, and often times she would say exactly what he'd been thinking.

Uncertainty rippled down his spine. She said she could see into the future. Was the woman a witch? Had someone else inhabited Elizabeth's body? Everyone from Mary, Elizabeth's most trusted servant, to the villagers commented on the radical change in her person, as though someone else had taken over her body. In truth, what had caused such a transformation from quiet and shy girl, to outspoken and bold lady?

He climbed the stairs to the second floor. Standing outside their bedchamber door, he lifted his hand to knock and hesitated. He heard singing, and he lifted the latch and opened the door.

Mary, busy tidying the room, turned to him. "Milord."

"Where is my lady wife?"

"I believe you will find her in the baker's hut."

Chapter Four

In the baker's hut?

What, pray tell, would Elizabeth be doing in the baker's hut at this time of night? He bent to enter the dwelling that was so hot as to be stifling, and squinted against the smoke, looking for her.

He found her, hair piled high on her head, a few strands escaping down her neck, caressing her hips and tiny waist. Her back to him, she stood before a large table, cutting apples. At her side, with matching apron on, stood his squire, Olivier. His blonde hair held back with a band, while he poured flour into a large wooden bowl.

The side of Kieran's mouth quirked. They were...baking?

All activity came to a standstill in the kitchen, all save the two at the table, their heads bent as they spoke to one another. Of what did they speak? The two had become as thick as thieves — one never far from the other. In truth, he believed Olivier ran to Elizabeth the moment Kieran released him from his duties. Instead of being jealous of his squire, he rather envied the boy for the time he spent in his lady's company. The two seemed to have an unspoken bond — one that Kieran yearned to have with Elizabeth, who had become as mysterious to him as she was the day he had taken Aedelmaer as his own.

Obviously sensing confrontation, the servants filed out the back door. Elizabeth finally noted the others had fled and she turned. She had flour on her nose, along her jaw, and all over the bodice of her gown where the apron did not cover. She smiled softly and Kieran's heart gave a jolt.

At her side, Olivier glanced over his shoulder and paled. He scrambled to get out of the apron, but Kieran held up his hand. "Your lady requires your services more than I, Olivier. Please finish what you started."

While Olivier reluctantly resumed adding ingredients to the bowl, Elizabeth walked toward Kieran and wrapped her arms around his shoulders. His horrible mood, nay—all the fear he had been feeling melted away with her hug. "You ruined my surprise."

Kieran buried his face in her hair—the scent of rosewood assailing his senses. God help him but he was lost to all thought when in her presence. She had dulled his wits to the point he had trouble keeping a single thought in his head save her. He yearned to take her here. He envisioned her flat on her back on the table, her legs spread wide to receive him.

"What wicked thoughts run through that head?" she asked, kissing him lightly on the lips.

"You can read my thoughts as well?" he murmured against her lips. "You truly are a witch."

"No, I'm not a witch. I just want to believe your thoughts mirror my own."

His cock reared at her words. He pressed his length against her, letting her feel what she did to him. She lifted a brow. "Don't tease me, milord. I've worked so hard to please you this day."

"You please me in every way."

"Do I?" She looked surprised. "And here I thought you were angry with me."

Olivier cleared his throat abruptly, and Kieran glanced at the boy, who in turn nodded toward the door.

Kieran turned. Hugh de Vesli stood with arm braced against the doorframe, his face devoid of expression. "Milord, the men are ready for you."

He turned back to Elizabeth whose smile had lost its luster. Every time Hugh came near, always she became tense. Could she be telling the truth? Could she in fact see into the future? Did she fear for his life? A part of him felt guilty for second-guessing Hugh's loyalty toward him, particularly when the one who accused him he'd only known for such a short period of time. Despite his desire to trust her explicitly, a little voice told him to be wary.

"I will be here when you return." She glanced at the table. "I'll be alone."

The sides of his mouth curved. "I'll be back soon."

* * * * *

The apple pie cooled near the window, where Lizzie had strategically placed the apron Olivier had used earlier. It served as a drape now. She had already cleaned off the table and now she sat on the hard wood, waiting expectantly for Kieran.

She had been relieved when he came looking for her. She had not been able to join him in the hall, especially so near Hugh without breaking down and crying, and she had not been able to wait for him in the bedchamber either. Antsy and completely bummed out, she did what she always did when she needed a lift. She baked.

She had found Olivier in the bailey and asked him to help her. He had readily agreed. At least a thousand times she had wanted to plead with Olivier not to leave tomorrow for Langaer, but she knew Kieran would be furious if she said anything to Olivier. Plus, she didn't want to scare the kid. There was no easy answer, but she had to stop both Kieran and Olivier from leaving tomorrow.

If Kieran insisted on going to Langaer, then she would talk him into taking her along. She wasn't sure how her going along would help him — she just knew her staying at Aedelmaer would be impossible while he left.

And Olivier. Her heart gave a little tug at the thought of the young man. In the past weeks he had become her confidante, her buddy and friend, and she wanted more than anything to see him grow to manhood, to become a knight, and fall in love.

She heard footsteps approach and she sat up tall, straightening the apron around her waist — the only clothing she wore. Her bare butt rested on the table, still warm from the pies. Nervous now that the time was at hand, she shifted and took a deep breath. She had never in her life done anything outrageous when it came to sex. The boldest she'd ever been had been the time she'd given Brent a blowjob while driving down the freeway. Other than that, she couldn't recall a single time they'd made love with the lights on, or without some form of clothing on, and the man didn't know what foreplay was. In all their years together, he'd only gone down on her a handful of times, and his technique had left something to be desired.

The man could have used lessons from Kieran.

Kieran didn't knock…he just threw open the door. Seeing her, his brows lifted, and he quickly shut the door, then latched it. He stood with hands on narrow hips, watching her, his dazzling blue eyes settling on her breasts and nipples that were tipped with apple pie filling. She took a deep breath, arched her back slightly, and spread her legs ever so slightly…enough to where he could get an enticing view of what was in store for him. His gaze shifted lower and he reached behind his head, ripped off his tunic in one fell swoop, and then started untying his braies. He yanked off his boots, slid his braies off and walked toward her, his huge shaft fully erect.

Red-hot desire flowed through Lizzie's veins, swooping low into her belly and between her legs. Kieran stood between her spread thighs with a positively wicked smile on his handsome face. He abruptly pulled her bottom to the very edge of the table and pressed his hard length against her. Glancing over at the bowl of apple-pie filling, he smiled devilishly, and dipped a long finger into the bowl. Lizzie's pulse skittered as he went slowly to his knees. She gasped when his fingers smeared the warm filling over her clit and hot cleft. Lizzie's heart hammered as he placed her legs over his shoulders and licked her slit, his tongue stroking her pleasure pearl.

With a contented sigh, Lizzie fell back on the table and closed her eyes as Kieran's tongue stroked her soft folds, laving her, lifting her clit with his tongue, teasing her relentlessly. Her entire body felt energized. Goosebumps covered her body that trembled with the impending climax. He stilled her with a firm hand to her stomach, pinning her there as he continued his onslaught. She lifted her head, watching him pleasure her. The sight of his dark head between her thighs was incredibly erotic, and as though sensing her gaze, he glanced up. His thick-lashed eyes held a devilish gleam as he sucked her clit hard. Her head fell back on the table, a hand grabbed the table's edge for support.

Heat raced through every inch of her body, and she jerked beneath his skilled tongue. The climax tightened her body and her heart fluttered as she fought for breath. Then it hit her like waves crashing against the shore, and she collapsed against the hard wood, trying to catch her breath.

She became conscious of his big hands stroking the insides of her thighs, the long tapered fingers gentle as they moved beneath to her bottom, squeezing, pulling her closer to his mouth as he loved her yet again. This man was too good to be true.

His tongue stroked and circled her clit then thrust inside her, and that's all it took. Lizzie's legs wrapped around his shoulders and she arched up off the table, her body humming from the release.

By the time she looked up Kieran was crawling up her body. His long hair tickled her legs, and then her belly as he kissed a path over her quivering stomach to her breasts where he licked the filling from one nipple then the other, his teeth and lips bringing her back up off the table.

With desperate fingers, she reached for his shaft, running her finger over the plum-size head that was already purple with need. She looked up at him, his eyes heavy-lidded, passionate, telling her without words what he wanted to do to her. She eyed the bowl of filling. She wanted to return the favor by taking him inside her mouth, to taste him, to lick him and give him the same pleasure he'd just given her. He knelt onto the table, using his legs to spread her thighs as wide as they would go. Apparently he had something else in mind.

He entered her, his gaze never leaving hers as he thrust into her slowly. Her head fell back against the table and she moaned in ecstasy. "Look at me when I love you, Elizabeth."

Her breath came in gasps as he thrust into her time and again. She clung to his broad shoulders, her stomach tightening as still another climax overtook her, her body quickening as she reached for the stars. His mouth slanted over hers, his tongue dipping and parrying, matching the thrust of his hard lance inside her.

Lizzie reeled with the force of the orgasm. She opened her eyes to find him watching her, sweat beading on his brow as he kept his desire in check. He smiled softly, then claimed her mouth with a kiss that stole the breath from her lungs. He drove his cock in deep for a final parry, then came with a triumphant roar.

* * * * *

Lizzie opened her eyes. She sat up abruptly and threw open the panel of the bed. Daylight streamed in through the open window, casting light on the empty space beside her. Her stomach clenched into a tight knot. She was too late.

Kieran had left for Langaer.

Last night they had laughed all the way from the baker's hut to their bedchamber and then made love again. It was early morning before they had fallen asleep in one another's arms.

All through the night she had begged him to take her with him to Langaer but he had shushed her, telling her that they would speak of it in the morning.

But they had not talked about it again.

"Mary!" Lizzie yelled, striding toward the wardrobe.

Within minutes, Mary's footsteps could be heard as she raced up the steps. The chamber door opened and Mary appeared wide-eyed. "What is it, milady?"

Lizzie threw a couple of gowns onto the bed. "Help me pack."

"Where do you go, milady?"

"To Langaer."

Mary gasped. "Nay, you can not. His lordship left this morning with the strictest orders for you to stay at Aedelmaer. I will not be responsible should anything happen to you."

Lizzie who had been throwing some chemises together turned to her. "Would you rather be responsible for *not* preventing his death, because you will be guilty if you keep me from leaving."

Mary's eyes widened. "What madness do you speak?"

"I have seen the future, Mary. Kieran is going to be killed if I cannot stop him. He's riding straight into an ambush."

"Milady, that does not make—"

"Olivier will be killed too."

Mary gasped, her eyes wide. "How would you know of such a thing?"

"I won't let it happen, and I believe you don't want his death on your conscience either." Lizzie glanced at the gowns — all of which would be too cumbersome to ride in. "I need squire's clothing. Anything that will fit. I'll need a hat as well. We'll pin my hair up so it won't be so noticeable that I'm female."

"I will go with you," Mary blurted, her face pale.

Lizzie turned to the maid and put her hands on her shoulders. She was ready to tell her no way, when a thought occurred. She had no idea how to get to Langaer. "Have you ever been to Langaer?"

Mary nodded. "I have been there on two occasions — one being your betrothal when you were but twelve."

Lizzie winced at the idea that children were betrothed at such a young age. Talk about a short childhood. "Good. I suggest you snag a squire's outfit for yourself."

* * * * *

Four hours later, cold and bitterly aware that she had only ridden a horse twice in her life, Lizzie stood in the stirrups and winced as every muscle protested. True, she had a young body, but mentally she was the same middle-aged broad of old. She glanced over at Mary and noticed her maid wasn't faring any better. The woman sat with back poker-rod straight, her thick dark hair piled under the hat she had pulled down low over her ears. "You make a nice-looking boy, Mary," she said, hoping to lighten the mood.

Mary frowned. "I do not see the humor, milady. I am tired and I believe we are hopelessly lost."

Those were not the words Lizzie wanted to hear. Rather than give into frustration, she prompted Mary to talk, but the maid was clearly disconcerted and pissed off. So they went along in silence.

Male laughter sounded in the distance, and Lizzie held her hand up. "I wonder if that's —"

The words had no more left her mouth when two men-at-arms appeared from the trees. Lizzie nearly sagged with relief recognizing Kieran's colors flying from the banner.

"Who are you and from where do you hail?" one man asked. He looked ominous, wearing chain mail from head to toe.

Lizzie sat up straight in the saddle. "We bring word for Lord D'Arcy."

One man nodded to the other, and obviously sensing no danger, they approached. An instant later the reins were unceremoniously wrenched from Lizzie's grasp, and likewise with Mary who looked at her pleadingly. Apparently the soldiers didn't recognize them with their hair up and dressed in squires' clothing. She opened her mouth to tell them who she was, but decided against it. If she was lucky, they would take her straight to Kieran.

Within ten minutes they came upon the camp where men lingered before a campfire. Three tents sat in the distance. Lizzie noticed Kieran immediately. Taller than everyone, he stood before the fire still dressed in full chain mail, looking very much the warrior. Olivier stood by his side. The young man said something and Kieran smiled. The gesture made Lizzie's heart jump in her chest. Oh but he was handsome. She had it bad for this man.

At their approach he turned. She tensed, feeling his stare.

"Dismount," the man at her side said, already off his horse, waiting for her to comply.

Lizzie nodded to Mary, who dismounted and pulled her hat lower, hiding her eyes.

Fingers wrapped around Lizzie's bicep. A knight pulled her forward. "Baron, we found these young men nearby. 'Tis likely they followed us."

Brows furrowed, Kieran approached, his gaze sweeping her from hat to the tips of her boots — then slowly back up.

Lizzie refrained from smiling as Kieran's gaze pierced hers. A dark brow lifted, along with the side of his lip. He glanced at Mary, but only for an instant before his attention returned to her. "I wish to speak with this...*squire* alone." The man-at-arms pushed Lizzie forward. Kieran looked sharply at his man. "Think you that is the way to treat a guest, Maubenc?"

The knight looked embarrassed. "Nay, milord."

Kieran glanced at Mary. "You must be tired from your arduous journey. Please eat and drink with us."

Mary nodded, pulled her hat low over her eyes, and went straight for the fire.

Lizzie entered the tent and turned, waiting for Kieran. She didn't have long to wait. He entered, secured the entrance and faced her. The smile on his face didn't quite reach his eyes. "Squire, you bear a striking resemblance to someone quite dear to me."

Lizzie lifted her chin. "Really? And who would that be?"

His lips twitched. "A blonde-haired witch who has ensnared me into her wicked web. I fear that I cannot get her out of my thoughts. Even now, when I look at you, it is her face that I see."

"Perhaps you hallucinate?"

He laughed under his breath. "Nay, I think not. I think said witch has followed me here." His gaze shifted from hers, to the snug surcoat, then down further to the tight-fitting chausses, which Lizzie knew emphasized her long legs. She shifted on her feet recognizing the passionate look in her husband's eyes. God help her but she wanted him here and now.

"Take your hat off, wife."

She feigned shock. "I am *not* your wife."

He growled. "I know that face, and I know those legs." He took the few steps that separated them, reached out and rubbed his fingers over her crotch. "And I know the feel of this sweet morsel here." He stroked her already wet cleft through the soft fabric of the braies.

"No fair," she said on a groan, going up on her toes to kiss him. He kissed her hard, pulling her up against him. "Your chain mail is kind of in the way."

He put her from him with a smile. "Before I forget how desirable you look, pray tell what you are doing here. Can I assume you missed me so much you could not bear the thought of being apart for a fortnight?"

All signs of playfulness were gone from his features, replaced by an intensity that kept her pinned to the spot. She swallowed hard. "I told you already. I feared for your life."

"Would you have me confined to Aedelmaer, Elizabeth? In truth, what would our enemy think? What would my *King* think? Nay, I will not live like a coward. I fear no man."

"Come home." The words were wrenched from her, and as tears burned the backs of her eyes, she looked away, embarrassed at cracking under the pressure. If she had to, she would physically drag him back with her.

"Shh," he said under his breath, pulling her into his arms. "Come now, Elizabeth. I am fine." He lifted her chin with gentle fingers. "I am flesh and blood as you can see and feel with your own hands. I have no intention of leaving you a widow for some other lusty Norman knight to take beneath him."

She knew he meant to humor her, yet his eyes lost their sparkle, and even his jaw had set in a grim line. "Nay, Elizabeth, I will not leave you. Not now, not until we have grown old together and had many babes."

Sweet Jesus let it be.

"I have sent Sir Hugh ahead to inform Richard of our arrival."

She tensed. "How long ago?"

The words had scarcely left her mouth when one of Kieran's men cleared his throat from outside the tent's entrance. "Milord."

"Yes?" Kieran called over his shoulder.

"Men approaching. We believe it to be Sir Hugh, for he flies your colors…yet there are more men with him than those who set out."

All her fears were coming to fruition. Lizzie started to tremble. A sense of dread fell over her, so intense she felt like she would throw up.

Kieran kissed her softly. "Stay here and I shall see what this is about."

She didn't stay, but instead waited a only few seconds before following him out of the tent. The group of a dozen men, all still wearing armor, took up their shields and weapons. Mary flew to Lizzie's side and linked arms. It was the first time the woman had ever shown fear. Olivier looked at her, his eyes widening in surprise. Obviously Kieran had been the only one to see through their disguises.

Kieran mounted his horse, his gaze on his squire. "Olivier, you will stay with my lady wife and Mary. Do not, under any circumstances, let them out of your sight. Do you understand?"

Olivier nodded and handed Kieran his longbow and shield. "God be with you, milord."

"And you, Olivier." Kieran turned in the saddle, his gaze intent. "Milady, I shall return."

Lizzie watched helplessly as Kieran and his vassals rode off, leaving she, Olivier and Mary alone. The darkness enveloped them to where she could hear nothing but the pounding of her own heart. Then voices raised in anger, followed by the clash of metal and the grunts of men. Elizabeth grabbed Mary's hand. "You will ride back to Aedelmaer and tell them his lordship is in trouble." She turned to Olivier. "And you will ride with her."

He shook his head furiously. "Nay, I will not, milady."

Lizzie took his head between her palms and looked up at him. "You will do as I say. You will leave with Mary. Your liege lord is in trouble. He needs your help — now! There is no time to waste."

Lizzie trembled from fear and from the obstinate stare of the young man before her. She knew it was useless to tell him to go. Olivier had given Kieran his vow to stay with her and he would not waver from that promise. He grabbed her hands, pulled them from his face and held them tight within his own. "Nay, milady. I gave my word to Lord D'Arcy, and I will not break it."

With a frustrated curse, Lizzie turned to Mary. "Go, now while you can. Ride as fast as you can to Aedelmaer. Tell them that Kieran and his men have been ambushed. Bring as many men as Aedelmaer can spare."

"Yes, milady." Mary ran for the horse, and within seconds she was on her way.

"Milady, I do not understand." Oliver's voice was full of uncertainty and something else. Fear?

She pulled him close, unable to keep the tears from falling. "Promise me you will do as I say. Promise me that no matter what—that no matter how much you want to deny what I say, that you will tell them it's the truth."

Olivier frowned. "I do not understand. Who is this 'them' you speak of?"

What was it with these soldiers? They continually questioned everything she said. "At this moment Kieran is fighting for his life, and God willing he will live to see tomorrow. But whatever happens to us, whoever comes over that bend, be prepared to lie. Our lives depend on it."

The words had scarcely left her mouth when the sound of horses' hooves approached. Never in her life had she been so afraid. "Promise me, Olivier," she whispered, the sound of the horses closer. "Whatever happens, do not say a word unless I tell you to. You will let me speak for us, do you promise?"

He looked scared to death, but to his credit, he nodded. "I promise, milady."

She sighed. "Stay alive, Olivier. Just stay alive."

Her breath left her in a rush seeing the unfamiliar men approach. The flag of D'Arcy flew on their staff, yet the men who approached were not Normans. They were bushy-haired, full-bearded Saxons, and they were bearing down on them…fast.

Lizzie wavered on her feet and she swallowed a scream. The Normans had been defeated. Why else would they be here instead of Kieran and his men? Pain and fury sliced through her, taking the breath from her as though she'd been knocked hard in the stomach. Dear God, how could she live without Kieran? The thought of him laying wounded nearby made her bite down hard on her lip.

The man at the front held up a hand. The knight looked down at her, the corner of his mouth lifting in a snarl. The man behind him lifted a bow, his target clear. She would die if she did not say something.

Her throat had closed from unshed tears, so she did the only thing she could think of. She ripped off her hat, letting her hair escape down her back.

The man lowered the bow, and the man in front laughed. "What have we here? The Normans dress their lemans as squires?"

Olivier stiffened at her side, and she squeezed his hand. "Nay, I am not a Norman's leman, but Lady D'Arcy of Aedelmaer."

The words hadn't left her mouth when the soldiers parted like the Red Sea, letting one man forward.

Lizzie's stomach knotted, knowing the man who came forward had to be none other than Richard, Elizabeth's jilted betrothed—and he wore Hugh's armor, and flew D'Arcy's colors. Hugh had *not* ambushed his liege lord after all. Rather, Richard had, dressed as Hugh.

Her stomach rolled. Hugh had suffered a traitor's death, going down in history as a traitor who had killed his liege lord in cold-blood, when in fact the faithful vassal had died in the line of duty.

Richard dismounted, took off his helmet and tossed it aside. "Elizabeth?"

"Richard?" Lizzie said, tilting her head back to look up at the tall Saxon who was almost the same height as Kieran, but not as brawny, nor as handsome. His chestnut-colored hair was matted close to his head, and he sported a beard like the rest of his soldiers, but his was clipped short. His brown eyes held hers, and he smiled wide, exposing a set of white, but crooked teeth. Lizzie wrinkled her nose. He smelled rank.

He pulled her into his arms and laughed. "Would that I had planned it any better. The heavens have indeed smiled upon me this day. Why else would milady be delivered to me moments after I have slain my enemy?" He turned to his men. "Tonight we celebrate, for not only have we bested these Norman bastards once and for all, but my woman will take her true place at my side."

Richard laughed under his breath, and he whispered into her ear. "Do not tremble, milady. I will protect you. You no longer have to fear that Norman beast. My archer shot for his heart, and he never misses."

Lizzie trembled, a little from fear, a lot from pain. He had just confirmed her worst fear. Kieran was dead.

He set her on her feet, and Richard's attention shifted abruptly to Olivier, who stood white faced and wide-eyed. Lizzie saw the confusion in his eyes. She saw him bristle in despair, but she caught his gaze and implored him with a look to trust her, and remember his promise to her.

Richard set her aside. "Who is this?" He drew his bloodied sword.

Lizzie placed her hand over Richard's, effectively sheathing the weapon. "'Tis my loyal servant, Olivier."

"He is Norman?"

"Yes, milord." Lizzie forced a smile. "He became a favorite of mine upon The Black One's arrival. He is like a brother to me, and hates the Normans as I do. For years his liege lord abused him…until I took him under my wing. I could not bear the thought of leaving him behind for those beasts to take their fury out on, so I brought him with me on my escape."

Richard glanced at her. "Your escape?"

She nodded. "Aye, The Black One never let me out of his sight, and when he left this morning, I found the opportunity to flee. I brought my trusted servant with me. I told Olivier that you were a gracious lord, and that you would treat him like family."

Richard eyed Olivier skeptically, then turned back to Elizabeth. His eyes searched her face, as though he could find the truth. She stared unblinking. Feeling uncomfortable under his regard, she threw her arms around his neck and pressed herself fully against him. "Milord, I can not tell you how happy I am to see you. I feared for my life every day, and prayed for the day we would be together."

Richard's hard sex probed against her and his hands clasped her waist. "I am pleased at this greeting, milady. I'm also pleased to hear you risked your life to leave the Norman." He lifted her chin with ungentle fingers. "You have nothing left to fear. We are finally together, our Norman spouses both dead, where they belong, and now we are with who God intended us to be."

Richard's eyes were dark with lust. She knew the look well, and realized that she might have bitten off more than she could chew. She had no idea how she would fend him off once they reached Langaer. He already looked ready to pounce on her.

"Let us return to the hall and celebrate our victory this day!"

The Saxon knights looted the campsite, taking everything they could carry. Olivier mounted a horse, and Richard lifted Lizzie up on the saddle before getting on behind her.

Lizzie's gaze scanned the surrounding countryside, looking for any sign of Kieran or his men. The moon was out, casting the landscape in shadows. They had not gone very far when she noticed the small alcove, a perfect place for an ambush, littered with bodies. Her heart gave a horrified jerk. Kieran and his men. She could not make her husband out amongst all the bodies since the men all wore chain mail. Every fiber of her being wanted to kill the man behind her and all the men that rode with him.

She glanced over and met Olivier's horrified expression. It was almost her undoing. He blinked back tears, his mouth open in disbelief. Lizzie shook her head in warning. He turned away from her, staring straight ahead, the nerve ticking in his cheek, and he flinched as though struck.

He was in pain and confused. How could he not be? She had no idea what she would do when she got to Langaer, nor did she care at this point. If she had her way, they could throw her in the dungeon and let her rot, but she had Olivier to think of. God willing, Mary would make it safely to Aedelmaer and alert the men. They would find Kieran and the others, take them back to Aedelmaer and bury them. Then, and only then would they come for she and Olivier.

Which meant she might be in the enemy's camp for a while.

She would have to live with the hope that she would return to Aedelmaer, to where she and Kieran had shared unbridled passion.

Chapter Five

Kieran opened his eyes and stared up at the night sky. The stars above blurred, so he closed his eyes for a moment to get his bearings. Pain lanced through him, burning deep in his chest, spreading into his right shoulder.

A wolf's howl filled the night, and he turned his head, the simple act making him moan in pain. At a glance he could see the bodies of his men laying scattered about the clearing. Memories of the attack came back swiftly. Hugh—or rather a Saxon dressed in Hugh's armor—had approached them, and out of the trees a group of thirty soldiers swarmed upon them, not to mention the archers who stayed back in the trees, firing away.

The attack had come suddenly, swiftly. Kieran, always ready for such an attack, cut through ten Saxons before the arrow had pierced his chest, another followed, deep into his shoulder, hitting him with a force that sent him off his horse and onto the ground. All around him he heard his men fighting for their lives, and then blackness claimed him.

The silence now was deafening. Elizabeth had been right. She had warned him, and yet he had ridden he and his men straight into an ambush. He cursed himself for not having believed her. Now many of his best soldiers had gone to their deaths—and only God knew what had happened to Elizabeth. An image of his wife just minutes before the attack came back to haunt him.

God, she had known all along, and tried to tell him as much, but he had not listened. A pain far worse than the wound to his chest and shoulder raced through him. If anything happened to Elizabeth, he would skin Richard alive. Hatred for the traitorous Saxon knight boiled his blood, making Kieran seethe with the need for vengeance.

Richard had killed his Norman bride because she'd gotten in the way of the wife he wanted. Now that he had Elizabeth, what would he do to her?

* * * * *

Lizzie sat in the tower, waiting for word. For nine days she had been held a virtual prisoner within the castle walls. Two guards stood outside the door, and an attendant, an old woman with fierce eyes stayed with Elizabeth twenty-four, seven, watching her every move, even going so far as to attend Lizzie while she went to the bathroom.

The first few days she was grateful to be left alone in her grief. She had to blink back tears and hide her anguish for fear the woman would tell Richard and he would question her about her loyalty to him, but every waking moment, and even in her dreams she thought of Kieran. He had left a big, black hole in her heart and in her life, and she wondered if she would ever feel the same again. Though she had no appetite, she forced herself to eat, knowing she would need the strength to escape with Olivier when given the chance.

If only she could get word to the poor kid. She had not seen Richard, and she wasn't sure what to make of his absence. She was too relieved to give it much thought. Instead, she spent the time looking out the window, hoping for a glimpse of Olivier. How did the boy fare in this den of their enemy? Her heart wrenched for the young man who had to mourn the loss of his liege lord alone.

"Who do you look for, Lady Elizabeth?" the old woman asked.

Lizzie glanced over at the woman, who embroidered a gorgeous pattern onto a deep-red surcoat. On several occasions she had tried to get Lizzie to help her, but Lizzie had told her she had no patience for such tasks. The truth of the matter was she couldn't embroider. Didn't have a clue how, and didn't care to learn, especially now when all her energy needed to go toward escaping.

Footsteps sounded outside the chamber, and a moment later the latch lifted and Richard walked in. His dark eyes found her instantly, and the corners of his mouth lifted in a wide smile. "Elizabeth, forgive me for keeping you here. I was called away from Langaer, and I did not trust my men to keep their hands off you."

His gaze raked over her possessively. "Have you enough to eat?"

She nodded and forced a smile. "Considering I've been locked away for nearly two wee—a fortnight, I'm relatively well."

Richard frowned as he walked toward her. "Think you that I willingly put you here?"

"Why else would you have guards at my door day and night? Why else do I have an attendant that does not even let me relieve myself without standing on the other side of the garderobe?"

He stopped before her, his eyes drifting to her breasts. She was relieved to have changed from the squire's clothes into the beautiful gown, compliments of his sister he said, though the old crone had mentioned Richard's voluptuous leman being of a similar size. Lizzie felt immense relief knowing the man had a mistress to keep him busy at night.

He reached out, took a lock of her hair and brought it to his nose. He inhaled deeply. "Lavender. 'Tis said you like the herb added to your bath. I am pleased you prepare yourself for me."

Lizzie flinched. How like a man to think she got freshened up for him. The only reason she insisted on a bath every day was to fill her time, and to hope the lavender would put her mind at rest to where she could finally sleep. Yet nightmares had kept her awake, and memories of her short time with Kieran made sleep almost as much of a nightmare. Thoughts of her fierce Norman knight filled her, causing her heart to ache yet again with the immense loss.

"Why do you frown, Elizabeth?"

Lizzie jerked her gaze back to his and forced a smile. "I'm sorry, Richard. I'm just bored. I've seen nothing but these four walls for nearly a fortnight. I don't understand why you keep me here, locked away, especially now that you're back at Langaer."

He lifted her chin with his fingers and bent to kiss her. She tensed, and seeing his brow furrow, she forced herself to relax. She lifted her chin to be more accommodating.

Richard smiled, and then his mouth slanted across hers. His lips were dry, and when he passed his cold tongue along the seam of her lips, she winced, but opened slightly.

He groaned low in his throat and pulled her up against him, grinding his erection against her. "Would that I could take you to our marriage bed right now," he whispered against her lips.

Revulsion swept through her and she abruptly put him at arm's length. "You forget we are not alone." She glanced toward the old woman who watched them intently, an amused grin on her haggard face.

"Ah, yes. Margaret," he said, releasing Lizzie. "You have been relieved of your duties for the day."

The old woman nodded, put her embroidery into a bag and left, shutting the door behind her. Lizzie became abruptly aware they were alone, and Richard took the opportunity to pounce.

He pulled her into his arms, kissing her fiercely, his tongue darting into her mouth, prodding her to return his kiss. With hesitance, she did, but she hated it. The man had no technique—all teeth and lots of slobber.

Despite her attempts at pretending to like his kiss, Lizzie pushed away from him. "Where is Olivier?"

Richard's eyes were dark with lust, his gaze devouring her. He grabbed her by the wrist, his fingers biting into her flesh. She winced, but didn't cry out. It was what he wanted, and she refused to give him the pleasure. His eyes brightened and she knew his rough treatment of her excited him.

"Where is Olivier?" she asked again.

He pulled her close, his gaze intense, his fingers tightening further. "What is the boy to you?"

She bit the inside of her cheek to keep from crying out. A second later she said in a cool voice, "I have told you. He is my friend."

He lifted his brows. "The boy is too pretty. He has even gained the affections of my sister, who nearly swoons whenever he comes near."

Lizzie hid a smile. Olivier would no doubt send many hearts beating, and he was still a young man. She had little doubt he would break his share of hearts one day. "Where is he? I have not seen him in the fields with the others."

"You look for him?" His tone was lethal. "'Tis unsettling you are so infatuated with the boy, Elizabeth. Do I need to worry about your obsession?"

She clamped her lips together, knowing she had already said too much. If his sister liked Olivier, then he would probably be safe. "I am so bored I have taken to staring out the window all hours of the day for having naught else to do. I am like a caged bird. I know no one else here, save for you and Olivier."

She saw the relief flash across his face before he masked it. If she could set his mind at ease, then maybe she would have a chance to get out and find Olivier. That would be the first step to escaping.

A knock sounded at the door.

"Who's there?" Richard asked.

"'Tis Betty. The one you asked for."

"Ah yes. Betty." Richard took Elizabeth's hand and brought it to his lips. "I've brought you a present. A woman who has vast knowledge of herbs and oils. Since Margaret told me of your interest in the healing arts, I thought you would enjoy this Betty as a companion. She will show you much."

Lizzie grinned, thrilled Richard would be leaving. Maybe this Betty would be a better companion than Margaret. Or better yet, an older woman prone to drinking. Whatever the case, Lizzie hoped the woman was not as loyal to her liege lord, and might even help her escape. "Thank you, Richard."

"'Twould please me for you to know the way of healing. In these times of war we have great need of such a gift. And who better to heal the people of Langaer than their lady."

She managed to keep smiling, when she wanted nothing more than to tell him to get the hell out already.

"Now, I have things to attend to." He kissed her soundly, then put her from him. "I would that our wedding night was this eve. I await word from King William. God willing, we will hear soon. How my loins burn to take you to my bed." He glanced down at his erection that strained against his braies and tunic.

Lizzie kept her gaze level with his chest, having already felt the erection, she certainly didn't need to look at it.

"I want you, Elizabeth."

For the love of God would the man just leave!

He sighed heavily, then walked toward the door and opened it. A woman carrying a large black bag walked in wearing a dark, threadbare cloak that covered her small frame. The door shut behind her and Lizzie approached her. The woman slipped out of her cloak and Lizzie gasped.

"Hello, Lizzie."

It was the woman from the exhibition hall!

The woman who had given her Kieran's sword stood before her in the flesh. She wore an old woolen kirtle, stained and well worn. Her big eyes twinkled with merriment and her frizzy white hair stood on end, looking ridiculous. Lizzie didn't know whether to laugh or cry. She hugged her.

"You've gotten yourself into quite a pickle, haven't you?" Betty said, keeping her voice low.

Tears clogged Lizzie's throat and she nodded.

Betty put her at arm's length. "We have much to discuss, but first I have to put forth a question and you must answer me in all truthfulness, for there are no second chances. You can leave this time without looking back. You will return to the future just as you were. Your mind will be a blank slate. Kieran and all of this," she motioned to the room, "will not have existed."

To be able to forget about Kieran's death and the horrible Richard who would marry her and do god knows what with her. Leaving would be a godsend, yet...

"What of Olivier?"

Betty lifted her brows. "What of him? His fate is sealed, Lizzie. You have done all you can for the boy."

Her shoulders slumped. "I haven't done enough."

"Lizzie, the only reason he lives now is because you made it possible. Once you are Richard's bride, he will dispose of Olivier, just as he will all Normans under his roof. He is threatened by all who are not Saxon. His hatred runs deep, and he wants nothing standing in his way to get to you. He feels Olivier is an obstacle to overcome."

Images of Olivier rose before her and Lizzie had her answer. "I have to stay."

Betty took a step closer. "You will never get another chance to return to your time. It is now or never."

Memories of her short time here filled Lizzie's mind. Kieran, Olivier, Mary, Hugh, the other knights, the serfs, villagers—they were a tight-knit family. So very different from the introverted, lonely life she'd lived in her own time.

Now or never.

A lifetime in this century without Kieran? What would become of her? She had endured the change in time because she had loved Kieran so much. She could go back to her life as though nothing had happened…back to her lonely existence where she worked seventy to eighty hours a week, ate frozen dinners, and chatted with friends on the Internet from time to time.

Suddenly the answer was clear.

This was her home now. She must think of all the people of Aedelmaer who she had come to love.

"I need your final word, Lizzie. I need to know right now."

Lizzie took a deep breath. "I want to stay."

Betty smiled. "As you wish." She dug into her bag and produced a vial of amber liquid.

"What's that?"

"Tonight, when the food is brought up, we will use this to drug the guards. They will both sleep until morning. Richard takes his leman to bed each night, and I will make sure that he has a potion to make him randier than usual—the woman as well. The two of them will spend the night in each other's arms, and God willing, we will all be safely back at Aedelmaer before they wake."

"All? You mean Olivier?"

"Hugh lives. He is to die on the morrow—death by hanging. Lord Richard desires his head to be impaled on a pike and displayed as warning to all Normans that he will not abide their treachery."

Lizzie nearly fell to her knees with relief. Hugh lived! She owed the man a *huge* apology for doubting him.

* * * * *

A few hours later the knock came. "Your tray is here, milady," a guard shouted from the other side of the door.

Betty who had been boiling herbs, poured the contents of the pot into two goblets, and nodded for Lizzie to open the door. She did as asked, and a page walked in, a boy of about nine who went directly to Betty's side. He placed the tray next to her, pulled a tunic, braies, chausses, and hat from his surcoat, and laid them on the table. With a nod, he took the goblets from Betty, and a vial, which he put inside his shoe…along with a handful of coins. He left as quickly as he appeared. Lizzie knew without asking that the clothing was for her.

"Now, we must hope the guards drink up."

Within an hour the guards snored outside the door. Betty, who stood near the window, called Lizzie over. "Look there," she said, pointing toward the hall where Richard strode across the bailey with his leman tossed over his shoulder. The woman's lusty giggles filled the night. "They will be occupied for some time to come. Let us wait and see."

Another hour passed in silence. Finally, when Betty thought it safe, she opened the door and the two of them tiptoed over the guards sprawled on the landing, and raced down the stairwell.

Instinct told her to turn right at the bottom of the stairs. Laughter rang out, and she had a feeling the Hall was nearby. Betty grabbed her arm, and whispered, "I will meet you at the clearing near the Witches' Elm." The Witches' Elm had been aptly named — an enormous tree with huge, sprawling branches that appeared like arms, and a huge round hole in the trunk that resembled a person screaming. Ironically, Richard had pointed it out on the way to Langaer.

"We'll be there. Good luck, Betty."

"God be with you, my dear." Without another word, Betty melted into the night.

Lizzie took a deep breath, and entered the bailey. Dressed in the page's too small clothing, she hoped she would pass as a young man. Kieran had seen through her squire's clothing, yet she hoped that these people wouldn't look close enough to figure it out. Thankfully, Richard was indisposed and would be for the rest of the night.

The hall bristled with activity. The voice of the herald telling a story of heroic strength and valor against Norman foes rang loud over the great hall. Every once in a while the crowd would clap and laugh at the feats the man spoke of. He mentioned a fair-haired Saxon princess and Lizzie had a feeling they spoke of her. They wouldn't think she was so fair when they realized she had escaped.

She slipped into the crowded room, standing beside a young page that looked no more than six years of age. He smiled at her, then turned his attention back to the herald.

Lizzie scanned the room, her gaze frantically searching for Olivier. With every minute that passed, she began to panic. Time was of the essence. The faster they made their escape, the better chance they would have of getting to Aedelmaer.

Then she remembered Richard's remarks and looked to the dais, where Richard's sister would sit. There on the far corner sat a girl of about three and ten. She sat on the edge of her seat, looking out into the crowd—not at the herald who gained all other attention. Elizabeth followed the girl's gaze and found it directed on Olivier. He stood near a table, holding a jug in his hands. Someone snapped their fingers and he went to do their bidding. His face was an alarming white tinged with gray, and his already lanky build looked even frailer. Dark half-circles made the green of his eyes brighter, and his blond hair looked dark and stringy. Her heart lurched. What had happened to him these past two weeks…and how could she gain his attention?

He poured the drink then returned to his place near the wall. He leaned back, his head resting against the stone.

Look at me, Olivier. Look at me. She stared at Olivier, willing him to look her way. He glanced toward the dais, obviously catching the girl's stare. She could not read his expression, but she did catch the telling blush that raced up his cheeks. He quickly looked away from the girl, his gaze wandering her way, skipping over her—and then ripped abruptly back to her.

The jug nearly slipped from his fingers before he caught himself. He stood ramrod straight, his gaze shifting from hers to the dais. The girl's brow furrowed as she looked to the far wall where Lizzie stood. She took a step back into the shadows, hoping the girl had not seen her.

Lizzie took a deep breath and made her way toward the back of the hall. She grabbed a jug off a table and filled a goblet or two along the way, not wanting to draw attention to herself in any way.

From time to time, she glanced at the dais to find Richard's young sister's gaze still riveted on Olivier. Thankfully, the herald had made his way to the girl's side of the dais, blocking a good portion of the lower tables from view.

Lizzie finished filling a goblet when she looked up and found Olivier on the opposite side of the table filling a cup. Their eyes met and she glanced at the doors toward the back of the Hall, near the servants entrance, then turned in that direction and made haste.

It was up to him now. He had to follow…preferably while the herald stood in Richard's sister's way.

He did not disappoint her. Within minutes he appeared, visibly shaking. "Milady, I had heard you were not well."

"I'm fine, Olivier. You are a sight for sore eyes, my friend."

He smiled and she gave him a quick hug. "Come on. We have to hurry to the Witches' Elm. Betty and Sir Hugh await us."

"Sir Hugh!" he said, wincing when he realized he had all but yelled the words. Assured that no one could hear Olivier over the herald's booming voice, Lizzie grabbed Olivier's hand and started for the bailey. Soon she was running to keep up to Olivier's long strides. A knight stood guard, and another stood not ten feet away. All around the wooden palisade it went— soldiers on alert. Lizzie focused on the closed gate.

"Where do you go, squires?" a voice boomed from above in the wooden tower. Three men stood lookout in the small structure overhead.

Olivier squeezed her hand, and Lizzie said, "Our master has had too much ale this night. He asks us to get his favorite woman who lives in the village. Please lower the bridge."

The knight and his cohorts eyed her keenly. Could they see through her disguise? He signaled to the man below. Lizzie held her breath as they waited for the bridge to lower.

Feeling the soldiers' eyes on them all the way down the rutted road, Lizzie wanted nothing more than to run, but waited until the castle was no longer in sight. She heard someone yell.

"Run!" she yelled, and they ran for their lives.

Chapter Six

Kieran sat atop his horse, his mouth set in a grim line. Richard had taken more from him than just the lives of ten of his best men. He had taken his wife, and for that he would pay dearly.

Aye, though he might be weak from the loss of blood and fever that had ravaged his body this past fortnight, he was strong of mind and he burned with the need for revenge.

He prayed that God would see to it that Elizabeth lived through the ordeal. A Saxon peasant had told one of his men that she had been kept in a tower room and had not been out since. Did she live, or did Richard deem her as traitor and deny her food and drink? Elizabeth had lasted a long time before without nourishment, yet her body had not returned to normalcy that long ago. His insides churned. What had been her fate at Langaer? Had she been alone for all this time?

"Milord, someone comes."

He glanced at his vassal and dismounted. The sound of footsteps came closer. Whoever it was, they were in a hurry and they were headed straight into their trap.

A man leaned heavily on an old woman, his hair matted to his head. His clothes as filthy as the rest of him. Kieran sat up straighter, a twinge of recognition setting in, and one he did not want to give to hope, lest he be disappointed.

The woman spotted them first. She hesitated, then looking straight at Kieran, she grinned widely, like an old friend.

He relaxed. No foe was this.

"'Tis your man—Sir Hugh," the woman confirmed, a kind smile on her face.

Kieran dismounted and rushed forward. At his approach the man's eyes opened, the familiar light eyes stared back at him in disbelief. "Do my eyes deceive me? I thought I was alive, and yet I stare upon the face of my liege lord, Baron D'Arcy. A man I was told died nearly a fortnight ago. Tell me, are you real?" Tears pooled in the other man's eyes and Kieran put his hand on his trusted vassal's shoulder.

Hugh cried out and embraced Kieran tightly. "Milord! I thought you dead."

Though Kieran was not one to show his emotions, his throat tightened as he awkwardly patted the younger knight on the back in reassurance. "Aye, it is I, D'Arcy, and we are both very much alive, my friend." He put Hugh at arm's length.

The man had tears streaming down his face, but he quickly snapped to attention. "Milord, I have heard rumors that your lady wife is held in the tower. I could not escape the dungeon to free her. They had me under guard constantly."

"You did well by staying alive."

"What of Olivier?"

"Olivier is at Langaer?" Hugh looked shocked. "I swear I know nothing of the boy. I've heard only rumors of your lady…and the upcoming wedding."

Kieran bristled. "The wedding?"

Hugh nodded. "Aye, Lord Richard seeks to take Elizabeth as his wife."

Kieran hissed in a breath. "By God, I will kill him with my bare hands."

The old woman stepped forward. A tiny thing she was, reaching barely to Kieran's chest. Her shocking white hair stood on end, and he would have been amused under any other circumstances. No matter the woman's amusing appearance, he could kiss her for risking her life to save his vassal. "Listen to me, Kieran. Richard believes you to be dead—but soon he will learn the truth, and he will stop at nothing to make Elizabeth his."

"He does not know me very well then, does he?"

The woman smiled. "Nay, he does not. Fear not, Lord D'Arcy. Your woman comes to you now—even as we speak."

Hope flared within Kieran's chest. "How do you know this?"

"I had been hired to watch over Elizabeth in the tower. Together we drugged the guards. My duty was to get Sir Hugh from the dungeon, while she found Olivier."

In truth, Kieran could strangle Elizabeth for risking her neck in order to save his squire, yet he admired her for her courage. "If she is kept prisoner, how can she walk about the bailey without risking her life?"

"She is dressed as a page."

"'Twould appear your wife enjoys dressing in male attire, milord," a knight behind him interjected, his voice laced with humor.

"She comes," the woman said, and true to her word, not a minute later, around the bend came Olivier—with Elizabeth flung over his shoulder. Kieran's heart dropped. An arrow arose from her back.

He raced to the pair, and immediately took Elizabeth from Olivier. "What happened?"

Olivier's eyes were wide as he stared open-mouthed looking at Kieran as though he were a ghost. Obviously the boy thought he'd not survived the ambush. Suddenly an enormous grin came to the young man features, but he sobered instantly. "Milord, the guards called out, and we ran. The next I knew arrows pierced her and she fell. I picked her up and ran. I do not know how far we came, but they will be in pursuit, of that I'm certain."

Elizabeth's head rolled back on her shoulders, and Kieran gingerly handed her over to one of his man-at-arms while he mounted, then reached out for her. Once he had her seated as comfortably as possible, he motioned for them to head toward Aedelmaer.

* * * * *

Lizzie dreamt that she had been hitched to a post and been given a hundred lashings while Richard watched. He stood, arms crossed over his chest, looking down at her with disdain. "Norman whore!" he yelled, along with the other Saxons who threw rotten cabbage at her. Horrible man!

She threw the blankets off of her. Damn, it was hot! Had Richard burned her alive as well?

She struggled against the bindings that held her pinned down.

"Shush," a familiar whisper crooned. "Milady, 'tis but a dream."

Lizzie tried to open her eyes but her lids were too heavy. She shifted abruptly and cried out from the pain that lanced through her back.

"She cries again, milord. She is talking gibberish." Mary's voice came from the blackness. "I will prepare another draught."

A large hand stroked her brow. "Elizabeth, milady wife, wake up."

His voice! His beautiful voice! She was in heaven. She had died, and she was in heaven with her Kieran.

She opened her eyes slowly, blinking against the brightness. The room spun, and she tried in earnest to focus.

Thankfully, the bright light diminished, and was soon replaced by the illumination of a single candle.

"Elizabeth?" Kieran's precious voice called out to her.

When her eyes finally focused, she consumed Kieran like a drunkard who craved drink. He looked gaunt, dark shadows beneath his blue eyes, and his already high cheekbones seemed even more pronounced. In her eyes he'd never looked so good "Am I in heaven?"

He smiled, his white teeth flashing in the dark room. "Milady, though you have been ill for a while. I assure you, you are not in heaven."

She glanced around the room, then at Mary whose eyes were filled with tears, and then finally looked at Kieran. This was real! Real! She threw her arms open and with a chuckle he went into them, laying his head against her breast.

Trembling, she pulled him close, dropping her chin on his head, inhaling the rich masculine scent that she had longed for since she thought him dead.

"Your heart hammers inside your chest, milady," he said, lifting his face to hers, and she stared at him, taking her fill.

"I never thought I'd see you again," she said, her voice cracking with the depth of emotion she felt for him.

He kissed her lightly. "We are both alive, Elizabeth. Both of us have outwitted the Saxon arrows and survived."

All the pain and anguish of the past weeks built up within her and she let it out. Kieran shifted to where he now held her in his arms while she gave in to her pain, frustration and happiness at having him back from the dead. Never had she been so happy, never had she felt so lucky. She could not get close enough to him, or listen long enough to the steady pounding of his heart beneath her ear.

When finally she had cried herself out, she looked up at him. "The next time I tell you I feel something is wrong, will you listen to me?"

He smiled softly, and taking both her hands within his own, kissed her knuckles. "Aye, I promise. Forgive me for not believing you. I felt your tale farfetched and I paid for that distrust with the life of my soldiers. You even risked your own life for my squire — who is most anxious to see you. In fact, he lingers beyond yonder door, waiting for word of your recovery."

Lizzie didn't want to let go. It was too soon. "Hold me a minute longer."

He laughed under his breath, and held her tight, his hand running up the length of her back, away from the wound. The touch reminded her that they had been apart for too long. Already she wanted him, despite the fact she had been wounded.

She lifted her face to his and he kissed her softly, but she would have none of it. She opened her mouth, her tongue thrusting against the seam of his lips. He pulled away. "Nay, milady. There will be time for that when you have healed. For now you will rest and recover."

He eased her back on the bed, and after making sure she was comfortable, he strode for the door. Her heart filled with love and intense happiness. "Thank you, God," she whispered.

"Do you wish to see him now, or later?" he asked, his dark brow quirked in the way she loved.

In truth, she was as anxious to see Olivier as he was to see her. "Send him in."

A second later Olivier walked into the dark room, his expression reserved. He came within a few feet of the bed and stopped. He nodded. "Milady."

Always so formal. She reached out a hand to him. "Come here, Olivier."

He hesitated, but did her bidding, taking her hand within his own. She felt him trembling. "What's wrong?"

"I thought you would not survive." His voice cracked and he coughed to hide it. If she wasn't mistaken she saw the light sheen of tears in his beautiful green eyes. Lizzie could not believe such a reaction was for her. She was touched by his concern and if possible he had just wedged himself even further into her heart.

"Would that I had taken the arrow in the back, I would have, milady. Gladly." He lowered his head. "I should have shielded you."

She pulled him down beside her. Sitting up against the headboard, she winced against the sharp pain. Olivier moved to help her.

"The only way you could have saved me was if you had eyes in the back of your head."

The sides of his mouth curved into a smile.

She punched him lightly on the arm, the slight movement sending a twinge straight to her back, but she smiled despite the pain. "You saved my life, Olivier. Even a noble knight could not have done more."

Two bright spots of color appeared on his cheeks. "Forgive me, milady. I doubted you for a while. I did not want to believe you had deceived Baron D'Arcy...yet I heard you were to marry Lord Richard. I thought you did not come to the hall because of me. I thought that you were too busy preparing for your wedding to give me any mind. I thought that you had forgotten me...and D'Arcy's memory."

She knew what it cost for him to say those words. They were not easy, and she had to confess she was surprised he had felt so deceived. Yet how could he not? The last time he'd seen her Lizzie was practically throwing herself at Richard. "Do you remember my words to you in the woods that day, Olivier?"

He nodded. "You said to stay alive."

"And you did. And now I live because of you." She squeezed his hand. "A more trusted squire D'Arcy could never have."

His face lit up at her compliment and she hugged him tight. She knew she could not love Olivier more had he been her own child. In that moment she felt like the luckiest woman alive. Her beloved husband was alive and she and Olivier had made it back to Aedelmaer. She had everything she wanted or needed right here.

The door opened and Kieran stuck his head in. "Olivier, let us take our leave and let my wife rest."

Olivier jumped to his feet. "Thank you, milady," he said, a genuine smile coming to his lips. Lizzie relaxed, knowing the old Olivier had returned.

Olivier strode toward the door in long strides, sharing a smile with Kieran who shut the door behind the younger man. Kieran leaned back against the thick door with a contented smile. "I have work to attend to, but I will visit you this evening."

Heat raced through her body, swooping low into her belly and between her legs. Her gaze ran over the length of him. She wished he could stay with her now, fill her with his great length. "Will you sleep with me tonight?"

He shook his head, despite the fire she saw in his eyes. "Nay, I would not hurt you."

"I don't ask you to ravage me. I just want to feel you in my arms. I want to feel the curve of your body against mine."

The side of his mouth lifted. "Aye, Elizabeth. I will come to you tonight, but only to sleep."

"Okay," she said, smiling, content to know that he would be back to hold her in his arms...and there was nowhere else she'd rather be.

Chapter Seven

Kieran took the stairs two at a time, his heart pounding in his ears. It had been not even two weeks since Elizabeth had escaped from Langaer. She had been abed for all that time. Mary had assured him Elizabeth had improved, and in truth she seemed to look better with each day.

Yet Mary had just summoned him to his bedchamber saying that Elizabeth needed him immediately.

He had asked the maid if she had taken to fever, but Mary only urged him to hurry. The guard keeping watch at the chamber door came to attention.

Kieran nodded and flung open the door to the bedchamber. The room was swathed in darkness; the bed drapes were pulled all the way around the bed, a flicker of a candle shone from within.

He frowned. What madness was this? He shut the door behind him and approached the bed, wary. "Elizabeth?" he said to the darkness.

There was no reply.

He reached out, took hold of the velvet hanging, and pulled it open.

His breath left him in a rush seeing his beautiful wife lying on the furs completely naked, a single candle illuminating her soft skin. His gaze shifted from the coy smile on her face, over her tightly budded nipples, over the smooth skin of her stomach, and lower still to the thatch of pale curls that guarded her most treasured prize.

With a groan, he ripped off his tunic, braies and boots, and climbed into the bed. He pulled the drape behind him, enclosing them in a world where only the two of them existed.

Her arms wound around him and her lips tentatively touched his. Though his body wanted instant gratification, he knew he had to take it slow and gentle for her sake. She had been through much these past weeks, and her body still mended.

Oh, but she felt good. He had held himself in check for so long, not wanting to hurt her. Now he could finally hold her naked body in his arms, stroke her soft flesh, and take her beneath him. His cock flooded with a need that made him tremble. He would make love to her until neither one of them could stand.

Her tongue stroked his, darting in and out. Her greedy mouth left his, drawing kisses against his jaw, and down his neck where the pulse beat rapidly.

His cock reared between them, as hard as steel and Elizabeth smiled down at him. "Now, milord. I want to try something. Lay back."

He did her bidding, saying nothing as she turned and straddled his chest, her back to him, her heart-shaped bottom just inches from his chin. He knew what she was about as she lowered her head and touched her tongue to the tip of his rearing cock. He almost bucked her off him. She clamped his thighs down with her hands and laughed, and then took him into her mouth.

With a groan, he lifted her hips so she was up on her knees and open to him. He licked her sweet folds, so open and accommodating to him. Her musky scent exhilarated his senses and he laved, while keeping his own hips pinned to the bed. Not the easiest of tasks when she took half his cock into her mouth, licking and sucking until he wanted to roar.

His hands clenched on the backs of her thighs as her mouth brought his cock near to bursting. When her mouth found his balls he about bucked her off again, but her hands tightened on his thighs.

"That's it, Elizabeth, give it to me," he said, before running his tongue over her sweet wet cleft.

They were the wrong words. While he teased the tiny nub of pleasure with his tongue, she sucked his balls hard, while squeezing his cock in her hand, stroking him into a frenzy.

With a curse, he grasped her waist and urged her up onto all fours. He went up on his knees behind her, his cock rearing as she arched her back and glanced over her shoulder at him. He leaned over her back, rubbing his hard length against her slick folds. She lifted her buttocks, prompting him to take her. Through the curtain of her hair, he could see the scar that marred her graceful shoulder. He kissed the wound gently, wishing he could take away the pain — and the mark.

He slipped inside her with a satisfied moan, filling her until he touched her womb. He closed his eyes and released a sigh. Finally! How long had he thought of this moment?

His hands found her breasts, teasing the diamond-hard peaks until she squirmed against him, her hot sheath clamping against him with each thrust. He tried to maintain a slow rhythm but she would have none of it. One hand trailed down her soft stomach, to the soft downy hair of her sex, and found the sensitive nub there. He stroked her softly, slowly, enjoying the soft groans coming from Elizabeth, the sound of his name on her lips, whispered in that husky tone he loved. He applied more pressure, his fingers teasing the swollen pearl. Her thighs opened wider and she lifted her hips, urging him on. Then her channel squeezed his cock tight, pulsing around his length as she climaxed hard. Holding her hips tight he thrust two more times and followed her over the edge.

She collapsed on the bed and he fell beside her. He went up on his elbow and looked down at his wife. One arm flung out to her side, the other lay on her stomach. Her face was flushed, her smile wide as she looked over at him.

"Vixen," he muttered, pulling her up against his length. "You have bewitched me."

She kissed him softly. "And you have ruined me for any other man."

He laughed under his breath and pulled her close. "Good. That was my plan all along."

* * * * *

Lizzie woke early in the morning, and immediately glanced at the man by her side.

Kieran.

Her heart constricted with love and desire. Last night they had made love like crazed people. It had been glorious, beautiful, and in the end, she had wept like a baby, grateful that God had given her this gorgeous man. Kieran had misunderstood her tears, thinking he had hurt her. When she told him that she cried from happiness, he had wrapped his arms around her and hugged her tight to his body, telling—and showing her, how much he cared for her. Cared, but did he love her as she loved him? He had yet to say the words.

"Come here, wife," he muttered, and she glanced at him, surprised to find him awake when he'd been sleeping so soundly.

"I didn't mean to wake you."

"How could I sleep with all that sighing?" He laughed under his breath.

She pursed her lips. "Is Olivier old enough to be a knight?"

Kieran groaned. "Elizabeth, you will not interfere with my affairs. Olivier is my squire until I see fit to make him a knight."

"But he's almost eighteen.

He sat up on an elbow. "You speak of another man while in bed with your husband?" He pulled her closer, and she snuggled up to his warmth and hard body.

"You know I think of Olivier like my own child. He risked his life for me."

"Aye, I know that." He wound a lock of her hair around his finger and brought it to his nose where he inhaled deeply. "You mentioned once that when we have a son you hope he is just like Olivier."

Lizzie nodded, hoping her infertility hadn't followed her into this century.

Kieran's gaze held hers. "I would like that as well."

She grinned, knowing what it had cost him to say those words. "He adores you."

Kieran's brows furrowed. "Truly?"

"Uh, yeah!" Lizzie laughed at his bewildered expression. The man thought too little of himself, clearly. "He thinks you walk on water."

He pressed his arousal against her. "And what does my lady wife think of me?"

She shook her head. "I think you are insatiable, milord, and that's just fine with me."

Lifting her thigh over his, he rubbed his cock against her wet cleft and slipped inside of her, his smile wicked as he filled her completely. She moaned in her throat as he moved in and out of her in tight, quick strokes. He reached between their bodies, his fingers finding her clit, which he stroked gently, tracing circles around it, then lifting it, teasing it mercilessly.

His other hand found her breast and he pulled on a nipple, squeezing it lightly between forefinger and thumb.

Elizabeth pressed against him as his fingers kept up the stroking and his cock moved in and out of her, so slowly she wanted to scream.

She urged him to quicken the pace, but he stilled her with a hand to her hip, his fingers making circles along the skin there. His lips moved to her ear, tracing the lobe with his tongue, laving the inside until she moaned low in her throat.

His hand moved to the other breast, taking the nipple between his fingers, rolling it. Her body tightened and she pressed against him, biting into his shoulder as the climax overtook her. "That's it, Elizabeth, reach for the stars."

She turned her head slightly and he kissed her, his tongue stroking hers. If only he would whisper that he loved her, that he had to have her with the same intensity she felt for him. His body tightened and she watched his face as he lengthened his strokes. His eyes, dark and heavy-lidded, were of a man pushed to the brink of desire. With a growl he pushed her onto her back and thrust deep into her. Her body quickened in response to the desire she saw in his eyes, and to the feel of his massive cock stretching her.

Digging her heels into the bed she arched against him, and she touched the stars.

* * * * *

Richard walked the length of the great hall. He had been made a fool by a slip of a woman and that hated Norman, D'Arcy, a man he had left for dead on a cold night not even a month ago. He should have sliced the man in two himself to make sure the job had been done.

Now, because of his archer's negligence, Richard had lost not only his prisoner, the Norman knight Hugh de Vesli, and his bride, but also the man who had taken the fair Elizabeth and made her his whore.

His spy who had infiltrated the Norman's lair at Aedelmaer had returned to the castle telling stories of Elizabeth, a woman so enraptured with her husband she rarely let him out of her sight. If what he heard was the truth, D'Arcy in return could not keep his hands off his wife. Once his spy had come upon D'Arcy and Elizabeth making love in a small alcove outside the Great Hall, and this while supper was going on. According to the spy, the two could not keep their hands off each other as the baron had taken her against the gray, cold stones, stilling Elizabeth's cries with his mouth.

Upon the telling Richard had shook with his fury, imagining the dirty Norman's hands on the woman who from birth had been slated just for him. Elizabeth had not escaped to Langaer that night. She had gone with D'Arcy. No doubt she could not stand to be kept away from her lover who kept her happy night and day. She probably lay in their chamber with legs spread wide just waiting for D'Arcy to return from his duties even now.

The slut!

And here he'd had Elizabeth within his reach. He had kept her under lock and key, fearful what his men would do. He thought she had *endured* the Norman's touch. In truth, the woman had the heart of a whore in a lady's body. Had he known then what he knew now, he would have taken her like the slut she was. His cock reared at the thought of the luscious Elizabeth lying on the bed, her pale blonde hair spread out on his pillow, her long legs spread wide for him.

She was a harlot, a woman that liked to be taken as a whore in the dark hallways of the Norman's castle. The spy had even heard rumors that Elizabeth and Kieran had rutted on the table in the baker's hut! By god, the stories that had burned his ears. The woman was shameless.

He glanced over at the servants busying the tables for the meal. His leman was not among them. She no doubt was at her mother's in the village. He spied a serf, dressed in a russet wool gown, filling glasses with a large jug. His gaze shifted over her rounded hips and full bosom. She glanced up, caught his hot stare and smiled. Richard glanced over his shoulder, and seeing none of his men about, he motioned her to follow him.

She met him just outside the door and he grabbed her hand and dragged her into the stables. His cock pulsed as she stepped out of the rough gown, displaying huge breasts with coral-colored nipples. Though she did not have a pretty face, her body pleased him and when he untied his braies and unleashed his shaft, she gasped in delight.

There would be no time for preliminaries. His need was too great, and the woman seemed not to care as she lay on the straw, her legs wide open. He fell on her, impaling her.

He closed his eyes, envisioning the lady Elizabeth beneath him, her blue eyes staring up at him, her sweet pink lips open in awe as he plunged into her time and again.

The servant cried out again and again, and Richard imagined it was Elizabeth crying out his name, her soft whimpers urging him on. The louder her moans, the harder his cock, until her sheath clenched around him and he came with a groan.

He rolled off the servant, pulled up his braies, and stormed out of the stables, swearing that next time it *would* be Elizabeth of Aedelmaer beneath him.

Chapter Eight

Lizzie wept with happiness as Olivier, dressed in resplendent white robes, knelt to take his oath of knighthood.

Kieran bent to whisper in her ear, "Milady, you do him an injustice by crying. Do not treat him as the boy you knew, but with the respect of the man he has become."

Lizzie lifted her chin and choked back the tears. Kieran was right. Olivier was not a child. He was a man—and this was his eighteenth birthday.

Kieran cleared his throat and looked down at Olivier with a smile. "Be thou brave and upright that God may love thee and remember that thou springest from a race that can never be false."

Olivier replied, "So shall I, with God's help."

Kieran was handed his sword and Olivier kissed the tip before it was placed on the top of his head, then the left shoulder, and then the right. "In honor of the Father, and the Son, and the Holy Ghost, I create thee a knight."

The ritual ended with Olivier executing feats of knighthood that left the other knights applauding. It was a proud moment for the young knight, and for them all.

The feast that night gave everyone a reason for celebration. Elizabeth toasted their newest and bravest knight, along with Hugh who stood nearby, looking fitter than he had since returning to Aedelmaer. Lizzie, still feeling horrible for having doubted Kieran's vassal, asked for a moment of his time.

The knight obliged, and extended his arm. They walked out into the bailey, the sounds of the celebration still boisterous behind them. "I feel I have done you a great injustice."

Hugh frowned. "You could never do me an injustice, milady."

"I doubted your loyalty to my husband."

He looked stricken but said nothing.

"I had a...dream that you killed Kieran and I told him about it."

"Olivier said that Richard wore my armor and flew the colors of D'Arcy." He shrugged. "Mayhap you saw a vision?"

She stopped in mid-stride and he turned to look down at her. "Whatever the case, I'm sorry. I was wrong, and I ask your forgiveness."

He opened his mouth to deny her and she shook her head. He smiled and nodded. "Very well, milady. You are forgiven."

She released the breath she'd unconsciously been holding. "Thank you."

"Your husband watches us," Hugh said with a mischievous smile. "I wonder if he does not trust his vassal. What think you, milady?"

From the corner of her eye, Lizzie made out the wide shoulders of her husband as he leaned against the wall of the great hall. Knowing he watched intently, she went up on her tiptoes and kissed Hugh on the cheek.

And Kieran was at her side before her feet were flat on the ground.

"Elizabeth," he said curtly. She turned to find Kieran's face void of all humor.

"Thank you, Hugh," she said, and then took her husband's hand in her own.

Kieran glanced from her to Hugh then back again. To his credit, Hugh did not even crack a smile before departing in seemly haste.

"'What are you and Sir Hugh about?" Kieran asked, pulling her tight against him.

The feel of his hard body pressed flush against her sent a wave of longing through her. "Let's go to bed," Lizzie said, nudging him toward the manor.

His eyes brightened. "Elizabeth, what did you speak to Hugh about?"

"Are you jealous, milord?"

He shook his head, then stopped, and nodded.

She laughed. "I knew you were there when I kissed him."

Kieran frowned.

"I asked Hugh to forgive me for misjudging him, and he accepted. That's why I kissed him."

Relief flashed over Kieran's face. "I wondered if my wife had found favor with another knight."

All humor left her and she pulled his face down to hers. "No one could ever take your place. I am spoiled, milord. I want only you, forever and always."

His throat convulsed. "In truth?"

She nodded. "In truth."

"Saxons!" The word was yelled from the wooden watchtower, sending fear through Elizabeth's entire being.

Men already rushed out of the Hall, straight for the armory.

Kieran took her by the hand and started toward the overhead bridge. "You will stay in the tower until I send word it is safe."

They raced up the bridge, and Elizabeth made the mistake of looking over her shoulder beyond the palisade. More than a hundred torches lit up the countryside, a steady stream of men coming their way. There were so many. Richard must have commissioned other Saxon lords to help.

Inside the tower, Kieran lifted her in his arms and took the steps two at a time. In the bedchamber that was just about ready to be moved into, he set her on her feet. "Do not leave under any circumstances!" He started back for the door.

Fear raced through Lizzie, paralyzing her. She couldn't stand the thought of losing Kieran again. She couldn't live through it. "Kieran!"

He turned and she flew into his arms, kissing him with all the fear and longing she felt. "Come back to me."

His eyes were fierce, glowing. "Aye, I will, Elizabeth. I will send Mary to you, with some furs to keep you warm. Be quiet and do not make a sound."

She nodded.

He lifted her chin with gentle fingers. "Promise me you will not leave this room, no matter what happens."

She released a sigh. "I promise."

He nodded, and kissing her on the nose, left her staring at the door, wishing more than anything Richard would just go to hell — literally. Minutes ticked by feeling like hours, and Lizzie did the only thing she could. She prayed.

When Mary pounded on the door, Lizzie welcomed her in, taking the furs from her and laying them on the floor. They waited in silence, the sound of war came all around. Mary brushed her hair, and Lizzie was grateful for the comforting gesture, yet she couldn't block out the sounds of war outside. Closing her eyes, she prayed for Kieran, Olivier, Hugh, and all the Norman soldiers she had come to love like family.

She felt nothing but intense hatred toward Richard. He had proven to be a ruthless adversary in war. He had pledged homage to William, then betrayed him and all the surrounding barons who held the neighboring land. He was a traitor and would be treated as such. He should have considered himself lucky to have been able to keep his castle and some of his lands. Many Saxons had not been as lucky and had been stripped of all their holdings.

Richard would get his...he would die today because of his betrayal.

Outside the stairwell a man's voice shouted a warning. Lizzie stood, eyeing the door. Mary backed away and took hold of Lizzie's hand, a second later a body slammed against the heavy wood.

Someone or something pounded the wood yet again and again. At each strike Elizabeth jumped, waiting for the inevitable.

Where was Kieran?

Lizzie ran to the window, her gaze straying out over the bailey, looking for the familiar figure of her husband. Bodies lay littered all over the ground, a few soldiers still fought with bloody swords and battle-axes swinging.

"Milady, the door is splintering," Mary whispered.

The door gave way. "Elizabeth of Aedelmaer!" Richard roared.

Lizzie's stomach fell to her toes. What had happened to Kieran? How had Richard made it all the way to the tower without Kieran or any of his men stopping him?

Richard crossed the chamber. His expression lethal. "You have made me look a fool, woman." His lethal gaze raked over her, filled with loathing. "Norman slut!"

The words were said with bitter cruelty, but Lizzie didn't miss the heat in his eyes as he said it.

"What do you want?" she asked, squeezing Mary's hand tight.

He pushed Mary away from them. "Leave us!" he shouted, and Mary sent her an imploring look before fleeing.

Richard pulled Lizzie up against him, grinding his hard sex against her. "By the end of this day I will have you beneath me, Elizabeth, screaming my name. I hear you like spreading your legs for the Norman. Just think what it will be like with a real man."

She pushed against him, but his arms were like steel bands, holding her trapped to his side.

"Lord Richard, they come." The yell came from the hallway.

Lizzie prayed Kieran would be among the men heading in their direction. The clash of swords could be heard from outside the door, and then the guttural cry of a man. A heartbeat later Kieran entered the room. A trail of blood stained his cheek, nicks and cuts could be seen through his chain mail. Blood dripped from his sword. His blue gaze raked over Lizzie, as though checking to see she had no wounds. He met her gaze, and she tried to keep from shedding the tears that burned her eyes. His eyes implored her to stay strong.

"Richard, let her go. This matter is between you and I."

Richard released a hiss, his breath hot against Lizzie's neck. "Nay, 'tis not about you and I, D'Arcy." Richard's hand cupped one of Lizzie's breasts and he squeezed. "You took a woman who was to be my wife and made her into your whore! Aedelmaer and all that is hers belonged to me!"

Kieran flinched, the muscle in his jaw tensing, his eyes fierce. "Careful—the woman you speak of so crudely, and hold with such familiarity, is my wife." His voice and expression turned deadly.

Richard reached down, near Lizzie's hand, and it wasn't until he withdrew a knife and held it to her throat, did she realize to what lengths Richard would go in order to get revenge. "Nay, she is not your wife. Well, she will not be your wife soon."

Kieran frowned. "Pardon?"

"She will be widowed, and I will marry her, D'Arcy. While you burn in eternal hellfire, know that Elizabeth will be my wife...*my whore.*"

A movement sounded behind them, and Richard tensed. Lizzie chanced a glance over her shoulder and saw Olivier move with amazing speed. One minute he sat propped up on the high window, the next he stood behind Richard, sword pointed at his back.

Richard did not move. He had Normans on either side of him, and he knew his position was precarious. The only problem Lizzie could see was the knife probing at her throat.

"So this is the way of it," Richard said, his voice deadly calm.

Soldiers ran into the room swords drawn. All were Kieran's men, Hugh leading the way. Seeing Lizzie at knifepoint, Hugh looked to Kieran who shook his head.

"'Twould appear we are at an impasse. I have your lady wife, D'Arcy, yet you clearly have won this battle since you have me surrounded."

"Let her go. This is between the two of us," Kieran said, taking a step toward them.

The point of the knife pushed further into her skin, and Lizzie felt the small stream of blood run down her neck and onto her kirtle. She bit her lip against the pain and kept her gaze riveted on Kieran.

Kieran turned to his men. "Leave us."

"Milord," Hugh argued, his expression pleading.

Kieran silenced him with a look and the knight backed out of the room after the men-at-arms.

"Mayhap you can call off this boy who stands to skewer not only myself, but your lady as well." Richard's voice held a tinge of amusement. Strange considering the situation he found himself in. Even if he killed her, Richard would never survive.

"Olivier." Kieran motioned him over.

Olivier stayed out of arms reach as he stepped around Richard and Lizzie and went to stand near Kieran. "Tell the others that we will be in the bailey momentarily. There, Lord Richard and myself will fight to the death."

"Milord!" Olivier implored.

Kieran looked at him sharply. "Go!"

Olivier cast a helpless look in Lizzie's direction and raced for the door.

Richard relaxed his grip. "Do you give me your word that when you die by my hand, your men will allow me to take my leave—and take Elizabeth with me."

The muscle twitched in Kieran's jaw. His expression became lethal. "Yes." The words were said between clenched teeth.

"How do I know you speak the truth?"

Kieran's bright eyes pinned Richard to the spot. "Because it is my word. I would die before I break it."

Everything happened fast. In the blink of an eye, Richard, still holding Lizzie pinned to him, made his way down the steps.

Every Norman knight stood back, battle faces on as they passed. She knew each one would love to skewer the Saxon lord, but they were defenseless, their frustration evident on their faces.

Kieran marched ahead of them in long strides, Olivier at his side. Kieran tossed his helmet at the young man, then began peeling off his chain mail. By the time they reached the bailey, Kieran wore nothing save his braies and his boots. His heavily muscled body flexed as he took the sword Olivier handed him. He turned and waited for Richard.

"I will claim my prize when this is finished. We will leave this place and we will not look back. Do you understand, Elizabeth? I would as soon burn Aedelmaer to the ground than to live in this Norman swinehold!" Richard's words dripped venom. Lizzie thought he seemed overly confident, considering the fact he was outnumbered and surrounded by the enemy, his men having fled.

The Norman knights surrounded the bailey, in the middle of the circle stood Kieran. He was magnificent in his anger, his bright blue eyes glowing, furious, and Elizabeth shivered, afraid of what was to come.

"Do not worry for me, Elizabeth," Richard crooned against her ear. "Soon we will be together." He shoved her away, and she ran toward Hugh, who quickly pulled her aside to safety.

"D'Arcy!" A knight yelled, and soon the chant took on a life of its own as soldiers, serfs and freeman alike filled the bailey.

Richard peeled off his chain mail, until he too wore just braies and boots. His long and lean body lacked the width and breadth of Kieran's, though corded muscle rolled beneath the skin with each movement of the sword.

Lizzie held her breath. One man would die, and she would bear witness.

She said a quick prayer for Kieran. She could not bear to lose him a second time!

The two men circled each other, their bodies tense, weapons drawn. The chant around them died down now, with only an encouraging word here or there. Lizzie swallowed hard against the lump in her throat.

Richard lunged and attacked, and Kieran jumped out of the way, the blade missing him by inches. He retaliated with a thrust of his sword, catching Richard's elbow.

The Saxon smiled cruelly, wielded his sword with the same grace as Kieran. Richard gave a war cry, and then with a sweeping arc, brought the blade down upon Kieran's, the clash of metal sounding like thunder. Kieran wrenched the blade up and away from his body with his own sword, his muscles bulging beneath the skin, showing the great effort it took to hold off such a blow.

Richard kicked a leg out, sending Kieran onto his back.

Lizzie cried out involuntarily, and Kieran glanced at her. The move gave Richard enough time to attack. The sword came dangerously close to taking off Kieran's arm when he blocked it once again.

Richard fell upon Kieran, straddling his hips, wrenching his sword up to give a final thrust.

Kieran bucked him off, sending the smaller man flying. Lizzie bit her lip to keep from crying out again. She could not distract Kieran from the fight. He must concentrate solely on the fight since Richard was proving to be a worthy competitor.

Richard stood, his chest rising and falling with his deep breathing. Kieran didn't even look like he'd broken a sweat. In fact, her husband appeared to be feeling a spurt of energy since he wielded the sword in a graceful arc, then charged.

With a battle cry, Kieran brandied his sword expertly and managed to knock Richard off his feet and pin him to the ground. Kieran kneeled above his enemy, hands clasped around the hilt of the sword, ready for the deathblow. Lizzie closed her eyes.

"Finish it!" Hugh yelled at her side. Soon it became a chant that roared in her ears.

Feeling Kieran's gaze on her, she opened her eyes. She sensed his indecision as their gazes met and held. She mouthed the words, *I love you.*

Kieran shook with his hatred, his enemy beneath him, his sword inches from sending him to hell. He looked up at Elizabeth. Her face was solemn, no fear, no judgment.

She mouthed the words, *I love you.* He wondered for an instant if he'd imagined it.

"Finish it," the Saxon said beneath him.

Kieran looked down at Richard, a man who had fought valiantly for not only his life, but for his land. Under any other circumstances, he would have liked to have Richard as a vassal rather than an enemy. But fate had a different plan for them and when two men fought for the love of one woman, only one could come out the victor, and he, Kieran the Black, had won the heart of Elizabeth.

"Do it Norman. I will not live in a dungeon."

"Mayhap you have no choice," Kieran replied. "You are a traitor to the crown. King William may have other plans."

"You said to the death. You are a man of your word. Now be done with it."

His men and people stood in silence around him, their stares boring into him, asking him why he waited to kill this man who only minutes ago had held a knife to his wife's throat. A man who had killed a dozen of his soldiers, imprisoned his most-valued vassal, made his squire live in the stables with the livestock, and taken his wife and imprisoned her in a tower with the intention of marrying her. What man would do such a thing?

A desperate man.

The man beneath him.

"I will kill Elizabeth if you do not do this. I will escape, just as she escaped me, and I will slit her throat and not—"

With a growl, Kieran thrust his sword through the man's chest.

The Saxon's dark eyes stared up at him. Blood escaped the mouth that moments ago had said the unthinkable.

Cheers of his men and the villagers rang out about him, yet he felt no victory.

Kieran stood on unsteady legs. He had lost his control. It had been the first time in his entire life he had let his emotions overstep his mind. Every part of his being had wanted to imprison the man, to make him die a slow, painful death— perhaps reward him to King William as a prize. Yet, when Richard had mentioned killing Elizabeth—*his Elizabeth*— Kieran's fury overtook his reasoning.

He grabbed the hilt of his sword and pulled it from Richard's body. Hugh was at his side congratulating him, Olivier's grin bespoke his happiness, yet he wanted, nay—*needed* to see the expression on only one person's face.

The crowd parted to let her near, and Elizabeth flew into his arms. He dropped the sword, encompassing her within his arms, pulling her near, as though he could pull her inside of himself.

"Thank God, you are all right," she whispered against his chest. "I feared for a moment that—"

"I am well, Elizabeth," he murmured, inhaling the soft scent of her, grateful that God had given this woman and this fief to him. She brought sanity to his world, and right now he wanted nothing more than to be alone with her.

"We shall celebrate this night," Sir Hugh said to the crowd, and a roar went up.

Two knights came forward to get Richard's body. "What shall we do with it, milord?"

Elizabeth pulled away from him a little and looked up into his face.

He turned to the knights. "Take his body to the gates of Langaer. You will take as many men as you see fit. They can bury him. We will send word to King William of Richard's betrayal, and I will send my request that Sir Hugh take his place as Lord of Langaer."

"Milord!" Hugh said, hand to heart. "I know not what to say."

Kieran glanced at Elizabeth who smiled like a fool, then back at his vassal. "Say that you will guard Langaer with your life."

"Aye, milord. You have my pledge," Hugh said, his voice booming.

"Sir Hugh, I will take my leave now." He turned to Elizabeth and took her by the hand. "Come, wife, I have need to hold you in my arms."

"What will everyone think, milord," she said coyly.

He lifted a brow. "That I wish to show my wife how much I need her. That is after I soak in the bath."

Her eyes lit up.

"'Twould milady like to bathe with me as well?"

She took his hand, and started toward the manor. "Aye, I would, milord."

Her eyes, bright with love and passion, said more than words ever could.

He pulled her back to him, his mouth slanting over hers, devouring her. His men cheered nearby.

"I love you, milord," Elizabeth whispered against his lips, and he stiffened. She pulled away, far enough to look into his eyes. "I love you, Kieran."

Hearing the words sent his heart racing, and hearing the endearment along with his Christian name made it even sweeter.

Feeling awkward and uncertain, especially with his men around, he just smiled down at her. Then he heard someone clear his throat, and it sounded much like Olivier.

"I love you," Kieran said, the words coming easy from his lips. He realized it was the first time in his life he had ever said them.

Her face lit up, her eyes searched his face, as though seeking the truth of his words. "Yes, milady. You heard me. I love you, Elizabeth. I love you." He put her from him, and turned to his men. "I love Lady Elizabeth!"

A roar went up all around them, and he lifted Elizabeth in his arms. Her arms encircled his neck and she nestled her head against his shoulder. He made haste to the manor, taking the steps two at a time. Hopefully Mary and the other maids were filling the wooden tub with hot, steaming water, as was the custom after a battle.

He set Elizabeth on her feet, and she smiled at him shyly.

"Nay, milady. No blushing miss are you."

She shot him a shocked expression and laughed.

He took a seat near the fire, and held out his hand to her. She took it and he pulled her onto his lap. They sat there in silence, both watching the flames. He watched her profile.

Elizabeth bit into her lip as she stared at the fire. He wondered what thoughts ran through her head. Seeing the welted mark on her neck, he winced, knowing that a small scar would always remain, reminding him of this day. His arms and torso were filled with deeper, broader scars from knives, swords, and arrows, but he would gladly take all the blows again to take away the pain of the one that marred her perfect flesh. He lowered his head and kissed the wound, tasting the metallic flavor of blood.

She squirmed. "What?" he asked.

"Your lips and tongue feel so good against my neck," she whispered, motioning to the maids filling the tub.

His cock filled with blood, pressing against her. He wished the women would hurry with the bath. "You like my lips on your flesh?"

She lifted her brows. "You know I do."

"What exactly do you like?" He nipped at her shoulder, his tongue running from collarbone, up to the lobe of her ear. His teeth grazed the lobe, gently sucking, then he darted his tongue into her ear.

Her breathing quickened and he smiled, glad she enjoyed his touch.

"Wait until they leave," she said, shifting on his lap again.

He stilled her hips with his hands and pulled her legs apart to where she rode one of his thighs. He lifted that thigh and he noticed her throat convulse as she swallowed hard. He could feel the heat of her mound against him.

With the maids behind him, he shifted slightly, so they could not see. He lifted a hand to Elizabeth's breast and caressed a nipple through the light fabric. Her legs spread wider. "Do you like that?" he murmured, his breath stirring the hair by her ear.

She nodded, and licked her lips.

His free hand flattened against her stomach and he felt the muscles clench beneath his hand. His fingers moved down, past her jeweled girdle to her woman's mound and the tiny bud that swelled at his touch. He stroked the tiny nub through the soft fabric of her gown. He smiled against her hair as her breath caught and her head fell back on his shoulder, leaving her throat open to his touch. His lips ran along her neck, stopping at the pulse that pounded there. He pulled harder on her nipple while increasing the rhythm and pressure of his fingers at her womanhood.

She moaned low in her throat and he felt the familiar pulsing of her body against his thigh. She turned her head and he covered her mouth with his, silencing her moan as she climaxed.

A minute later, still shaking, she pulled away slightly. "You are wicked."

He grinned, feeling more alive than he ever had. He had never known that bringing a woman to climax could bring him so much pleasure. Always it had been about self-gratification, about the moment and nothing of emotion. But fate had a different plan in the way of Elizabeth, and he was a changed man for it.

Thankfully, the maids left within minutes, and when Mary shut the door, Kieran prompted Elizabeth to stand. She stood before the fire, waiting for him to take off his braies and boots.

It took but a second. Her gaze drifted over him slowly, a long passion-filled look that told him she was pleased with his body. Her lips twitched when his cock bucked and reared. "I want you," he said needlessly.

"I can see that," she said, a lazy grin on her face as she went to him. Her fingers splayed against his chest, then moved down over his stomach. She slowly went to her knees and wrapped her hands around the base of his cock. Her hot lips wrapped around his shaft, taking him deep into her mouth. His head fell back and his hands weaved through her hair, pulling her closer, loving the feel of her fingernails biting into his buttocks as she pulled him nearer.

She sucked and licked, her tongue encircling the head time and again, before taking him into her mouth again and again.

He could not take it. He pulled her to her feet and had her gown off before she could blink. She glanced at the bath, and then at the rug before the fire. Taking her meaning, he pulled her down to the rug, and climbed between her thighs.

"I love you, Elizabeth," he said, kissing her hard while entering her slowly. He groaned low in his throat as her hot sheath surrounded him.

Her head fell back on the rug and she closed her eyes.

"Elizabeth," he whispered, and she opened her eyes, the blue orbs dark with a passion he knew well.

He pulled out of her, just the head of his cock inside her. Her brows furrowed and then he plunged in. Her mouth opened and she released a soft cry. It was his undoing. Though he wanted to take her slowly, he could not, and it seemed she would not allow it. She met him thrust for furious thrust, her body tightening and clenching, crying out his name as she climaxed.

He watched in wonder at this gorgeous, passionate creature beneath him moaning his name. *His woman. His wife.*

Slowly, he started the pace again, sweat heavy on his brow, his cock impossibly hard. The side of her mouth lifted, and then she looked down between their bodies, watching his shaft as he entered her.

His gaze met hers. "I love you, Lizzie," he whispered, and she went still.

"What did you say?"

"I love you."

She smiled. "But what did you call me?"

His brows furrowed as he watched her. "Lizzie."

She bit her bottom lip and tears came to her eyes. "I like when you call me that."

Lizzie could not believe Kieran had just whispered her name. Her *real* name. Love for this man overwhelmed her and she kissed him with everything she felt for him—all the love and desire that had been pent up while he and Richard had fought.

Sweat beaded his brow and she knew he held off his climax for her. She lifted her hips, increasing the rhythm, and he smiled against her lips. "Come with me, Lizzie," he whispered against her lips.

She hooked her legs around his waist and raked her fingernails across his shoulders as he pistoned against her. "That's it, Kieran. Fuck me."

With a growl, he came, pouring his seed into her, and a second later she followed him, her tight sheath pulsing around him with an intense orgasm that had her heart pounding out of her chest and her body humming.

Kieran rolled onto his back, taking her with him. His hand ran up and down her back lazily. He kissed the top of her head. "*Je vous aime de tout mon coeur, Lizzie.*"

She smiled against his chest, and then looked up into his beautiful blue eyes. "And I love you with all my heart, Kieran."

* * * * *

Outside the manor, Betty smiled to herself knowing that this night the Lord and Lady of Aedelmaer had successfully made an heir. The baby girl, later a young woman with fiery red hair and temper to match, would be the first of many children born to Kieran the Black and his soul-mate Lizzie.

Betty whistled to herself, glad to be on her way, off to another time, another place, to help yet another poor soul who had ended up in the wrong time.

GOD OF FIRE

Written by

Jaid Black

To my daughters:
For the daily gift of unconditional love,
For overlooking my faults and quirks,
For letting me cuddle with you even though you're growing up,
For keeping my sense of humor in tact,
For never doubting me when anyone else would,
And for making me believe magic is real...
I love you.

"Each friend represents a world in us, a world possibly not born until they arrive, and it is only by this meeting that a new world is born." – *Anais Nin*

Prologue

Valhalla (The Hall of the Slain)
Somewhere in Time

Frigg was friggin' pissed.

She glowered at her husband from across the room as she stabbed at a piece of mutton with her bejeweled gold dagger and knifed it into her fashionably pouting mouth. Odin was at it again, the lecherous swine, screwing half of the goddesses in the hall. Even now the big jerk was throwing a meaningful glance with his one and only eye toward Jorth, the airhead who had birthed his beloved first son, Thor.

Frigg could stand to see no more. She threw her golden dagger down onto her golden trencher and stomped out of the hall with the regality of a queen, or in her case, a goddess. She marched past the slain Vikings who stood guard at the Valgrind gate and indignantly made her way toward the River Thund.

It was time for a little revenge.

Frigg fumed through her entire trek, a journey that took her all of one magical second to accomplish. She decided, with much exasperation, that a mere second wouldn't give her enough time to cool down this go-around, so she threw her simmering self to the ground and onto her stomach, beating and kicking the riverbank like a spoiled child.

It wasn't fair.

She, Frigg, was Odin's wife. Not Jorth — *never* Jorth. She had given Odin Balder, the most beautiful of all of his sons. She had graced the Viking god's hall for more millenniums than she

133

cared to dwell upon, and she had remained steadfast and faithful to him for the duration.

Sort of. Well, most of the time.

She frowned. Okay, so only when she felt like it.

But that wasn't the point!

The point was that her husband, one-eyed bastard that he is, should have eye for no goddess but herself. She was Frigg, damn it. Not some half-witted Jorth who wouldn't know her head from her arse if her son Thor shoved a lightning bolt up it and twisted painfully.

Frigg hoisted her elbows up onto the bank of Thund, plopped her weary head into her palms, and contemplated her pitiful options. She sighed. There was only so much a goddess could do to retaliate against Odin. He was a sneaky god-king, that husband of hers.

Frigg gazed down into the icy waters, placing her hand within the river and swirling it about as her mind reeled through the possibilities. Her revenge had to be subtle. It had to be noticeable, but it had to be subtle. She smiled slowly as an idea came to her.

Odin had been prattling on, excited of late over the impending arrival into Valhalla of his son Thor's favorite human warrior, Ragnar the Feared. The Valkyries had decided just a few days past that Ragnar was to die on the field of honor whilst raiding a Celtic village a fortnight hence.

Frigg was having none of that.

True, the warrior maidens were the ones who chose who would die in any given battle and who would remain on the earth, but the Valkyries couldn't bring a man into Valhalla who hadn't been injured in battle to begin with.

Frigg smiled, her immortal eyes merrily twinkling. She would see to it that Ragnar never made it to the Celts' shores during the upcoming raid, let alone find righteous death in glorious battle.

Ragnar was young at thirty and two, and could therefore wait a little longer to see Valhalla. Frigg, on the other hand, was not willing to wait. She was beautiful, aye, but older than dirt, and she steadfastly refused to wait any longer to see her revenge through to its fruition. Enough was enough.

Frigg winked a smile into the River Thund, happier than she'd been in ages. It felt good, revenge. In fact, it felt damn good. She clapped her hands together and laughed, growing more excited by her plans every moment.

And then she frowned.

A thought occurred to Frigg that she didn't care for at all. She might be able to stop Ragnar from participating in the upcoming Celtic raid, but she couldn't be there to watch over him and impede him always. She needed something more, something that would make her revenge last longer. A distraction that would keep Ragnar the Feared from her hall of slain warriors for many, many years to come. Nothing would irritate Thor, and therefore Odin, more.

Frigg tapped her long, elegant nails on the bank of Thund and wracked her immortal brain for an answer to her predicament. She squealed in excitement a minute later when the answer of all answers came to her.

But she would need aid.

She grinned provocatively into the waters, feeling every inch the goddess to be reckoned with. The god Loki would help her. He owed her one.

Besides, that little twit would do anything for a good blowjob.

Chapter 1

Stavanger Region of Norway, 820 AD

Every warrior seated around the long table watched the Jarl in anticipation as he paced the length of the *thing's* meeting place. The *thing* hadn't planned to assemble again until a fortnight hence, but Erik the Wise had sent messengers to each of the council's judiciary members this rising, summoning them to the hall in posthaste.

Ragnar Valkraad, the first-born son and heir to the great Norwegian Jarl now pacing before the assembled men, gazed upon his father with a sense of trepidation. 'Twas never good news when Erik the Wise called upon the council to come together unexpectedly.

Two female Celtic slaves appeared in the doorway carrying pitchers of freshly brewed mead toward the Jarl's seat. They placed the drinks deftly upon the long table, then scurried from the hall as quickly as they'd arrived.

Ragnar slowly smiled. The slaves were not ignorant of the goings on inside of the *thing*. 'Twas apparent neither of his father's thralls wished to be used as bed sport for the gathered Viking men. Yet Ragnar knew that wenching was the furthest consideration from the minds of all present. They had far more pressing matters to contend with.

The murmurs of the councilmen could be heard throughout the longhouse, all of them talking amongst themselves at the table, speculating as to why the Jarl had called upon them in the first. Ragnar the Feared considered it as well, but arrived at no conclusion. 'Twas not like his sire to be so secretive.

Ragnar watched in silence as his father, Erik Valkraad, ran a weary hand through his long silver-yellow mane of hair and paced the dirt floor of the assembly hall. He was a tall man, still thickly muscled and well-honed at the age of two score and eight. He was an impressive warrior, an intelligent jarl, and Ragnar respected him very much.

"Thor's teeth, Valkraad!" the Jarl's brother-within-the-law, Leif Boerge called out. "You are making us all fretful with your pacing in silence. Tell us now the matter you seek to put before us this day."

A chorus of approval went up like wildfire, inducing the typically stoic Jarl to wince. He sighed, but relented with a nod, then strode toward the long table to take his seat of honor.

The room grew immediately quiet. Ragnar stirred atop the wood bench, his sense of foreboding deepening.

Erik the Wise took a long, healthy swallow of mead, swiped his hand across his mouth, and set his tankard back down upon the table. He belched for good measure. (This was, after all, serious business.) The Jarl sat straight up in his chair and harshly gazed into the eyes of all present, making the members of the *thing* realize in no uncertain terms that whatever he was about to say would be countered by no arguments to the contrary. "The Celts shan't be raided by us a fortnight hence."

Shouting broke out amongst the members of the council, all of them speaking louder than the next, vying to be heard above the din. Ragnar raised a battle-roughened palm, inducing the councilmen to silence. "Father," he began, the agitation in his tone apparent, "why wouldst we abandon this trek? We have planned in earnest for three fortnights." He shrugged a broad shoulder. "Our people gain much good fortune when we prey upon the weak-kneed Welsh."

A choir of "ayes" rang throughout the assembly hall like songs offered up to the gods. Sven Haardrad slammed his hammy fist upon the tabletop and glowered at the Jarl. "Your son is correct, Erik. You wouldst make the time and planning we have already expended for this journey all for naught?" Shouting punctuated the gathering once more, all men present sorely unhappy.

Erik the Wise raised his hand to silence the noise, a hush falling over the *thing* in the process. "Loki the Trickster has appeared to me in a dream."

Startled gasps rose up, permeating the silence and all but causing chaos to erupt. Every man present believed wholeheartedly in the Jarl's visions, for 'twas his second sight and useful premonitions which had earned him the name of the Wise. But never before, not as long as Ragnar had lived, had he ever heard his sire make a claim to have had visions of the fire god himself.

Ragnar squirmed ever so slightly on the bench, excited yet apprehensive to hear the rest of his father's tale. The appearance of Loki could mean naught but trouble.

Erik the Wise lifted his heavily muscled arms, calling silence down upon the assembly. He cleared his throat to speak. "Loki has declared that Frigg, the omnipotent wife of Odin, is sorely displeased with us and commands that we make recompense to her. He has said that we have offended the goddess-queen, and all manner of ills will befall our people if we do not obey her decree."

The Jarl peered into the eyes of all assembled, demanding they realize the seriousness and severity of Frigg's displeasure. "The trickster god has promised to aid her in her bid to keep our warriors from reaching Valhalla if we fail to do as we are instructed."

Distraught "nays" echoed fearfully throughout the longhouse. When a warrior's sole purpose in life was to die during battle that he might take up residence in the Hall of the Slain, 'twas a fate far worse than death being barred from glorious Valhalla.

The men of the *thing* didn't want to believe the Jarl's words, yet knew Erik the Wise was speaking in earnest. His visions were accurate, always had been. Ragnar made not a sound, though his insides were in turmoil. He feared beyond reason what Frigg's recompense would entail.

The Jarl stood up and circled the long table slowly. All eyes were transfixed upon his formidable person as he made his way around the group. "We are to call off our raid on the Celts, the loss of the riches we wouldst have obtained a small punishment for offending Odin's wife."

A collective breath of relief let loose throughout the meeting place. Erik shook his head and smiled humorlessly. "I wish that 'twas to be the punishment in full, yet is there more."

Twenty apprehensive Viking marauders watched the Jarl circumnavigate the long table, all of them dreading his next words. They knew not what he would say, yet all present were certain they wouldn't care for it in the least.

Erik continued to walk, circling around them as he spoke. "Instead of journeying to the land of the Celts, one of us will make haste to the River Thund on the morrow. Upon the northeast bank of the river, the chosen one shall find a woman sleeping and bring her back to our lands with all speed.

"The woman has been branded by the god of fire, thus she sports the image of the dragon upon her right ankle. She shall be recognizable to the chosen one by her unusual, yet comely looks. The wench is gold of hair, gold of skin, and gold of eyes, created in the likeness of Frigg's favorite material possession."

Murmurs and excited chatter rose up throughout the *thing* yet again. Ragnar made a disapproving face at the men, wanting them to quiet so he could hear the rest of his father's tale.

"What are we to do with this woman once we find her?" Sven asked thickly, his tongue all but wagging.

Ragnar rolled his eyes, knowing the lecherous boar was nigh unto erect from the possibilities swimming about his empty mind. He had the urge to thump him on the empty head in question, but his father's voice rose above the shouts, distracting him.

"The golden woman will be sent by Frigg on the morrow as both punishment and second chance," Erik clarified. "She will come to no harm at our hands. Verily, she will know no man's bed except that of the chosen one." The Jarl cleared his throat, his eyes glaring daggers at the Vikings. "We must treat her with every kindness, show her every consideration, *serve her every need*."

Ragnar sensed the gathered men's disapproval as much as he felt it festering within his own body. By Thor's teeth, they were warriors, not serving wenches! 'Twas women who had been sent from the gods to serve men, not the other way around. Ragnar sighed. Frigg must be sorely displeased indeed to bring upon them such punishment as this.

"We are to serve *her*?" Sven asked incredulously. "By Odin's eye, see if I will!"

All Vikings present turned to the wayward Sven and grunted. Ragnar's uncle Leif jabbed an ominous finger toward him. "You will quiet your tongue anon, lest Frigg hears you and brings us added bad fortune."

"Furthermore," Erik expounded, effectively ignoring Sven's blasphemy as though it had never been uttered, "no Viking of our lands shall see Valhalla unless certain events come to pass."

"What events?" Leif asked warily. He took a deep breath, wishing he had never bothered to crawl out of his godsforsaken bedfurs this morn.

The Jarl stopped his circling and stood before his warriors. "We are given one year from the morrow to see Frigg's stipulations carried out." He placed his fisted hands on his hips and glowered at the men before him. "The chosen one," —he looked pointedly at Sven—"and *only* the chosen one, will wed and breed with the golden woman branded by fire. She must bear a golden son within the year, do any of us wish to see Valhalla. The child shall be called Balder, in deference to Frigg's beloved, departed son."

"That shouldn't be o'er difficult," Aran Boerge, Leif's eldest and Ragnar's cousin, called out with a bellow. "We are Norsemen, the lot of us. Our seed is potent."

Lusty laughter rang throughout the hall. Even Ragnar had to crack a small grin at his cousin's words.

Erik the Wise, however, was not amused. "Ah, how right you are nephew, and yet is there more." The Jarl shook his head in resignation and not a little irritation. He took a deep breath and expelled it on a groan. "The golden woman cannot be forced abed."

The hall of twenty smiles evaporated into the hall of twenty frowns. Vikings were known for force, for taking what they would when they wanted it. They did not woo. Not a man amongst them was fit to don tights and spout poetry.

Ragnar ran a frustrated hand through his shoulder-length sunny blonde hair and grimaced. "By Thor's hammer, please be kind, father, and tell us that Frigg desires no more of us."

Erik the Wise smiled kindly at his son, wishing he could say it 'twas so. "There is still more. Though not much, I'll grant."

"Good gods above!" Leif hammered out. "What have we done to offend her? You wouldst think we had spat and peed upon Frigg's image as bad as this is! Tell us now the whole of it, brother."

Erik nodded, as eager to end this tale and begin the preparations as the rest of the warriors. "The golden woman is ignorant of Frigg's stipulations and will remain thusly. None amongst us shall enlighten her of the fact that she must bear the golden son. She can only be told her part after 'tis done."

"Then how do we get her to breed?" Ragnar asked, somewhat stupefied. The wench couldn't be forced abed and yet she couldn't be told how vital it was to their people for her to bear a son either. This was madness!

The Jarl grinned, the first sign of good humor any of the assembly had witnessed in him thus far. "'Twill be up to Frigg's chosen one to woo the woman into the marriage bed, to coax her into spreading her legs, and allowing him to get her with son."

Erik shook his head, as bemused by the situation as he was terrified of it. "The chosen one must couple with her, must plant his seed deep in her belly, and he must do it quickly, yet with the wench's permission." He shrugged. "The fate of every warrior in this room, verily every warrior in our lands, rests in the seed of the chosen one."

"I could coax the golden wench to open her legs," Sven bragged as he stood up and flexed his muscles. "Let her behold this body nigh unto its perfection and she will more like than not force *me* abed."

Leif rolled his eyes and shook his head in exasperation. "'Tis more like than not that the only wench you could get abed a'tall is one both blind and unable to smell." He scratched his beard and contemplated the situation. "Mayhap it should be me who goes. I could bed her did I try. They do not call me Leif the Wench-Wooer for naught."

Ragnar chuckled as he stood up and stretched out his back muscles. "I cannot say I was aware that you were named thusly, uncle."

Leif shrugged. "'Tis a name from my younger years."

The Jarl frowned, crossing his arms over his chest. "My sister called you by that daft name only to cater to your pride, you lack-wit." He grunted and waved his hand tersely through the air. "We stray from the topic. All of this talk is for naught, as Frigg has already decided who the chosen one is."

Ragnar felt a chill creep down the length of his spine. He was afraid to ask the next question, but knew that he must. "Who is the chosen one, father?" he quietly asked.

Erik the Wise surveyed the room, his eyes making contact with each and every warrior. Finally, his gaze came to rest upon his own son. "'Tis you, Ragnar. You are Frigg's chosen one," he said softly.

"We are dead!" Sven cried as he clapped a hammy hand to his distraught forehead.

"Valhalla will never be ours!" a warrior called Selik predicted forlornly.

"Is this a quest Frigg knows we cannot succeed in?" Aran demanded, his fist thumping on the long table.

The room broke into fits of outraged temper, all of the warriors furious with what they were certain was no escape from their mutually impending doom. Ragnar took his seat at the long table again, plopping down onto the bench with a weary sigh.

He was a warrior through and through, six feet and five inches of raw power and steely muscle. There was little he couldn't accomplish, yet was he fearful that this task set before him, the most important task ever given to any mortal as it had been issued by Frigg herself, was the very feat he would be unable to master.

He knew little of wooing wenches and even less of impregnating them. Ragnar's seed was, after all, the only of the adult males' in the village that had not yet bore fruit.

Chapter 2

Frigg and Loki, naked and spent, gazed into the River Thund and laughed. The woman they had decided upon would never lower herself to sleep with a man she would surely consider a primitive. She was from the future, for Odin's sake! She was used to men who were weaker, less surly, and more obliging. And even if she did succumb to the bed of the Jarl's son, Ragnar the Feared would never impregnate her.

Ragnar had known two wives, yet neither had produced an heir. True, they had both died of fevers before the first year of their respective marriages had been spent, but if Ragnar's loins had proved fruitful, they would have carried his issue at some point before their untimely demises.

Frigg rubbed an impatient hand along Loki's chest. She scratched her tapered nails across his flat nipples, causing him to suck in a pleasure-filled breath. "Go fetch the wench, my dearest. I am anxious to let the show begin."

Loki settled himself between Frigg's thighs and entered her immortal pussy with one powerful thrust. "Anything for you, my pet. You know I cannot resist you."

Chapter 3

Cuyahoga Falls Ohio
The United States of America, 2003

Dara Sabine bolted upright in bed, her eyes glazed over with unquenched arousal. Her silk nightgown was drenched in her own sweat, beads of perspiration covering her body like a wet second skin. She glanced around her bedroom.

She had been dreaming. *It was just a dream.*

She took a deep breath, feeling strangely disappointed. Just a dream. Lately, she sighed, it seemed as though all of life's finer offerings were dreams and fantasies. Nothing was turning out like she had thought it would—hoped it would.

Realizing it would be a long while before she could fall back to sleep if at all, Dara threw the goose-down covers off her legs and planted her feet on the cold oak floor. Pulling on a robe and slipping into her fuzzy slippers, she padded downstairs.

Ten minutes later, she sat before her TV eating a bowl of cornflakes with one hand and channel surfing via the remote with the other. Her mind was like a blank television station—fuzzy and unfocused. She didn't want to think about the dream, nor did she wish to dwell on the current status of real life. Paul—things just had to work out with Paul. She sighed, refusing to deal with the uncertainty she had in regards to her upcoming nuptials. Certainly there had to be something worth watching on TV no matter how ungodly the hour...

Romper Room (what four-year-old kid would be up watching TV at three a.m.??), an old rerun of a popular show from the late seventies, and she frowned, some boring show about an old Viking queen on the History Channel. She sighed, deciding to watch the show about the Norsewoman.

...an interesting fact about the jarl's wife, the show's host pontificated in his sophisticated English monotone, *was the legend surrounding her arrival into Valkraad lands. The widely believed consensus at the time was that she had been sent by the gods themselves and was the key to the survival of not only their people, but later their mystics would believe, to all people. How and why is not known by historians as records dating that far back are scarce.*

What is interesting to note, however, is that she encouraged her husband to build and live *below the ground following a Celt raid some ten years after her marriage...a very early example of bunkers and safe houses military historians find intriguing. The elders of the clan believed the Viking queen, Dara, to be a time traveler...*

Dara smiled. "Hey we share the same name," she murmured. "Pretty neat."

But not neat enough to keep her attention. She gave the program one last cursory glance, then sighed before switching off the TV, dismayed that nothing good was on the tube at three o'clock in the morning.

Dara heaved another dramatic sigh as she drew her spoon up to her mouth and plunged a huge bite of cereal between her lips. Since there was little else to do at three a.m., her mind drifted back to the dream that had awakened her so abruptly this morning. She grinned, thinking to herself how idiotic she'd been to get worked up over a silly dream about a fabled Norse god.

He had called himself Loki, the trickster god, the god of fire.

Devastatingly handsome, this mischief-maker had been. Tall and well muscled, as sexy as sin itself, and a very good kisser. He was the god of fire all right, she wryly admitted. She had felt his fire right between her thighs.

Loki threw her down onto the bed and made love to her with his mouth, his tongue flicking over her clit in rapid darts. When Dara had almost reached climax, she begged him to fill her up, to thrust inside of her. Loki licked her nipples then devilishly smiled down to her. "I cannot, lovely Dara, though I wish I could."

"Why not?"

"You are to wed another."

"You mean Paul?"

The trickster god laughed uproariously, as if she'd just told the joke of a lifetime. "Nay, love. You will not wed with Paul. You will be given to a real man, to a warrior some might say can rival even me."

"No one can rival you," she purred as she reached up and licked his chin with one seductive swipe..

Loki basked in the feel of her mortal tongue against his immortal skin, relishing the silky feel of her body beneath him. He trailed his kisses downward, ending at the wet place between her thighs. He splayed her legs wide and groaned, coveting what would never be his.

Loki took her into his mouth, teasing her clit with his tongue and lips. He brought her to the brink of completion once more, then stopped.

Dara ran her hands through his hair and groaned with need. "Please don't stop again."

"I must."

"But why?"

"You will know pleasure at the hands of your husband and no other. The course has been set."

"I want you to be my first. You will bring me more completion than Paul could ever hope to."

Loki grinned. "I told you, you will not wed with Paul."

"Then whom?"

"You will wed a warrior."

Dara threw her head back and laughed. "A warrior, eh? Too bad there haven't been any around in…oh…I don't know…hundreds of years?" She reached out and brushed her fingers through Loki's mane of hair again. "Please take me," she whispered thickly.

Loki lowered his head, drew her clit between his teeth, and sucked amorously. When Dara began to thrash around on the bed in her passion, he stopped, again not bringing her to completion. He looked up at her and grinned. "Warriors do not exist in your time, but they exist in mine. 'Tis my time to which you will come."

"Your time?"

"Aye. When people still believed. When the gods of Valhalla still ruled."

"You can rule me." She pushed him from between her thighs, sat up on her knees, and drew his hard shaft into her hands.

Loki sucked in his breath as the mortal woman stroked him back and forth. Her caress could only have been borne of him — fire.

He removed Dara's hands from his erection and pushed her back down onto the bed. "Give yourself to your husband." He sighed and shook his head. "I want the mortal Ragnar to win."

Dara knit her eyebrows together, shaking her head ever so slowly. "I do not understand."

"Don't try. I have already said too much."

"But Lok — "

"Nay, love. You cannot know me. Your husband will come for you on the morrow and take you to his bed. Make haste and enjoy the journey. You will know much happiness do you submit to him."

And then the god of fire shape-shifted, evolving into a dragon before her very eyes. "Loki?" she asked breathlessly, somewhat frightened.

He ignored her fear, boring her with his heated gaze. "Lest you believe this a dream, feel my mark upon you." The dragon breathed out fire, singeing her ankle with flames that branded her, yet caused no pain.

And then he was gone.

Dara gazed down at her foot and smiled. Upon her ankle was a tiny and perfect image of Loki as the dragon…

Dara sat on the couch frowning, knowing full well why she'd had such an erotic dream to begin with. It was because she didn't love Paul. She was going to marry a man who brought out none of her passion and her ever-efficient subconscious was merely trying to point out as much. She set down her bowl of half-eaten cornflakes and sighed. Passion or not, she *would* become Paul's wife.

But the passion, the ache…good god! Was it possible for a real man to make her feel the way her dream lover had? She grimaced, realizing that the man she was about to marry never would.

Dara shook her head, clearing it of the last remnants of her dream. There was no way in heaven, hell, or Valhalla that she was going to stop the wedding now. She'd be insane to do so. The man was as rich as a Trump and as powerfully connected as a Bonaparte.

She sighed a bit dejectedly as she picked up the remote and switched the TV back on. This was no time for her subconscious to kick into overdrive. Not when the wedding was within spitting distance. "Hell," she muttered to herself, "at least *The Galloping Gourmet* is on now."

* * * * *

After lunch, Dara strolled toward the bank of the Cuyahoga River telling herself that she felt better than she had in years. She all but skipped down the leafy path of the lush forest nestled deep into the gorge, doggedly convinced she had done the right thing. She was going to marry Paul. Yeppers. She was sure it was the way to go.

Paul D'Abois was wealthy and sophisticated, everything Dara's doting mother had ever wanted for her in a husband. He had his own lucrative engineering firm, several advanced degrees, a summer home in the Hamptons, and a yacht most women would kill to call their own.

Dara snorted, effectively dismissing her misgivings as trivial. So what if Paul was a little boring? Who should care that he was a proverbial wuss among men? So what if he spent more time preening in front of a mirror than she did? Dara Sabine was going to be rich! Loki be damned!

Dara sank down to the ground a moment later, the weight of her weariness getting to her. She shook her head and sighed, not wanting to contemplate the matter further. And yet thoughts continued to plague her as she slowly undressed. Her fingers absently worked at the buttons of her cotton dress, her mind in turmoil.

She had given up an entire two years of her twenty-six year old life in pursuit of making her mother's dreams for her a reality. She would not, under any circumstances, question the value of the prize she had finally claimed as her own. Paul D'Abois would become her husband.

An hour later, Dara laid by the riverbed as naked as a jaybird, enjoying the feel of the suns rays beating down upon her. It was her own privately held land, so why not? It's not like anyone would ever see her.

She smiled as she closed her eyes and the seconds turned into minutes. Her sun-kissed skin grew more golden as the minutes ticked by, which would draw out the color of her tawny-gold eyes and golden, sun-streaked hair.

Dara told herself over and over again how elated she was at the prospect of her impending nuptials, of how perfect she would be in the role of *the* Mrs. Paul D'Abois.

And then she gave up with a sigh.

Who was she kidding?

She didn't love Paul, and it wasn't fair to use him to achieve her mother's goals. Hell, they weren't even her own goals. They were the desires and dreams of a woman long dead. A woman who had known far too much heartbreak and poverty in her own short lifetime.

Dara knew what she had to do. Her dream lover Loki had been right. She had to end this farce of an engagement once and for all. Paul wouldn't be devastated, thank God. He was far too rich and had too many willing women surrounding him, ready to jump in and take her place at first opportunity.

Besides, Dara could take care of herself. She didn't need a man to do that for her. She'd worked herself up from nothing to gain scholarship into Harvard. She'd plowed through her courses and bulldozed her way into the halls of Yale graduate school. She was a self-sufficient, modern woman. Not at all the sort of female to entertain the notion of marrying a man because he held clout.

And money. Yes siree, there were quite a few buckaroos the wuss boy she was giving up could call his own.

Dara resigned herself to the inevitable, knowing that when she rose from the riverbank she would do the right thing and call off the engagement. Paul would never make her feel the way Loki had. The closest she would get to climaxing in Paul's bed would be arguing with him over the significance of Gauguin's contributions to Impressionism while watching the History Channel.

Okay, okay, she was definitely going to dump Paul. But before dealing with that unpleasant business, she would allow herself to luxuriate in the sun's heat just a few minutes longer. She arched her back, a feeling of pleasure cascading throughout her body as the rays of the hot sun reached down and caressed her nipples, elongating them into tight peaks.

Loki was right. She *could* find herself a warrior among men.

And then she fell asleep, enjoying every moment of nature's erotic kiss.

Chapter 4

Ragnar Valkraad made his way through the forest, walking swiftly alongside his mount. He was well aware of the fact that he was feeling sorry for himself and wasn't ashamed to admit it to man, beast, or fowl.

Why had Frigg done this thing? Why did she hate the name Valkraad so much that she would forsake an entire clan of warriors, barring the lot of them their entry into the much-coveted Valhalla?

He meandered through the forest, his sense of keen awareness telling him he would arrive at the northeast bend of the River Thund at any given moment. *And into the sights of the sleeping golden woman.*

Were it not for the impossibility of the task set before him, Ragnar knew he would be beyond himself with excitement. As it was, he couldn't help but to wonder what the wench would look like and if she was to be as comely as his father's vision. He felt a tremor of impending conquest course through his veins, realizing without any doubt that he was closing in on her. He brought his mount to a halt, commanding it to stay put and not follow behind him.

Ragnar sighed. 'Twas as fruitless as his loins, this mission. He had wed two wives, dallied with every female slave in his father's house, yet to the best of his knowledge he had never been the cause of a single pregnancy. Any wench within the whole of Norway would have run to him in delight were she to breed his child, for they all knew he would wed the woman who could give him an heir, whether she was a free woman or a thrall. Then all the riches of the Valkraad holdings would be hers — and her babe's — to one day command.

He shook his head and frowned. 'Twas useless, this.

Ragnar stealthily crept into the thick of the trees, making not a sound as he approached the bank. He sighed with deep resignation, knowing full well that no matter how ill-fated this quest might be, 'twas still one he must give his all toward achieving. He parted a swaying branch and stepped to its other side, then looked around for his prey.

There she was.

Ragnar's breathing momentarily stilled as he walked toward the woman and knelt down beside her slumbering form. His father had been right, he thought, his cock growing hard. Comely did not begin to describe this naked wench. His thick shaft grew painfully erect just gazing upon her slumbering form.

The wench was long and voluptuous, her hair the color of spun gold, her skin glowing like the sweetest of summer's honey. Her eyes were closed so he knew not their color, yet was he certain they would be as golden as the rest of her.

He came down to his knees beside her. The wench's mons was covered with a triangular patch of silky gold, the same shade as the satiny hair pooling about her head. Ragnar ran a large, callused hand over the curls between her thighs, splaying his fingers in the silken nest.

'Twas hard to believe that a woman so fine had been given to him by Frigg for a wife. Of course, he thought with down-turned lips, that would make the goddess's revenge all the sweeter—give him a comely woman to mount day and night, but a woman he could never give heirs to.

To be certain he had acquired the correct wench, Ragnar sought out her right ankle and looked for the mark of the fire god upon her. He took a deep breath and blew it out. Sure enough, the tiny image of a dragon graced the wench's sexy little ankle, proclaiming the sleeping woman to be his betrothed.

Ragnar let his eyes roam the length of the wench's body, appreciating her beauty more and more with each passing moment. His cock ached for her. He wanted to take her, to ride her this very moment, yet he knew 'twould be a foolhardy breaking of the rules.

Still, she was to be his wife. 'Twas not foolhardy to gentle the golden woman to his eager touch.

Ragnar beheld the sight of her plumped breasts as long as he could without making a motion toward them. Finally, he relented. He had to touch them, needed to know the feel of this body that would belong to him irrevocably. Her nipples were large and puffy, peaked off at the crests with hard pink berries. He ran his roughened hand over her silky smooth chest, feeling first one breast and then the other.

The golden woman moaned softly in her sleep.

He drew a nipple between thumb and forefinger and pulled gently but firmly at its crest.

She moaned again.

His jaw clenched. At least one part of this task wouldn't be overly difficult, he absently thought, his cock so stiff it ached. He was a good-looking man, willingly received by free-women and slave wenches alike, and this golden woman lying beside him was naturally passionate.

Ragnar ran his hands over her breasts once more, then over her stomach, and finally back to the pelt of curls covering the place between her thighs. He worked his strong fingers between her legs, found her woman's bud, and wiggled it around as he watched her face.

The wench moaned again. Ragnar's manhood engorged painfully.

The golden woman writhed just a bit, a small groan in the back of her throat, as he rubbed her swollen clit with one hand, then reached out and stroked and tweaked her nipples with his other. He watched in fascination, wanting her to reach her peak before she opened her eyes and realized him a stranger to her. 'Twould help gentle her to his touch did she find pleasure at his hands.

And he would be touching her a lot.

Mayhap he could not mount her without permission, but nowhere in the rules was it said that he could not touch her as much as he desired. Eventually, with enough prompting, the golden woman would spread her legs eagerly and willingly for him. 'Twas then the real quest would begin. Hope swelled inside his chest as he prayed to Odin that the wench would favor him with a son. Mayhap she wouldn't, but he would enjoy the trying immensely.

The wench's golden eyes flew open as she loudly groaned, her climax relentlessly boring down upon her. She looked disoriented for a few moments as her golden honey eyes met Ragnar's vivid blue ones. And then they looked frightened.

She screamed. A bloodcurdling, high-pitched, Odin-cursed scream. Ragnar released his hold on her clit and nipples and covered his ears.

* * * * *

When Dara's eyes had flown open during the most devastating orgasm of her life, she had half expected to see the handsome Loki hovering over her body and loving it. She had certainly never expected to see the scraggly bearded face of a man whose facial hair bore a disconcertingly strong resemblance to Grizzly Adams staring back at her.

A panic like she'd never known coursed throughout her body. It was like being in the middle of a really bad acid trip. Of course, she had never tried acid, but she was certain that this must be what it felt like.

A quick glance over the man's body told her that he was a huge, hulking giant of a beast. His muscles were thick and steely and covered every square inch of his solid frame. Though kneeling, the length of his thighs told her he'd be formidably tall when standing upright. The man was the embodiment of power and strength.

A heady reality had he been Loki. A terrifying reality considering his resemblance to Grizzly Adams. And the fact she wasn't dreaming.

Dara gazed up into the stranger's face and took note. She was good at note taking, she hysterically reminded herself. She'd worked her way through college doing secretarial jobs on the side. The notes she now gathered didn't set well with her.

She wanted to crumple them into a ball and toss them into the nearest trashcan. *The man was frightening looking.*

True, his eyes were the most beautiful sea blue she'd ever beheld, and his body was something to be reckoned with, but the man's full blond beard—which he wore partly braided, no less!—covered the majority of his face and was not a turn-on in the slightest. Perhaps if he'd shaved…well, it was hard to tell. The man was simply too hairy of face…

Arrg! What was she thinking?!

Dara suddenly became aware of Grizzly Adam's hands clamped onto her nipples and clit. Good God, she was going to be raped! She was going to be raped by one of those crazed, lonely mountain men she'd heard about on Oprah. She had no idea what a mountain man was doing in northeast Ohio, but her hysterical mind supposed anything was possible.

This close to fainting, she opened up her mouth and screamed bloody murder.

Chapter 5

Ragnar removed his hands from his ears and used them to cover the wailing wench's mouth. By Thor's hammer, the woman knew how to kill a fair mood. "You will stop this noise anon," he commanded her sharply.

When her eyes rounded with a mix of anger and confusion, he had to wonder if the golden woman spoke his people's tongue. By Odin's eye! 'Twould be just like Loki to add yet another complication to this already impossible task.

Ragnar looked down at the wench quizzically, then released her mouth and ran a soothing hand through her hair. "Do you speak my tongue, woman?"

Dara gazed up into the giant's eyes trying to make sense of his words. His voice was stern and booming, and much out of character with the tender manner in which he was caressing her. She took a deep breath, absently thrusting her breasts upward in the process. "I do not understand what you are saying. Can you speak slower, please?"

Ragnar cursed. He wanted to spit nails. The wench definitely did not understand Norwegian, but he most certainly understood her tongue. 'Twas Saxon she spoke! A badly mauled and much butchered version thereof, yet Saxon it 'twas.

He shook his head in disbelief. The woman was too fine of form to herald from the race of little smelly people who were useful to the Vikings as naught but slaves. And yet Frigg had given the golden Saxon for him to take to wife. Surely his people's sins did not warrant this!

Ragnar stood up and sighed as he intently studied the wench. He mentally shrugged, knowing he must wed with her whether she was Saxon, Celt, or a hoof-footed troll. He held out his hand and spoke to her soothingly in her own language. "You will come with me the soonest. Rise up, wench."

Dara blinked. *Wench?*

She shot up to her feet and threw the giant a wary and hopefully intimidating look of undisguised contempt. "I have risen, mountain man, but I am not going anywhere with you." She took a few steps back, growing more and more frightened as the seconds ticked by. She prayed she looked more self-confident than she felt. "I am going home. *Now*," she nervously stuttered out as she spun on her heel and tried to make a run for it.

Ragnar put out a hand to stop her, whirling her around to halt her leave-taking and face him once more. "You will go no further, Saxon. We leave for Valkraad lands anon where we shall be wed upon our arrival."

Dara blinked a few times in rapid succession. She shook her head as if to clear it, then peered up into the face of the man with the scraggly half-braided beard. She frowned. "First of all, I am not a Saxon. I don't even know what a Saxon is, unless you mean those people that have been dead for hundreds of years. And second," she announced with more courage than she felt, "I wouldn't marry you if you were the last man crawling around on God's green earth. I am already engaged to be married to Paul D'Abois. Yes that's right," she swiftly informed him with a wave of her hand, "*the* Paul D'Abois!"

Ragnar hadn't the slightest notion who or what this Paul D'Abois was, but little did he care. He was pleased to learn that the wench wasn't a Saxon, but the rest of her tirade he dismissed as trivial—the parts of it he'd taken the meaning of anyway. "Mayhap you *were* betrothed to this man called Paul, yet has it been decreed by the gods that you will now wed with me, Ragnar Valkraad, known throughout Vikingdom as Ragnar the Feared."

Dara didn't know whether to laugh or cry. She was standing next to the river as naked as the day she was born, listening to some deranged man who fancied himself a Viking tell her of his designs to marry her. And worse yet, his name was downright awful. And he looked like Grizzly Adams. She couldn't believe it. It was just too much.

"Listen Mister Valkraad, I am flattered to no end by your wish to marry me," — that was a lie — "but as I have already indicated, I am set to wed another." She straightened her back and thrust her chin up with a lot more staunch than she felt. Good lord, this was the weirdest conversation she'd ever had! "Now if you will excuse me, I will be going back to Paul immediately."

She spun on her heel and marched off, hopefully this time for good.

Steely arms coiled ominously around Dara's belly from behind. She gulped, wide-eyed. This escape might not prove to be as easy as she was hoping it would be. Oh God, he was crazy. A crazy, psychotic, totally deranged mountain man. Panic and fear engulfed her.

The owner of the powerful arms leaned closer into Dara's backside, pulling her tightly against him. He craned his neck down, whispering softly near her ear. "'Tis best not to fight me, sweet. I hold no desire to bend you to my will by force, yet will I if I must."

"Are you saying you mean to r-rape me?" Dara whispered, shaking at the very thought of it.

"Nay," Ragnar denied as he stroked her hair in a placating manner. "You will know my bed only when you come to it willingly. On that, you have my word."

She let out a breath of relief. At least that was a start. She'd *never* go to the mountain man's bed willingly. "Then you will let me go?" she breathed out.

Ragnar shook his head, slowly, definitively. "Nay. That I cannot do." He cupped her breasts from behind, stroking her nipples as he spoke. She gasped. "You belong to me now, sweeting. Best accept it and move forward."

* * * * *

Half an hour and many horrible thoughts about what he meant to do with her later, Dara decided that she wasn't going to accept jackshit. She frowned down at the apple the giant had handed her, then pelted it at him. "I'm not hungry!" she seethed. "And I want to go home!"

True, she had realized this past half-hour that the ogre was rather okay as ogres go, but she refused to let herself warm up to the man. She was, she reminded herself, a prisoner. Prisoners don't have to like their captors.

It didn't matter how nice he was to her, she knew. She wanted to go home. *Home.*

Ragnar, reclining on the ground hoisted up on one elbow, raised his eyebrows. She was sitting on her knees before him, granting him an enticing view of the slippery folds of pink flesh between her legs. He was certain if she'd realized as much, she would have closed her splayed knees abruptly, so he said nothing. "We've a journey that might take a few hours. Best eat now."

"I don't want to eat. I want to go home!"

"And you will," he returned calmly, "to your new home, to my home."

Her jaw tightened. "You do realize this is called kidnapping, don't you? When the authorities find you, you'll do hard time."

"I imagine much of the time I spend with you will be spent hard, my sweet." He glanced toward her slightly spread knees and grinned mischievously.

Dara gulped. Much to her dismay, her nipples tightened and elongated at the mental image the mountain man was painting. She closed her eyes and mentally groaned. She was his prisoner, for crying out loud! People don't fantasize about their captors! Especially not ones with yucky beards, she admitted forlornly.

Dara looked away from the giant's gaze and sighed. "Can I at least have some clothes to wear?"

"Nay."

"Why not?!"

"Because I enjoy looking at you." Ragnar pulled her to the ground on top of him, rolled over to reverse their positions, and settled himself between her thighs. Dara gasped. "And because t'would please me did you grow comfortable with me and my touch the soonest."

"I thought you said you wouldn't rape me," she said wide-eyed.

Ragnar grinned. "And so I shall not, yet still will I touch you."

"What do you mean?" she asked warily.

Ragnar shrugged. "I must gentle you to my touch, else will it be too long before you come to me willingly." He leaned down and kissed her softly on the lips. "I will not force you to accept my cock inside of you afore 'tis time, yet will you never deny me the right to look upon you and to touch what belongs to me."

Ignoring her startled gasp, he lowered his head to her breast and drew a plump nipple into his mouth. He sucked on the tightened flesh long and wickedly, knowing she was already responding to him.

Dara shifted beneath him, closing her eyes against the pleasure. Why wasn't she objecting? She should be yelling and screaming at the top of her lungs! She should be, but she wasn't. She didn't know what was going on, but everything felt surreal.

Oh God, she mentally groaned, she had to fight him...

Seeking to remedy the situation, she raised one hand to ward him off, realizing a moment too late that she needn't have bothered. Ragnar had released her nipple and was now drawing his giant-sized body off hers.

Ragnar gazed down at his betrothed. Her breathing was heavy, her nipples hard. It wouldn't be long before she gave herself to him. "I am going to ready the mount," he murmured. "We leave at once." Standing up, he walked away without looking back.

Dara sat up and watched Ragnar stroll into the thick of the forest. She could scream. She could run. She could try to escape. But...she didn't move. She stayed there and waited for him in silence, as unable to make a decision as a deer caught in headlights. She was going crazy!

Dara shook her head, completely irritated with herself. She gathered her common sense together as she drew herself up, preparing to dash into the trees. It was one thing to behave so recklessly in a dream and quite another to...the dream! Yes of course, she thought, her eyes widening, the dream!

She thought back quickly on everything that Loki had said to her last night, trying to decide if this was the man he had spoken of.

Impossible! She'd never had a psychic dream in her life, so why start fortune telling now?

Dara gulped in wide-eyed dismay as something else the fire god had said came back to her. *"Lest you believe this a dream, feel my mark upon you."*

She closed her eyes, refusing to look at her ankle.

"'Tis my time to which you will come," he had said. *"When the gods of Valhalla still reigned."*

Dara vigorously shook her head back and forth, knowing what she was thinking wasn't possible. No way—no damn way.

When she could endure the suspense no longer, her eyes flew open and she glanced down at her ankle. She closed her eyes again and cried out helplessly, having seen the fire god's mark upon her. Shrugging off the perversely eerie feeling that she'd just been catapulted through the annals of time, Dara stood up and dashed for the trees.

She had to escape.

* * * * *

Wide-eyed, she ran faster. She could feel him gaining on her, could hear leaves crunching under his boots as he drew closer and closer and...

Please! Please! Please! she silently begged the heavens as she blindly ran. *Please let me get away from him!*

Dara glanced over her shoulder, the look of determination on her captor's face enough to give her the chills all over again. She turned her gaze back in front of her, running a zigzag through the dense trees as fast as a barefoot woman could possibly run. Her heart was pounding in her chest, her naked breasts bobbing up and down. She just had to make it to safety — just had to! She dared another look over her shoulder.

Nothing, she mentally gasped. He was gone. Had she been dreaming? Had Ragnar even been real? "What the — *oomph*," she muttered as she collided with a very hard chest.

The wind knocked out of her, Dara fell onto her backside, her heart rate over the top. "Go away!" she rasped, scooting away from him. She wanted to cry as she watched him watch her. His face was so stoic, so unrelenting. "Please just go away."

Making one last attempt at freedom, she shot up to her feet and tried to run past him. Dara screamed when he caught her by the foot, then pulled her back to the ground and toward him. "Let me go!" she wailed, hitting him as hard as she could on the chest. "Go away!"

Ragnar laid down on top of her, pinning her flailing hands above her head as he did. "Nay," he said calmly. He pressed his very noticeable erection against her belly. "Nay," he said again, his voice thick.

Dara's eyes widened. She wet her lips. "Don't rape me," she whispered, her voice shaky. "Please."

His eyes gentled. He said nothing for a long moment and then, "What is your name, wench?"

She closed her eyes briefly, long enough to take a steadying breath. She had lost, she realized, resignation settling in. For now she had to go with him. "Dara," she murmured.

* * * * *

"Can I please put some clothes on?"

"Nay."

"*Why not*!?"

"'Tis only you and I here, sweet Dara. What need have you for clothes?"

"You're not naked."

"Wouldst you like for me to remove my clothing as well?"

"No!"

Ragnar chuckled. He was enjoying the company of the golden wench much more than he had expected to. She sat before him, her rounded buttocks pressed against his groin, his right hand wrapped around her belly to steady her and hold her close as they rode astride his mount toward Valkraad lands.

He was taking no more chances. The willful wench had already tried to escape him once. She would never get a second opportunity to do so.

Ragnar knew he would have to clothe Dara before they approached the fjord, so he intended to enjoy the feel of her smooth skin against him for as long as possible. He rubbed his hand across her belly and smiled. "You've the skin of a babe," he muttered more to himself than to his betrothed.

She responded anyway. "And you have the manners of a pig."

Ragnar laughed, but he didn't disagree.

Dara sat in a daze before the giant, not knowing what to think. For the past two hours they had ridden through forests and over lands which should have been familiar, yet weren't. She had lived in the valley all of her life, grown up by the river, and was as knowledgeable of the terrain as she was the back of her own hand. But now as they cantered along, everything familiar was eerily foreign.

The man had said his name was Ragnar Valkraad. Loki had spoken of a Ragnar. The man believed himself to be a Viking, even going so far as to dress the part of one. Ragnar was wearing a long sleeveless tunic with crossed garter hose and both of his heavily muscled biceps were clasped about the middle with ornately bejeweled golden armbands. Thor's hammer was centered upon the left band and a dragon upon the right one.

Loki had also said that she would marry a warrior. And indeed, this man looked every inch the capable warrior.

Dara closed her eyes as a sense of foreboding stole over her. She was beginning to fear that this was no longer a dream, but a reality from which there was no escape. She sank deeper into Ragnar's arms, unthinkingly seeking comfort as she spoke to him. "What will we do when we reach your home?"

"You will meet the *thing*."

Dara harrumphed. "Look buddy, I will not be meeting anybody's thing. Get that thought out of your head right now."

Ragnar chuckled. "Not that thing. The *thing* is what Norsemen call their council. 'Tis a body of lawmakers over which my father rules and over which I will one day rule. My father is Jarl there."

Dara nodded. She hadn't the slightest notion what a jarl was, but decided to explore that issue more in depth at a later time. She had enough on her plate as it was. "And after I meet the...uh..." she cleared her throat, "*thing*?"

"Then we shall be wed."

She nodded like a marionette, a dazed feeling creeping up her toes and settling into her body proper. Unconsciously, she snuggled against Ragnar, seeking a comfort from him that she couldn't name.

Ragnar smiled. His wench was gentling to his touch already. 'Twould be soon enough he could claim her as his wife in truth. In a few hours, the jarl would say the words that would bind them together by law, and then within a few days, Dara would bind herself to her husband in every way. Ragnar was certain of it.

Dara closed her eyes and laid the back of her head against his steely chest, no longer wishing to have any of these scary thoughts she'd been entertaining. Thoughts like, the Viking was really a Viking. Thoughts like, she had been whisked through time by a handsome god with a wicked sense of humor. Thoughts like, the Viking's hand had moved from caressing her belly to caressing her breasts. She gasped when she realized that the latter was more than just a thought.

Ragnar heard her sharp intake of breath, but ignored it. 'Twas time to accustom Dara further to his hands, that she would no longer fear his exploration of her body. He released the hold he'd kept on the mount's reins with his left hand and used both of his large palms to cup her breasts. His horse knew exactly where home was, so it wasn't necessary to lead him.

Dara sucked in her breath as Ragnar's fingers began tweaking her nipples back and forth with fluid strokes, inducing them to swell into painfully erect points. His touch felt so good. So impossibly good. She should stop him but she didn't. She couldn't.

What was she doing? She didn't want him to make love to her…did she?

Dara took a deep breath in an effort to clear the cobwebs from her brain. She grabbed his hands and pushed them from her body, then folded her own arms over her breasts, making it difficult for him to resume his touching.

Ragnar merely chuckled. He used one large hand to gather her hair and brush it to the side out of his way. When he secured a direct path to her neck, he bent his head and nibbled upon her sensitive skin there. She moaned, as turned-on as she had been when he'd played with her nipples. Her hands dropped defenselessly to her sides as she closed her eyes and felt arousal overwhelm her body.

He continued to kiss and nibble upon her neck as his hands sought out the nipples she'd tried to deny him. He pinched them between thumbs and forefingers, grabbing each one at the root and pulling upward toward their tips, over and over again. Dara bucked against him, her buttocks grinding into his erect groin.

Ragnar released one of her nipples, freeing a hand to roam down her belly and toward her mons. She whimpered out a ragged breath as his callused fingers ran through her pubic hair, petting her down there like a favorite kitty cat.

"'Tis like silk, your pelt."

She moaned at his words, then groaned when a large callused finger found her clit and began massaging it.

He rubbed her pussy in agonizingly slow motions. She wiggled in front of him astride the horse, trying to stop the inevitable from happening. But eventually she reached the point of passion overwhelming sanity, of her body's need no longer caring what her brain had to say concerning the situation. Her clit was pulsing. Her nipples were diamond-hard. "Faster! Rub faster!" she thoughtlessly groaned.

Ragnar smiled, and complied. He increased the speed of the circles, his hand growing drenched from the downpour of honey between her legs. She would burst at any moment.

Dara had never felt so excruciatingly aroused in her life. She threw her head back against Ragnar's chest and screamed in ecstasy as her orgasm ripped violently throughout the whole of her body. She shuddered and convulsed, writhing against her captor as the waves of pleasure rippled through her. Oh lord — oh sweet lord.

Ragnar ran his fingers through her velvety pelt, petting her like he had before. "Good girl," he thickly murmured, his deep voice husky with lusty approval. "Good girl."

One hour and three orgasms later, Dara laid face down and exhausted across the horse, feeling anything but a good girl. Her arms were stretched up toward the mount's neck, her nipples still aroused from the feel of the horse's coarse hair brushing against them below.

Ragnar rubbed her buttocks from behind, kneading them like two silky balls of golden-honey dough. He slipped a large finger from one hand into her climax-flooded flesh, while his other hand continued to rub her lush derriere.

Dara bucked up against his hands, closing her eyes against the inevitable. She wondered vaguely as her fourth orgasm roared through her belly just how many climaxes she could possibly endure before dying of pleasure. She smiled into the night, knowing that her Viking would find out.

Why not smile? This *had* to be a dream.

Chapter 6

"Wake up, sweet Dara. We are almost home."

"Hm?"

Ragnar grinned as he pulled his sleeping betrothed up tighter against him. He nudged her chin up so he could gently force her to awaken. "Open your eyes, sweeting. We will be in the heart of my sire's lands the soonest."

Dara sleepily forced her eyes open long enough to smile up to him. She closed her eyes again, unable to stay awake. She was so exhausted from the endless stream of orgasms Ragnar had given to her that she felt as though she could hibernate for a week straight.

He possessively cradled her against his chest, but did not back down from his command. "Wake up, Dara. You can sleep in our bedchamber when we reach it."

That woke her up. Her head poked up. She gazed at Ragnar with rounded eyes. "But I thought—" She looked away, saying no more.

Ragnar rubbed her back soothingly, crooning to her as though she were a small child. "Have I not gentled you to my touch yet, sweeting?"

Gentled her? Was he kidding? She was as gentle as Jell-O at the moment. "Yes, but it's just that I—I am not ready for the other yet."

"Why not?"

Dara shrugged, but said nothing.

He lifted her chin and surveyed her expression. "What do you fear from me? You must realize by now that I wouldst never hurt you."

And this has got to be a dream. "Perhaps not intentionally," she heard herself mutter.

"What do you mean with those words?"

Dara pulled away from the hold Ragnar had on her chin and looked away. She sighed. "I've never been with a man before."

"Never been where with a man?"

"To bed!" she yipped, embarrassed he'd made her spell it out.

Dara broke from his hold and turned her head. She simply couldn't hold his gaze after having admitted to being a virgin. How embarrassing, admitting something so personal to a man she'd known only a day! Of course, this was also the same man who had brought her to orgasm more times than she could count in the past few hours.

Ragnar sat behind Dara atop the mount, his shaft swelled with desire and near to bursting, his eyelids heavy with arousal. *She was a virgin.* No warrior had ever claimed the golden Dara before. She was unused, untouched. And she was all his. His was the only cock that would ever take her. He was the only man who would ever pour his seed into her belly…

Ragnar gripped Dara's nipples between thumbs and forefingers and possessively clamped down on them. She gasped a little, from surprise he supposed, but otherwise said nothing. They rode that way in silence for another ten minutes before Ragnar released his hold on her nipples and stroked her thigh. "I will give you my tunic to wear until we reach our chamber."

Dara's head whipped around, her gaze piercing him accusingly.

Ragnar sighed. "I will say this once more, but then I shall never repeat these words. You shan't be forced, Dara. I will wait until you are ready to give yourself to me."

"Then why are we sharing a bedroom?"

"Because 'tis what married people do. And make no mistake, sweeting, we *will* be wed on the morrow."

"I thought you said we were marrying tonight?" Dara gulped, wondering if it had been foolish of her to remind him of something she didn't particularly want to do. A little sexual touching in a dream was one thing, marrying him was quite another.

Ragnar shrugged as he pulled his tunic from over his head and put it on her for covering. "I rode slow so you could sleep peacefully, thus are we arriving late into the night. All will be abed by now."

Dara let out a slow breath, feeling both relieved and anxious. Relieved because she wasn't prepared to meet anybody new, anxious because it occurred to her that this dream was a bit too detailed to be a dream. "Good," she said weakly, "I'd like to have some decent clothes on before I am forced to be introduced to anybody."

Ragnar nodded. "Even though we are not yet wed, you still will share my bed for sleeping tonight, Dara. I will take no chances that another might steal you away and claim my prize."

"Your prize?"

Ragnar smiled humorlessly. "Your virginity."

* * * * *

Fifteen minutes later, Ragnar and Dara stole into the longhouse and crept soundlessly down the corridor leading to Ragnar's private chambers. He had insisted he didn't want anyone to hear them come in, not even a slave, for he wanted to keep her all to himself this night. He refused to have her expend even a moment of her time or attention on another.

That was perfectly fine by Dara. She had no desire to meet up with any strangers tonight anyway. She was having enough trouble adjusting to Ragnar. And to the discomfiting thought that Loki's appearance hadn't been a dream. And to the equally horrifying thought that even now, she was wide awake. It was a fact that was getting harder and harder to deny.

As soon as they were safely squirreled away inside his bedchamber, Ragnar walked toward the sconce on the wall nearest the door and lit a single beeswax candle. That done, he pulled his tunic from over Dara's head and discarded it into a nearby chair, leaving her fully naked in his presence once more. He turned away from her and strode to the side of the huge, plush bed, then patted it, smiling at her. "Come, sweetings, and get your rest."

Dara nodded, glancing around at the furnishings in his bedchamber to see what the big room looked like. To her utter dismay, she couldn't make out much. Perhaps Ragnar could divine details by the light of only one candle, but she couldn't. If it hadn't been for the moonlight pouring into the room and resting upon Ragnar's form, she wouldn't have even seen him pat the bed and beckon to her.

When Dara reached the bed, she climbed on top of it and made her way slowly toward its center on all fours. Ragnar reached out and patted her bottom as she crawled, then slipped his hand lower and stole a quick feel of the swollen flesh between her legs.

Dara sucked in her breath, but kept moving. She fell to her side, curling up like a cat, and faced what she strongly suspected was one of the chamber walls. She felt dazed. Completely overwhelmed.

Ragnar climbed into bed beside her a moment later, reaching out for her as he laid down. "Come and sleep near me."

Dara nibbled on her lower lip, eventually releasing it to sigh in resignation. If she didn't go to him, he'd simply come to her. Huffing, she sat up on the bed, turned toward him, then plopped back down facing him.

He patted his chest. "Lay your head here."

She did so stoically, too drained to argue.

And she was scared, more frightened than she'd ever been before in her life, for she'd come to realize that this was no dream. Ragnar was very, very real, and she didn't know what to make of that fact.

She also didn't know what to make of her own behavior. She hated how compliant she'd been acting these past several hours. Dara had always been one to stand her ground, yet in the Viking's presence she found herself merely relenting to his demands without protest. Of course, it was one thing to form an opinion on how one *should* behave in such a situation and quite another reality when faced with it.

She sighed. This was the most confusing and frightening day she'd ever lived through.

She was a prisoner, a captive of a huge man who had decided to marry her upon first sight. Furthermore, she didn't know where she was or if she'd ever see her own home again. But by far the most frightening concept for her to come to terms with was Loki's ominous prediction, his insistence that she was to be wed to a warrior from the fire god's time.

Dara had never been much of a European history buff, but she'd retained enough information from her requisite courses in world history at Harvard to realize that the Vikings had ruled mainly in the 800's and 900's.

She firmly closed her eyes against her fear, snuggling closer to Ragnar's side. Odd, but the very man who had captured her was the same man who was able to breach some of her unease. Burrowing into his warmth somehow managed to make this fate more tolerable. A fate she had slowly come to fear over the past several hours might just be inescapable. She closed her eyes in confusion of her feelings, her hand absently resting on his washboard stomach, her face near his flat male nipple.

Ragnar placed his hand over Dara's, holding it firmly but gently against his stomach. It felt good, cuddling with his woman. Her body was finely sculpted — lush, soft, and pillowy, just as a warrior preferred. He couldn't have chosen a more desirable mate for himself had he tried.

Ragnar yawned in contentment and offered up a silent thanks to the gods who had brought his Dara to him. If she was to be his punishment, he couldn't ask for a better sentence of judgment. He nestled himself against her and smiled.

He had almost drifted off to sleep when his father's words from the last rising echoed through his mind. *"The chosen one will wed and breed with the golden woman. She must bear a golden son within the year, do any of us wish to see Valhalla."*

A year.

And his beautiful wench was a virgin.

Ragnar couldn't have been more delighted by Dara's innocence, yet did he also realize 'twould cause much apprehension of mating on her part. For one thing, the size of his cock would likely intimidate her. 'Twould make it more difficult to get between her legs if the sight of his manhood frightened her needlessly. He would have to accustom her the soonest. He grew immediately erect just thinking about it.

Ragnar gripped Dara's hand more firmly, then slid it slowly down his heavily muscled stomach and onto his jutting shaft. At her intake of breath, he knew she was not yet asleep. "Ragnar, I—"

"Shh, love," he whispered. "'Tis best to have you know what will be inside of you, that you grow to not fear it." He leaned down and placed a soft kiss on her furrowed brow. "Just touch me," he commanded her hoarsely. "No more will be asked of you this night." He released his grip on her hand, wanting her to explore him of her own will.

After what seemed to Ragnar to be endless moments of hoping, he at last felt Dara's fingers curl around his thick shaft as best they could, accepting him. He let out a sigh mixed with relief and longing.

Dara had to admit that she was wickedly curious about Ragnar's body. She'd never been in the presence of a naked man before, Loki aside. She knew now, without a doubt, that Ragnar's entire body was built on the same massive scale. The Viking was *huge*. She secreted a smile into the dark, perversely curious as to whether it was his sword-wielding or lovemaking that had earned him the nickname Ragnar the Feared.

Dara curled her fingers around his cock tentatively at first, but grew bolder when she heard him suck in his breath. She stroked him slowly from root to tip, exploring the sensuous feel of rock-hard muscle covered in satiny silk. Ragnar moaned as Dara continued to fondle him, his body tensing at her touch. Her nipples grew tight in response to the sounds he elicited, the power she felt over him quite heady.

She picked up the speed of her perusal, stroking up and down the length of his shaft with greater urgency. She could feel the tip of his penis growing wet with pre-ejaculate and she knew she was close to taking Ragnar to the same heights he'd taken her so many times today.

She drew her head up from his right bicep and licked one of his nipples as she masturbated him, her strokes getting faster and faster. Ragnar growled, no longer caring if he woke up his entire household or not.

And then he burst.

Ragnar groaned out his satisfaction as his orgasm exploded and spurted out all over Dara's hand. He breathed in long, deep breaths as he steadied himself from the impact of his climax. By Thor's hammer, if he burst like this at the touch of his betrothed's hands, he could well imagine what it would feel like whilst inside of her.

Ragnar reached for a piece of woolen cloth sitting near the bed and cleaned up his wench's saturated arm. He then patted his chest, directing her to lay her head upon him once more. He held her close, enjoying the cuddling more now than he had before.

He smiled wryly into the night as he drifted off to sleep, his last coherent thought a beatitude of thanks to Frigg for cursing him.

Chapter 7

When Dara awoke the next morning, the first thing she realized was that Ragnar wasn't in the bed with her. She was alone. Naked and alone.

She glanced down to her ankle on the off chance that the Viking had been a dream, then sighed in acceptance when she spotted the dragon still branded upon her. No dream.

Now that daylight was pouring into the room, Dara was able to see the contents of the chamber quite clearly. She wasted no time in her inspection. She drew herself up from the bed and stood up to have a peek around.

The first thing Dara noticed was the elaborate paintings and artwork that donned every wall. No, she thought as she examined the wood closer, the artwork didn't merely don the walls, but was an ingrained part of them, etched by a master artist. The scenes depicted hunts and what she gathered to be raids. There were also creatures she didn't recognize, carved and painted into the walls, along with a few that she did. It was the gold-gilded dragon that called out to her, beckoning her closer.

Dara strode closer to the symbol of the dragon and ran her hand over the intricately detailed carving. The creature was etched deeply into the pine log wall, then painted with magnificent colors and gilded with a gold overlay. It was beautiful, simply breathtaking. And it resembled the one upon her ankle down to the most minute of detail.

She walked toward the hearth next and admired the fine tapestry that had been woven and placed above it. It was bright and bold, magnificent with color. And like the walls, it depicted a hunting scene. She grimaced when she realized that the prey was a woman. She could only assume that this was the medieval equivalent to porn.

Dara walked toward Ragnar's side of the bed and took note of the massive gilded and bejeweled chest laying on the floor beside it. She was no more a medieval history buff than she was a European history buff in general, but she knew enough of it to realize that a chest served the dual purpose of closet and dresser drawer in this time.

Her perusal of the chamber was cut short when a knock sounded at the door a moment later. Her eyes widened in dismay, realizing immediately that she was naked and had no clothing here to speak of. She reached up onto the bed and pulled an animal skin off of it to cover up with, then quietly told the intruder to come in.

A short, round woman of middle years waddled into the room a moment later. She closed the door firmly behind her, then turned to study Dara. She eyed Dara up and down, beaming a brilliant, toothless smile her way. "Me name is Myra. The master did send me to ye because I am the only slave here that speaks yer tongue."

Dara snorted. She could hardly agree that they spoke the same language, as she could barely understand a word the woman had said. Wait a minute! she thought in dismay, had she heard the word… "Slave?"

Myra shrugged, seemingly not bothered by her status. "Aye. I was thrall to the jarl, yet now do I belong to his son." She grinned, patting her belly. "When Ragnar took to his own lodgings, he refused to give up me cookin'."

"Slave?" Dara repeated, still trying to get beyond that fact of early medieval life.

Myra frowned, shaking her gray head in puzzlement. "Do ye not have slaves where ye come from, milady?"

"No! That's awful! Barbaric! Uncivilized! You should run away!"

"Run away?"

"Yes! Run away!"

"And go where, pray tell?"

Dara sighed as she contemplated the matter. Hell, *she* didn't know where to go. How could she tell Myra here to do the impossible. "Let me get back to you on that one."

Myra dismissed Dara's ranting with a wave of her hand. "Ye do that, mistress. Now as to the reason I'm here..."

"Yes?"

"I will have the Celtic thrall Maron bring in yer tray of food and the Finnish thrall Brun will bring yer bath."

Dara sighed, hating the idea of anyone in bondage serving her. She was an American, for goodness sake! Americans don't like to think on that hideous part of their own past, let alone have it confront them in the flesh. She sighed, realizing that nothing she said or did would make a difference to Myra. "Fine. And then?"

"After ye have finished, I will bring in a dress I've been sewing for ye for two risings, then Brun will escort ye to the *thing*."

She thought to ask Myra how she could have worked on a dress for her for two days when she'd only just met her, but found herself distracted by the last bit of information the older slave had imparted. "The *thing*? Is that where Ragnar is?"

"Aye, milady. He awaits ye with the jarl and the rest o' the council at the long house."

Dara visibly gulped, not at all pleased with the notion of meeting more men of this time. She'd read the stories. The word "gang-bang" echoed morosely throughout her rattled brain. She felt dizzy, realizing that this situation was just too much to take in all at once. Still, this was no fault of the older woman's. And the slave was not likely to help her find a way out of it. "Fine. Thank you for coming to explain things to me, Myra."

Myra beamed another smile her way, putting Dara more at ease. If she hadn't missed her mark, and she was pretty sure she hadn't, she'd just made an ally of the older woman. And heaven help her, she knew she'd need all the friends she could muster around this place.

"Think nothing of it, milady," Myra insisted as she waddled toward the chamber door. "I am always here do ye have need of me."

An hour later, Dara was fed, bathed, clothed, and more afraid than ever before. Now she would have to deal with an entire hoard of Vikings and not just with the one she'd grown semi-accustomed to. It was enough to drive her to drink. Realizing that was the best idea she'd entertained all morning long, she picked up the tankard of ale Maron had left on her tray and emptied it. It tasted awful, but it would have to suffice for the moment.

Myra knocked on the chamber door, calling out to her that the *thing* was anxious to make her acquaintance and that she and Brun needed to depart the soonest.

"I'll be there in a moment!" Dara shouted back, as she turned to a gleaming silver platter to study her reflection. She sighed in distaste, thinking the metal plate was the poorest excuse for a mirror she'd ever encountered. The only aspects of herself she could make out for certain were the ones she could look down and see with her own eyes.

Her gown was a long, silk green that she had to admit contrasted brilliantly against her skin. A gold chain was roped about her belly, riding just below her hips and clasped at her mons with a gold and ruby dragon. Her shoes were leather half boots that were designed to fit either foot and were well hidden under her dress.

She had no idea what her hair looked like, but gathered from Myra's preening eye that Maron had done a good job with it. It was unbound, yet secured away from her face by a gold headband that sported rubies, emeralds, and sapphires all over it. She didn't have to see her reflection to know that Ragnar had made certain she would look good on her wedding day.

Wedding day.

Good grief! How could she marry a man she'd known barely a day? Of course, how could she not? He'd left her with little choice, she thought anxiously.

And at some godforsaken point during the night—perhaps when Ragnar had climaxed on her hand!—she had arrived at the irrevocable conclusion that she was definitely not dreaming. This was real. Very real. Dreams were broken and bizarre, lacking detail. They weren't vivid and colorful, depicting huge Vikings and toothless slaves. Dara mentally winced, realizing she'd been left in a year she didn't know the date of to wed a man she barely knew.

And she didn't have the first clue how to escape.

Like an idiot, she'd slept through over half of the journey to Ragnar's house, so she hadn't any clue how to make it back to the magical river if she tried. It was hopeless. Purely hopeless. For now she would simply bide her time.

Dara sighed, supposing she should be grateful that she'd been brought here as a bride-to-be instead of as a slave. That's right, she was slated to become a wife. She could only assume that becoming a wife ruled out gang-bangs, she prayed. And speaking of becoming a wife…

"Sorry to take so long Myra. I'm a little nervous."

"Not to worry, milady," the older thrall called from the other side of the door. "Ye will not be spillin' yer virgin's blood until the sun sets."

Dara swallowed roughly, her mouth having never felt quite so dry. Good God. Now she had even more to worry about!

Chapter 8

Ragnar paced back and forth in front of the long table as he waited for Brun to bring his betrothed to him. Only members of the *thing* had been invited to witness the impending nuptials. The celebratory feast to follow would take place afterwards in the jarl's home where one and all of the village would attend. 'Twas a time of great revelry for slaves and freemen alike, for no work would be done this day. The village would feast until the wee hours of the morning, carrying on for the higher-ranking families of the village for three full sennights.

Ragnar continued pacing as he scratched his beard in thought. He was nervous, restless, and he couldn't contain his reaction. The fate of an entire clan of warriors rested in his hopelessly inept seed. It was enough to drive him daft. He just prayed to Odin that the gods would see fit to grace his future wife with his babe.

That thought only served to lead him to another nerve-racking one. His bride was a virgin and he couldn't force her to submit to him. Thor's teeth, between one dire predicament and another, he would soon be as crazed as a frothing mouthed boar!

"By Balder's toes, son, would you quit your pacing?" Erik the Wise frowned over to his heir as he watched him prowl back and forth on the dirt floors.

"Aye, cousin," Aran grinned, "I have never seen you so worked up o'er a mere wench afore."

"She is not *mere*!" Ragnar bellowed in her defense as he quit his pacing and went to stand next to his father, cousin, and uncle. "Indeed, she is the loveliest creature I have ever laid eyes upon."

"'Tis your good fortune," Leif announced. "My first wife—not your aunt Brekkhild mind you—was chosen for me. The woman was nigh unto a pig with her eyesore of a build."

Erik snorted. "You didn't say that whilst you courted the wench."

Leif shrugged, dismissing his observation as trivial. "Her father was as rich as you, brother. Besides, she was the only free wench in yon village that wouldst spread her thighs awillin'."

"Ah," Erik grinned as he reminisced on the days of youth gone by, "the low depths a young man will sink to whilst in the fever of his need."

The laughter in the *thing* was brought to an abrupt halt when Brun knocked on the door and entered. He searched out Ragnar, smiling when he noticed how nervous his master appeared to be. "Yer betrothed is just outside, master," he offered in Norwegian. "Do ye bid her to enter anon?"

"Aye," Ragnar confirmed as he let out an anticipatory breath. "Bring her in the soonest."

Brun bowed low, then turned around and scurried outside.

"By Odin's eye!" Sven exclaimed as he walked closer to the conversing group of four nearest the long table, "I am nigh unto bursting with excitement! I cannot wait to see the woman created in the likeness of gold!"

Ragnar frowned, giving Sven the thump on the head he had wanted to give him during the meeting where his father had first announced his dream of Loki.

Sven rubbed his temple and grunted. "All I wanted to do was see her," he muttered.

A few moments later, the door to the long house opened up to reveal the golden woman of the Jarl's dream. The warriors stilled, the Jarl's prediction as accurate as usual. They watched her enter the meeting place, as nervous as she was comely.

She was just as he'd envisioned, Erik thought to himself. Golden of hair, golden of skin, and as she drew nearer, he realized she was also indeed golden of eyes. The trickster god had revealed to him the truth. He walked up to her and smiled, then spoke to her in Saxon. "I am Ragnar's father Erik, milady, and soon to be your father as well. 'Tis an honor to make your acquaintance."

Dara let out a breath of relief, pleased as punch that the jarl could communicate with her. She was still quite nervous about marrying a man she barely knew, but she forced her skittish thoughts from her mind and dealt with the reality of the situation. She smiled a bit weakly up to the huge Viking, who looked just like an older version of Ragnar, and nodded. "Likewise, sir."

She braved a quick look around, her gaze finally settling on Ragnar.

He grinned as he scanned the length of her, liking very much what he saw. "The gown becomes you, Dara."

"Nay, 'tis she who becomes the gown."

Dara shifted her gaze to the man standing next to Ragnar and offered a dazzling, pearly smile his way. Here, after all, was another man who could communicate with her.

Ragnar frowned, not caring at all for the predatory gleam in his cousin's eye. He knew Aran would never dare to touch what belonged to him, yet realizing that he even harbored such a thought was enough to put Ragnar in a jealous rage. He clamped his arm possessively around his betrothed's shoulders and stared daggers at his bemused cousin.

The men of the *thing* bellowed with laughter, thoroughly enjoying Ragnar's show of jealous temper. Dara scanned their faces, curious as to what had made them all laugh, then shrugged, realizing that she was unlikely to figure that particular puzzle out. The Vikings had an odd sense of humor, she decided.

Ragnar's father smiled down to his soon to be daughter-within-the-law. She was a fetching wench, this woman. He almost envied his son the task Frigg had set before him, but relented with an easy grin, remembering that there was no other love for him save his sweet Jaron. "Tell us, Dara, was your journey here a pleasurable one?"

Dara blushed profusely, remembering all too well how pleasurable it had been. Ragnar caught her reaction and winked at her. "Yes," she admitted weakly, "it was."

"From where did the gods bring her?" another warrior asked Ragnar in Norwegian, as he looked Dara up and down. The remaining members of the *thing* encircled the couple, curious as to what his answer would be.

Ragnar shrugged, just now realizing he'd never gotten around to asking. "I cannot say," he admitted. "I have not yet asked her."

Erik the Wise shook his head in amusement, his eyes twinkling. "You must be besotted indeed, my son, for it wouldst have been the very first question I put to the wench."

Leif and Aran nodded their agreement.

Erik the Wise turned his attention back to Dara and inclined his head down to her. "From what land do you herald, daughter?" he inquired in Saxon.

Dara swallowed roughly, her eyes wide with apprehension. How exactly was she supposed to answer that question without them thinking she was insane? Did they have madhouses in Viking times? She shuddered as she envisioned herself locked away in a foul smelling chamber with nothing to eat or drink save stale cheese and old mead for the rest of her natural born life. She wrung her hands together, her nerves overpowering her sensibilities once again. It was an action that didn't go unnoticed by the assembled warriors.

Ragnar squeezed Dara's shoulders, knowing instinctively that she was riled and needed to be calmed. "It matters not from whence you came, sweet. Tell us the truth of it."

Wide-eyed, she looked up at Ragnar and realized then and there that he'd never allow these men to harm her if they thought her crazy. That was comforting. Disconcerting to think she'd come to trust him in less than a day, but comforting nevertheless. "I'm from…someplace else," she quietly offered, losing her nerve to tell the truth as quickly as she'd gathered it.

The warriors of the *thing* who spoke Saxon laughed gaily, joined in by the ones who didn't after Dara's words had been translated for them. Erik the Wise shook his head and grinned. "We have figured out as much, Dara. But from where did Loki bring you?"

Her head snapped up. "You know about Loki?" she breathed out, not quite believing the jarl.

"Of course."

"But how?"

Erik Valkraad shrugged his broad expanse of shoulders, not minding the telling of it in the slightest. "He did appear to me in a dream to tell me of your imminent arrival."

"He appeared to me in a dream before Ragnar brought me here as well!" Dara spouted out excitedly, happy and relieved to not be the only loony-toon around here that had been visited by the god of fire.

Dara's comments elicited a round of excited chatter amongst the councilmen. All of them were even more interested in her tale now than they had been before. "Truly?" Ragnar asked as he gently squeezed her shoulders again. "And what did the trickster god do in your dream?"

Dara shifted on her feet, instinctively realizing that she had better stick to what Loki had *said* and not to what he had *done*. Otherwise, the man she was about to be forced into marriage with would want to kill her.

Ragnar raised an eyebrow at Dara's telling anxiousness, but said nothing because he wasn't certain what to make of it. "Well?" he asked when she made no move to speak. "Tell me the whole of it."

Dara lifted one shoulder in an absent shrug, feigning her innocence to Ragnar. She frowned up at him when she realized what she was doing, angry with herself for acting as though she had betrayed the Viking when she hadn't even known him at the time. Besides, she had thought it was a dream. And she was a prisoner for crying out loud! Still, for some reason she couldn't name, she didn't want to hurt Ragnar's feelings.

Now where did that thought come from? she wondered idly. Here she was, having been plummeted through the veils of time, captured and brought to the village naked, forced to marry her gigantic captor, and she was worried about *his* feelings? Geez, she was an idiot! And yet the concern she felt for Ragnar didn't lessen.

Dara forced her attention toward the jarl and smiled. "The fire god told me he was bringing me here." She tapped her finger against her cheek and squinted her eyes in contemplation. "Come to think of it, he even mentioned Ragnar's name specifically."

The chatter in the long house erupted immediately.

"He did?" Ragnar asked.

"Yes."

Erik the Wise impatiently waved his hand through the air, demanding with the gesture that the room revert back to silence. Satisfied, he nodded down to Dara. "What did he say to you of my son?"

Dara shrugged, knowing that Loki hadn't said much of him. "Not a lot. Just that he wanted Ragnar to win. I didn't understand what he—"

Dara was cut off by the loud cheering that rose up throughout the meeting hall. She nervously glanced up to Ragnar to gage his reaction, and felt immediately calmed by the look of triumph smothering his features. "That was a good thing I take it?" she asked, thoroughly bewildered by such a loud response.

"Aye," Ragnar laughed as he bent his neck and craned down to kiss her atop the head. "'Twas a very good thing."

The cheers and shouts in the long house grew to pandemic proportions once the warriors who didn't speak Saxon had been filled in on Dara's announcement. She clapped her hands over her ears, suddenly feeling very frightened. The jarl noticed her action and immediately raised his hands to silence the gathered men. "You are scaring the tiny woman," he shouted in Norwegian. "Command yourselves."

Leif, for one, couldn't seem to get his eagerness under control. He was too cheered by the news to pay heed to the unwritten decree that 'twas the Jarl's right to question the wench and not his own. He spoke out of turn. "What else did Loki say? Anything of us going to Valhalla?"

"No," Dara slowly denied. "He said nothing of it. Why do you ask?"

Erik jabbed his brother-within-the-law in the ribs, frowning at him for asking questions before thinking. "You forget the rules," he chastised Leif in Norwegian. "She cannot know that our fates rest in her womb."

Leif frowned, but nodded.

Erik the Wise smiled down at Dara and reverted his speech back to Saxon. "Do go on. What else did Loki say?"

Dara felt inexplicably skittish. She couldn't place a finger on the why of it, but something inside her was screaming out that these men were hoping to hear something specific from her lips, some sign of…something. She flushed awkwardly on her feet, wishing she had more to tell them, but knowing that she didn't. Unfortunately, Loki had said little about them. "All he said was that I was going to be brought here to his time and that I would be married to Ragnar."

The groans of disappointment throughout the meeting hall were so loud and noticeable that Ragnar was the only man present who immediately picked up on what his betrothed had just thoughtlessly uttered. "His time?" he asked as the room finally quieted down again. "What mean you, Dara?"

Dara's head shot up, her wide golden eyes meeting Ragnar's blue ones. She sighed, shrugging her shoulders with as much nonchalance as a woman frightened out of her wits could summon. "I don't know," she said quietly.

"You don't know?"

"No."

"*Dara*," he gritted out, more exasperated than she'd seen him yet. "From what time do you herald?"

She straightened her back, nostrils flaring. "I refuse to answer that question!"

Ragnar narrowed his eyes into menacing slits as he regarded the tiny golden wench next to him who dared to refuse him anything. "Why?" he asked quietly. Too quietly.

Dara braved a glance his way and visibly gulped when she took in how irritated he had become with her. "Because," she protested in barely a whisper.

"Because why?" he prodded.

"Because," she admitted as hysteria overwhelmed her, "because if I tell you what year I am from and you tell me it is that year no more, I will probably cry!" She sagged against Ragnar's hard body, the admission behind that truth hitting her weary mind full force.

Ragnar felt immediately contrite, sorry that he'd gotten a temper with her when she was obviously very frightened and mayhap confused.

And it was true. Dara *was* frightened. Somewhere in the back of her mind had been the hope that she was in some distant land she'd never seen, but still in her own time. Until she actually heard the damning words that would reveal otherwise, she carried that tiny kernel of hope deep within her.

Ragnar smoothed his large hand down Dara's back, letting her know without words that she could depend upon him always. Odd, but the small token of caring comforted her. "'Twill be all right, sweet," he coaxed. "Now tell us from which year Loki brought you."

Dara folded her arms across her chest and rubbed the goosebumps from them. She slowly averted her gaze from the floor of the hall to the man looming above her. She lowered her eyes to his chest and admitted aloud, "2003."

Chapter 9

Ragnar had told her that the year was 820. *820*? God in heaven! A series of chills raced down the length of her spine.

Dara stood stoically at Ragnar's side, pale as a sheet (or as pale as a woman with a golden tan was likely to get). She listened with half an ear to the words of the ceremony that were even now legally binding her to Ragnar for life. Laws that gave the Viking absolute power over her life and livelihood, at least within the confines of this time and place. When it was done, Ragnar and her new father Erik took to either side of her, led her from the meeting place of the *thing*, and into a procession that led the entire party to the jarl's longhouse.

The Viking version of the wedding reception took Dara by complete surprise. Fighting amongst the men was commonplace and seemingly encouraged, wrestling bouts and sword matches breaking out over the tiniest of perceived offenses. Dara tucked herself closer into Ragnar's side as a match of sword-fighting broke out behind them. The warriors were cursing each other in Norwegian, so she hadn't the foggiest notion what they were dueling over.

Ragnar, much to her amazement, didn't even seem to notice. He was laughing and jesting with his father and the other warriors seated closest to them as he ate the foods set out before them. Chagrined and more than a little peeved, she elbowed him in the ribs to gain his attention.

He cocked his head in her direction and raised a brow. "Aye, sweeting?"

Dara huffed. She cast her gaze nervously behind them, then narrowed it at her husband. "What if one of them trips and accidentally severs my head from my body?" she hissed under her breath.

Ragnar turned on the bench to behold the battling warriors for the first time. He shrugged his shoulders dismissively. "Both Aran and Selik are skilled with the sword, my love. No harm shall befall you."

She frowned. She didn't care how skilled they were. The men were fighting right behind her, and on her wedding day no less! Besides, accidents do happen. And any accident with a sword was bound to spell death.

She was about to point out as much when Ragnar's mother came to her aid. Until that moment, Dara hadn't even realized her mother-in-law could understand her English, or "Saxon" as they called it. "Instruct your cousins to be seated, son." Joran smiled welcomingly at Dara as she set her dagger down to rest upon the trencher she'd been eating from. "'Tis upsetting to your lady wife on this the most important day of her life."

Dara didn't know if she'd go so far as to call it the most important day of her life—perhaps the strangest one—but she smiled at Joran nevertheless.

Ragnar sighed, but relented. He had much work ahead of him this night and desired to concentrate his energies on thinking up a plan to woo his wife into spreading her legs for his pleasures when they would take to the bed later. Still, he wanted Dara's happiness as well as her prize, so he rose from the bench and turned to deal with his sparring cousins.

"Aran!" Ragnar barked. "You and Selik will cease your battling anon, for it distresses my lady wife sorely."

Surprised by the interruption, after all 'twas common to sword-let whilst feasting, Aran tripped over Selik's foot, fell back into Ragnar's arms, and did the Feared's face a harm by scratching it with the point of his sword. Ragnar cursed and let Aran fall to the ground as he clutched at his bloody face.

"By Odin's eye, cousin!" Aran accepted Selik's hand up as he took to his feet. "You could have been killed whilst sneaking up upon me in such a manner!"

Ragnar muttered something in Norwegian under his breath as he glowered at his wide-eyed wife. Good. At least she looked sorrowful over the agony she'd unwittingly caused him. "'Tis naught but a scratch, cousin."

"Oh my God, Ragnar!" Dara jumped up from the bench to appraise the extent of his injuries. "It's bleeding very badly," she said sympathetically. "You could have lost your eye!"

If Ragnar didn't miss his guess, his captured bride actually cared that he'd been injured, though in truth 'twas just a bad scratch. Still, knowing as much did wonders for soothing his ill mood. He returned her gaze and smiled. "'Tis naught to trouble yourself over," he murmured.

Dara, however, was paying him no mind. She forced him down onto the bench where he no longer towered over her to such extremes and she could more readily surmise the damage that had been done to him. She shot a look that spoke volumes toward Aran and Selik, causing the warriors to look chagrined. "We really need to get something on this so it doesn't get infected." At Ragnar's bewildered look, Dara tried to explain. "A salve or healing ointment?"

"Ahh." He nodded. "'Twould be Myra who knows what I've the need of." He scanned the room, then motioned for a young — and gorgeous — female slave to come forward.

The girl, Karil, who was eighteen if she was a day, smiled coyly and immediately rushed toward Ragnar's side. Her large breasts jiggled seductively from beneath her rough, low-cut dress as she threw him a look that Dara immediately guessed meant that the two of them knew each other intimately. She shook off the pang of jealousy she experienced, telling herself she didn't care who Ragnar took to his bed.

The other warriors present noticed the slave's jiggling assets as readily as Dara had. Leif, now her uncle by marriage, patted the thrall on the bottom then reached up, drew the top of her dress down and cupped a breast in his palm. He rolled the nipple between his fingers and laughed before he released her.

Rather than appearing offended or even worried by what might next transpire, the slave girl giggled. Not even bothering to draw her dress back up to cover her exposed breast, she sauntered up to Ragnar's side and bowed her head reverently. Dara rolled her eyes.

Grinning, Ragnar shook his head. He knew Karil was a lusty piece, as he'd ridden between her thighs more times than he could count, so he could not blame his uncle for wanting to get inside of her. His aunt, a lovely woman he held in much esteem, would care not a wit. She preferred for Leif to find his pleasures elsewhere, as she'd never carried a fondness for the bed sport.

But Ragnar had been taught differently. He'd had the example of his parents set before him the whole of his life and wanted the closeness with his own wife that they shared. Neither of his parents took to the beds of another and neither ever would. The closest Erik had ever come to being with one of his thralls was in accepting a suckling from Karil, the lusty piece standing before Ragnar now.

That cock-suckling had almost cost his father a happy marriage, so Erik had never allowed as much again. It had taken many sennights to coax Jaron into forgiveness and his sire had vowed to never touch another thrall again. He had even gone so far as to give Karil to Ragnar, so now she was thrall to him instead of his father.

Ragnar inwardly sighed at the sly look Karil was giving him. Was she daft, making eyes at him in front of his lady wife? He could feel Dara stiffening up beside him, and although it did his heart good to know that she was afflicted by jealousy, he didn't wish to start out married life on so bad a foot. 'Twould bring naught but trouble. "Karil, send for Myra that she might tend to my wounds." He kept his voice short and clipped, not wishing to hurt her feelings, but neither wishing to cause bad tidings with his wife.

Karil raised a brow, but said nothing. She turned on her heel and made to find Myra.

Dara visibly relaxed, even going so far as to release a pent-up breath without realizing she'd done so. Ragnar held back a smile. "Do not fret over me, sweeting," he said, pretending that her concern was over his scratch. "Myra will see to it."

Dara glanced up at his face, remembering the scratch. She grimaced. "I hope so, Ragnar. It looks pretty deep."

He shrugged, but didn't comment.

Ten minutes later, Myra stood at one side of her master and Ragnar's mother Jaron at the other. Dara smiled at her husband from over her shoulder as two thralls led her away to prepare her for the wedding night, a thought that caused butterflies to do a number on her belly. Ragnar winked back, shooing her away with his hand, letting her know there was nothing to worry over. He had, after all, promised not to take her unwillingly.

Myra clucked her tongue, worrying over Ragnar like a grandmother would. "'Tis too deep to leave be with naught but herbs, master. Ye needs must remove yer beard, leastways then I can better get to the cut."

Ragnar groaned. "Remove my beard? Nay! I will not!"

"You will," Jaron said forcefully. "Warriors have been known to expire from less than a cut such as this one."

Myra harrumphed. "'Tis true."

Ragnar slashed a hand through the air. "'Twill give me the face of a babe, not that of a man!"

"Why the worries, master?" Myra asked, dumbfounded.

Jaron made a sound, half snorting, half laughing. "He worries what his bride will think, I imagine." She shrugged dismissively. "Dara seems a lovely girl, but even should she spurn you, take heart, my beloved. She is yours now. You captured her in fairness and she belongs to you. Her body is your vessel, made by the gods to ease your needs. You need not her permission to make use of it. This you well know, Ragnar, so why thrash yourself for naught?"

It was on the tip of his tongue to tell his mother she was wrong, that such was not the way of it, but remembering the rules, he held his own council. His mother believed Dara to have been captured through raiding. She knew naught of anything else and never would. Leastways, not until Dara had bore his son. Seeking to end the conversation, he nodded. "Aye, of course, mother." He then turned to Myra. "Tend to my beard anon."

Chapter 10

Dara bit down hard on her lip as two beautiful, not to mention very naked slaves, went about the task of removing her clothing. She understood why they were trying to remove her wedding dress, so Ragnar could claim "his prize", but she didn't understand why the thralls were naked. Nor did she care to contemplate the matter to any great extent. She had enough on her mind as it was.

Namely, how was she going to get through her wedding night with her virginity intact? And then again, should she even try? The feel of her nipple being rolled between the fingers of one of the slaves pulled Dara out of her musings. Her head snapping to attention, she sucked in a sharp breath as an unwanted tendril of desire passed through her body.

A beautiful red-headed thrall with pearly porcelain skin and large, creamy breasts met Dara's bewildered look with a grin. Pushing Dara's naked body gently back upon the bed covers, she explained. "I am Brenna, milady, and this is Ana" — she indicated the voluptuous naked blonde on the other side of Dara — "'tis our duty to prepare ye for the lord's penetration."

"P-penetration?"

Brenna threw her an odd look. "Aye." She cocked her head as she accepted an opened vial of exotic oil from Ana and emptied part of its contents into her palm. It smelled of mints. "Do ye understand what will happen this eve, milady?"

Dara ran a tongue over her suddenly parched lips. Her voice quivering a bit, she admitted, "Um, yes. I'm supposed to make love with Ragnar."

Brenna nodded. "He has a very long and thick rod, the master does. Ye will be glad we've prepared ye when he dips it between yer legs."

Dara's spine went rigid. She cocked a golden eyebrow. "Oh? And you've seen his penis many times to know this?" she sniffed. The thought was not a pleasant one, though she couldn't say why.

Brenna squinted, shaking her head slightly. "His what?"

"His penis," she repeated. At the thrall's confused look, she sighed. "His cock," she blushed.

Brenna waved that away. "Oh, aye, all his thralls have suckled and ridden the master to pleasure. Though I am thrall to him no more, for he gave me as a gift to his uncle," she added. Brenna shrugged dismissively. "'Tis Master Leif's cock I suckle and ride every night now."

Dara shook her head and sighed. "I see." The way Brenna had said that, as if it was an accepted duty no different than making breakfast or ironing, well and truly rankled. Her jealousy was forgotten as her feminist instincts became utterly offended. "That's just awful that he makes you do that."

Brenna shrugged. "In truth, I love him now. Leastways, he's good to me and does not let his friends put their cocks inside of me as is the fate of so many other thralls captured in battle." She tapped her cheek thoughtfully. "The only other warrior he allowed to touch me was his father whilst he lived, but how can a man say nay to his own sire?" She grinned. "Leastways, all I ever did was suckle his father. The master never allowed his sire to poke me with his cock."

"How thoughtful of him." Dara rolled her eyes, then sighed. The year 820 was deplorable! "You know something Brenna? I—*ohh*."

Whatever she had been about to say was forgotten as Ana drew Dara's breasts up into her palms and began massaging the exotic, minty smelling oil into them. Paying special attention to Dara's nipples, the slave tweaked and pulled at them as they grew elongated and hard. Shocked, and not having the first idea what to make of this, Dara sucked in her breath, trying in vain to stave off the feelings of pleasure Ana's hands were giving her. A moment later when Brenna's oiled up fingers found Dara's clit, she gave up altogether and moaned.

"Open yer legs wider," Brenna whispered. "'Twill feel so good, milady."

Dara did as she'd been bade, spreading her thighs open, moaning as Brenna's fingers expertly massaged her labia and clit. Ana continued to roll Dara's nipples between her fingers, causing the climatic feeling to heighten.

Just when Dara was about to come, Brenna eased up on the pressure she'd been applying to her clit and rimmed the folds of Dara's labia instead. The intensity immediately lessoned, causing Dara not to orgasm.

Panting heavily, she eyed Brenna speculatively.

The thrall grinned. "Not yet," she whispered. "'Tis a beautiful berry indeed, yet does it need further ripening." And with those words, her head disappeared in between Dara's thighs.

The first touch of Brenna's tongue to her swollen clit caused Dara's hips to rear up off of the bed. It felt so wonderful. So wicked and wonderful. Ana's lips and mouth found one of her nipples as Brenna continued to tease the nub of her womanhood with her teeth, lips, and tongue.

"Mmm," Brenna praised, "'tis a tasty berry too, milady." Grinning, she flicked her tongue across the hardened bud.

It occurred to Dara—somewhere in the back of her aroused mind—that she shouldn't desire this. She shouldn't want this. It should feel dirty, awful. Not like the next best thing to ambrosia. "Oh God," she sighed. Arching her hips, she closed her eyes tightly as her climax drew nearer.

But then Brenna stopped, frustrating her orgasm once again.

Dara's eyes flew open. She grunted. "Why do you keep stopping?" Blushing, she realized she'd just all but admitted that she wanted Brenna to continue to give her pleasure.

Brenna stifled a smile as she kissed the inside of Dara's thigh. "'Tis the job of the thralls to prepare ye, milady, not to complete ye. The master will do that."

Dara's eyes widened. She was afraid to hear the answer to her next question, but knew it needed to be asked. "Wh-what do you mean?" she breathed out.

As an answer, Brenna's head disappeared in between Dara's legs once more. She groaned, both from the exquisite feeling, as well as from the knowledge she now harbored.

So *this* was how Ragnar meant to seduce her, to get her to come to him willingly. If things were as she suspected, then what her husband had done was commanded the slaves to work her up into a sexual frenzy with strict instructions to allow her no release.

Oh, he was wretched! she thought, her hips rearing up seemingly of their own volition to give Brenna's mouth better access. By the time this torture was over, she'd probably screw anything that walked upright! He was evil incarnate, the devil's own son. And, she conceded with a frown, he was also incredibly intelligent. "*Oh God.*"

Splaying her thighs as wide as they would go, Dara arched her back and allowed the slaves to fondle her. They continued down the path of Ragnar's choosing, bringing her to the brink, then allowing her no release. Over and over. Again and again. The feel of tongues on her clit, her nipples being sucked on, hands everywhere.

A half-hour ticked by. And then another. Tears of frustration welled up in Dara's eyes. She needed release like she needed to breathe. She needed to come and she needed to do it now. Arching her back, she closed her eyes and moaned as she used one of her hands to shove Brenna's face in closer to her clit.

This was how Ragnar found his bride.

Motioning to Ana to help him remove his tunic and braes, he devoured the sight of his wife's needful body until he was drunk with it. "Fear not, sweeting," he murmured from just beside the bed as Ana dropped to her knees to remove his crossed garter hose. "Your lord husband will take care of your need." He paid no attention to Ana, who was clutching his thick shaft by the base while removing his pants, mindful not to let the material chafe him as it gave way. He stepped out of them, then absently patted her on the head before making his way to the bed.

Dara clutched her eyes shut tightly, refusing to look at her husband. Damn the man for knowing exactly what he was doing! Her resolve firm, she pinched her lips together in a gesture of disapproval as she continued to keep her eyes firmly closed. "I will not," she said acidly, "make love with you."

Ragnar shooed away the slaves with a flick of his wrist, indicating it was time for them to take their leave. Giving them no more thought than he'd given his wife's proclamation, he climbed up on top of the bed and settled himself between her legs.

Dara gulped.

Ragnar grasped his erection by the base and swirled the tip of it across her swollen clit. She whimpered.

"*Spred lårene dine,*" he murmured. "Spread your thighs."

"N-no." Dara bit down hard onto her lip.

Ragnar retaliated with another swirl across her clit. She groaned, but quickly stifled it. He grinned. "*Spred lårene dine,* sweeting. And spread them wide."

The tip of Dara's tongue darted out to moisten her lips. "N-no," she squeaked.

Grabbing a heavy breast in either palm, he proceeded to roll both nipples between his fingers. She moaned, her hips arching upward even as she sought to keep her legs from widening further. "Ragnar, damn it!" Indignant, her eyes flew open. "I said n—"

Dara's eyes widened. In shock, in desire, and in more than a little dismay. Good God in heaven, she thought forlornly, realizing she was a goner, the man was gorgeous. More handsome than she didn't know what! Resisting him had been difficult at best when he'd been sporting that atrocious mountain man beard. Resisting him now would be impossible.

"I said…" She began to pant as her thoughts seem to elude her alongside her willpower. "I said…" She gulped, her panting growing worse. "Shit," she muttered under her breath.

Ragnar raised an eyebrow at the strange word, but chose not to comment. His wife wanted him. This he knew. 'Twas all he cared to know. "*Spred lårene dine,*" he said firmly, definitively. "*Now.*"

Dara's thighs immediately opened, giving her husband the access to her body that he'd commanded. She felt her body stiffen as he lifted her hips and poised the tip of his erection at the entrance to her vagina. She'd never done this before. And he was huge. Her gaze shot up to meet her husband's. "Ragnar," she breathed out, "I..."

"Shh, sweeting, 'twill be naught but a pinch, then 'twill feel like bliss." He penetrated her with his gaze, his jaw rigid, his ice-blue eyes unrelenting. "I will take my prize now," he informed her. "'Tis mine."

Dara's breathing grew shallow. She was experiencing mixed feelings of desire and fright, a powerful combination. When she found the nerve to make eye contact once more, she could see that Ragnar was waiting for her to give him approval. And it wasn't easy on him in the least. His muscles were bunched and corded, his nostrils flaring, a sheen of perspiration covered his face. For some reason or another, knowing that she held a degree of power over the situation did much to calm her nerves. She relaxed her muscles, her breathing growing calmer. "Yes."

"You want me?" he asked in low tones.

Her resolve strengthened. She nodded briskly. "Yes."

Ragnar smiled. The gesture was one of arrogance, dominance, and accomplishment. "'Twill be bliss," he said thickly. Grabbing her hips, he resituated the tip of his erection at the entrance to her vagina, then with one powerful stroke, surged into her, ripping through her hymen in the process. Dara screamed.

"Shh, shh, little one. 'Twill be bliss."

"Bliss?!" she sputtered. "That hurt! It was awful! It—*ohh.*"

Ragnar grinned down at Dara as she welcomed the rubbing of her clit with a look of rapture smothering her face. When he felt her vaginal muscles relax around his shaft, he began to slowly move within her. She moaned, then arched her hips and splayed her legs wider, inviting him to take what he would.

"Mmm, 'tis good, your sheath." His words were thickly whispered, his eyelids heavy, as he rotated his hips and slowly sank in and out of her. "Mmmm…"

"Oh wow," Dara breathed out, her nipples stabbing upwards. "Oh."

Picking up the pace of his thrusts, Ragnar grabbed her hips and stroked in and out of her in long, deep movements. His teeth gritted as he rode her, his cock sinking in and out of her tight pussy in fast thrusts. The feel of her tight hole suctioning him back inside made his jaw clench, made him want her impossibly more.

"*Oh God, Ragnar.*"

"*Ja, småen elsk med meg.*" He thrust harder, his orgasm drawing nearer. "Aye, little one, make love to me," he hoarsely ground out.

Dara reached up toward his face and pulled it down to her own. Opening her mouth, she invited him inside, accepting the thrusts of his tongue even as her body accepted the thrusts of his cock. Ragnar picked up the pace of their lovemaking, giving her everything. Their slickened skins made slapping sounds as their bodies grinded into one another's.

"*Ja,* sweeting." Pulling his mouth from Dara's, Ragnar breathed heavily as he reached once more for her clit and began circling it with his thumb. He continued thrusting, possessively pounding into the depths of her body. Her moans of pleasure made his climax draw closer. "Give me everything."

"*Oh God.*" Dara threw her head back and groaned as her orgasm ripped violently through her body. Moaning, she gave herself up to the pleasure. It seemed to go on forever, the intensity of her climax all-consuming and powerful. She reached for her husband, drawing his body down to cover her own even as she screamed from the pleasure of it.

Ragnar's thrusts became lightning quick, deep and primal. Burying his face in his wife's neck, he gritted his teeth and fucked her hard. "*Dara,*" he hoarsely shouted as his own climax exploded. His heavily muscled body shuddered as he spurted himself deep within her womb.

He had come so hard he felt close to dizzy. Panting, he held her tightly in his arms while his body came down from the high. "Mmm, wife. *Jeg elsker deg.*"

Dara turned her face to meet his gaze. Not understanding what her husband had just said, she shook her head slightly to indicate as much.

Ragnar's face colored. He looked away and cleared his throat. Turning back to his wife, he smiled. "We will talk of that later," he mumbled.

Dara nodded. She really wanted to know what he had said, but decided to be patient and ask him later. Besides, her husband had been right. It *had* been bliss. Once she had gotten passed the feeling of being split in halves anyway. It had been bliss and she wanted more.

Grinning, she entwined her arms around his neck. "I don't know about the pinch part, but you were right about the bliss." She arched her hips and rotated them, pleased to find that he was already growing hard for her again.

Ragnar kissed the tip of her nose, then grinned back. "'Twas a worthy prize, little one." Thrusting deeply inside of her, he groaned. "And 'twill like as naught be the death of me."

Dara giggled. "But what a good way to die. Beats the heck out of dying in battle."

"Aye." Ragnar laughed, a rich booming sound. "Valhöll can wait."

Chapter 11

One month later

Satiated, Dara smiled sleepily as her husband's face emerged from between her legs. He'd spent the better part of an hour down there, licking and sucking on her until she'd come so many times she could scarcely hold a thought in her head. Now she needed to feel him buried deep within her.

Luckily, Ragnar agreed.

Dara moaned as he slid inside of her, then grinned up at the face she'd grown to adore over the past month. Pulling his body down to cover hers, she kissed him sweetly on the mouth. "You know," she whispered, too exhausted to do much else, "we've spent practically every hour of every day in this bed since our wedding night."

An arrogant eyebrow arched. "You are complaining of this, sweeting?"

She half laughed and half groaned. "No."

He snorted. "I thought not." When his wife rolled her eyes, he countered with a chuckle. "'Tis a Viking you have as husband. Our needs are great."

"Oh? How great?"

"Very great." He craned his neck to gently sip from her lips. His expression turning serious, he raised his face to meet her gaze. *"Spred lårene dine,"* he murmured. "I want you to take all of me inside you."

Dara readily complied, spreading her legs wider, then wrapping them around his buttocks. He rotated his hips, grinding his jutting cock deeper inside of her. She moaned. "Oh God," she whispered, her breath hitching, "you always make me feel so good."

Ragnar rotated his hips again, hitting a particularly sensitive spot. Her groan of pleasure made his nostrils flare. "'Tis naught," he rasped out, "compared to what you do to me."

Situating his body so he could grab a breast in either palm, he plucked at her erect nipples while he sank into her slickened flesh. "Ah, little one, *Jeg elsker deg.*" Picking up the pace of his thrusts, he bore into her mercilessly, branding her with every stroke. The muscles in his arms and neck bunched and corded as he groaned. "*Jeg elsker deg.*"

Moments later, Dara was orgasming yet again. She dug her nails into the flesh of his buttocks, branding him in her own way. And then he was climaxing with her, hugging her body tightly to his as he emptied himself in her womb.

A few minutes later, when the couple was lying together, holding one another, Dara ran her hand over Ragnar's jaw. "What does it mean?" she murmured.

He didn't pretend not to understand her. He knew precisely what she'd meant. "*Jeg elsker deg.*" He cleared his throat. "I love you."

* * * * *

Dara stood outside the longhouse staring at seemingly nothing. She absently watched the goings on of the village, concentrating more on her own thoughts than on her surroundings. Not that she particularly cared for the events unfolding around her anyway. It wasn't a sight she wished to dwell upon, but a fact of life in 820 nevertheless.

There was a celebration today, twenty warriors having just returned from battling in Saxony. The Norseman brought with them hordes of gold and jewels that had been confiscated from "one God" churches, as well as thirty new slaves to add to the already impressive number cloistered within Valkraad lands. Dara could live with the thieving of material possessions...material possessions didn't have feelings, nor did they have families worrying over what had become of them. It was the slavery that bothered her more than words could express.

A chill raced up and down the length of her spine as she watched a slight girl, a maiden that couldn't have been more than thirteen, weep into her hands as Ragnar's uncle attempted to remove her dress. Dara closed her eyes, not wanting to watch, feeling powerless to stop it as a child was mauled before her eyes.

"What troubles you, daughter?"

Dara's head shot up. Startled, her eyes momentarily widened. She hadn't realized that Joran was just behind her. Grimacing, she threw her hand toward the offensive scene. "That," she said wearily, looking away. "That."

"Ah." Sighing, Joran placed a gentle hand on Dara's shoulder. "He will not rape her if that is your fear. Leastways my youngest brother Leif has never been one in need of taking what women so willingly give to him."

"Then why is he removing her clothing?"

"Lice. The Saxon prisoners tend to come to us filled with the vile things." She smiled. "If you would but look, you would know that my words are true. Leif will bring the child no harm. On this you have my vow."

Reluctantly, Dara raised her gaze to where her uncle-in-law was struggling with the child. And indeed, now that her clothing had been removed, he was handing her over to an older Saxon thrall, instructing the slave to have the child cleaned up and attired. Absently throwing the frayed sack-like garment the girl had been wearing onto a lit pyre, he turned to the next prisoner and repeated the process.

Dara expelled a breath of relief. She could never condone keeping other people as property, yet knowing that the girl wasn't about to be raped did much to alleviate her anxiety. Of course, there was no guarantee that whatever man she became a slave to wouldn't take her virginity at whim once he owned her. And that was one of the reasons she was standing outside today, looking but not seeing, hearing but not listening, a prisoner of her thoughts. As much as she'd come to care for Ragnar, this period in time was brutal, harsh, and far from ideal. In love with her husband or not, she wanted to go home.

In love? Was she truly in love? Dara sighed, her eyes absently flicking over the revelry taking place but a short distance away. She knew she was in love. There was no point in denying it.

"Dara, are you listening to me?"

"Hm?" Shrugging off her dismal thoughts, she turned to face her mother-in-law. "I'm sorry Joran," she apologized, "I guess I have a lot on my mind."

Her smile was understanding. "Mayhap so."

Silence ensued for long minutes, neither of the women speaking. Both of them turned to watch the unfolding festivities, but made no effort to join in with them. There was music, laughter, dancing, and food galore.

Young maidens flirted coquettishly with young warriors they hoped to entice into marriage. Young warriors showed off their prowess, impressing the girls with their manly ability to excel at sword-letting, as well as demonstrating their ingenuity while playing the favored board game of *Hnefatafl*. Slaves scurried about serving meade, trenchers of mutton, and honeyed sweets. But all Dara saw was the little girl, now cleaned and clothed, and still looking utterly frightened and helpless. Her heart wrenched painfully just looking at her.

"Did you know," Joran murmured from where she stood adjacent to Dara, "that before I was wed to my husband, I had been naught but a thrall to him?"

"No I didn't." She cocked her head to study her mother-in-law. Her forehead crinkled. "I thought it was against the law here for a man to marry a slave?"

Joran shrugged, her gaze never wavering from the sight of the little girl. "So it is." She turned her head at last to study her daughter-in-law. "Think you the law matters to a warrior besotted?"

Dara had the feeling that they were talking about more than Joran and Erik, more even than what might become of the little girl. She sighed and looked away. "What is it that you are trying to tell me?"

"I love my son," she said simply, quietly. "And my son loves you. There is little a man in love won't do for the object of his affection and desire. Leastways, if you want the child given to you as a gift, simply ask Ragnar for her. But don't," she said pleadingly, "leave him."

Dara closed her eyes briefly, opening them as she took a deep breath. She spoke not a word for a suspended pause, her gaze flicking back and forth between the child standing with a group of thralls at one end of the celebration and her husband sitting at a wooden bench laughing and jesting with his father and friends amidst the revelry. "I love him, Joran," she murmured, breaking the silence, "but I'm frightened."

A soothing hand found Dara's shoulder and remained there. "From what time do you herald, daughter?"

Surprised, Dara whirled around to face her mother-in-law. Joran chuckled. "I am like as not many things, yet never the fool." She searched her gaze. "You haven't the speech of a Saxon, yet 'tis the only tongue you speak. Your thoughts are odd, your grievances misplaced—leastways for a woman born to this time." She cocked her head to regard her. "From what time, daughter?"

Dara cleared her throat. She studied the regal image her beautiful golden-haired mother-in-law made as she considered how it was she could have known. Lots of people had to have noticed how different she was from the other women of the village, yet Joran was the only one to have picked up on the why of it. "2003." She smiled, showing off her pearly teeth. "But really Joran, the way I speak and behave aside, how could you have known?"

She chuckled. "Because I prayed every night to Freya that she might bring you here. I love my son. I want his happiness. I cared not where Freya found it for him so long as she did indeed find it."

"Freya?"

Joran nodded. "Aye. The goddess of sex and fertility." She shrugged. "Leastways, 'tis well known throughout the Norse lands that Freya is the possessor of a magical feather coat."

Dara smiled. Rather than acting as though Joran's religious beliefs were unfounded or ridiculous, she took a genuine interest in them. Besides, after dreaming of Loki, being branded by fire with the image of a dragon, and catapulting over one thousand years into the past, she was hardly in a position to say it wasn't possible. Eyeing Joran quizzically, her nose crinkled in thought. "What can the feather coat do that makes it so special?"

"'Tis what enables Freya to travel between worlds," she stated matter-of-factly. "'Tis what enabled her to find you."

Dara chuckled. "And do you think that's what happened? She brought me through the River Thund with her feather coat?"

"Mayhap."

"Hmm."

"Leastways, Freya appeared to me in a dream." Joran tapped her cheek, her eyes squinting reminiscently. "She assured me that my diligent devotion wouldst be rewarded and that my son wouldst receive a wife he treasured dearly." She shrugged bemusedly. "She said something about tricking Frigg and Loki into doing her bidding."

Dara's face drained of color. "L-Loki?"

"Aye." Joran waved dismissively. "Some call him the god of fire, some the god of mischief-making, and some call him both."

Dara snorted. "That's understandable," she muttered under her breath.

"No matter." Joran smiled over to Dara, her blue eyes searching. "My point in telling you all of this is simple. I see in your eyes the desire to flee, to run from all in this world you do not approve of." She shook her head. "Ask Ragnar for your heart's desire. Ask him for the moon and the stars if you will, but give life here a chance. Do not seek out Freya's feathered coat just yet."

Dara closed her eyes and sighed. When she opened them, she gave Joran the respect of her honesty. "I cannot make any promises to stay here if given the chance to return home," she said quietly, "but I can promise to give it a lot of thought."

Joran nodded, expecting as much. "'Tis all I ask."

* * * * *

'Twas a long day indeed, Ragnar thought to himself as he shrugged out of his tunic and braes. Naked, he padded over to his and Dara's bed and plopped himself tiredly onto it. Fully erect, he placed his hands behind his head, closed his eyes, and awaited the ministrations of his wife. He fell asleep that way, waiting for her to come to him, but she never did.

An hour later, Ragnar awoke to the feel of a warm hand wrapped around his jutting erection. Smiling, he kept his eyes closed and enjoyed the experience. He sucked in his breath as the hand began to masturbate him up and down. "Mmm. 'Tis good. I missed you, sweeting."

"I missed ye too."

Ragnar's breathing stilled. His eyes flew open. That voice didn't belong to his wife. It belonged to Karil. Regarding the naked thrall in his bed, he attempted to sit up, only then realizing that she still had his staff in her palm. Reaching toward her, he gently removed her hand. "What do you here?" he asked. "I am wed now. This you know."

Karil smiled impishly as she shrugged her shoulders. "It has been two full fortnights since ye've wed, master. Ye waited not this long to return to me the other two times ye took a wife." She cocked her head. "Why wait now?" she murmured.

Ragnar sighed. Running a hand through his long sunny blonde hair, he shook his head. Thinking better of it, he threw an animal pelt over his groin as covering. "'Tis different this time, Karil. The other unions were arranged." He smiled. "Mayhap this one was to an extent as well, yet am I content with my wife." He met her gaze directly, definitively. "'Twill be no more rutting with you. Not now or ever. On this, you must understand."

Karil's eyes narrowed, but she looked away from him, conceding—for now. "Ye will change your mind," she haughtily returned. Standing up, she made for the door to the bedchamber without looking back. "Ye will change your mind."

Ragnar shook his head as he watched the lusty Karil exit his rooms. Beautiful she might be, but Dara she was not. And Ragnar knew he wanted none but his wife.

* * * * *

Dara exited the longhouse quietly, closing the door behind her. Shutting her eyes, she rested the back of her head against the pine door and inhaled deeply, attempting to steady her breathing.

Ragnar had done the right thing, she reminded herself. He hadn't touched Karil. Her husband had no idea that she'd came upon them, that she'd seen everything, witnessed the entire attempted seduction, yet still he had done the right thing.

This time.

But what if Karil was correct in her self-important assumption? What if Ragnar eventually did tire of Dara and turned to Karil for his pleasure in the process? Could Dara stand that?

No, she told herself, as she sucked in a breath of air, she couldn't.

Anything could come to pass if she continued to remain in 820. What, for instance, would happen if she was to become pregnant and *then* Ragnar turned to his oh-so-willing thrall? Her nostrils flared as she considered the answer to that all important question. She would be stuck in the year 820 with a philandering husband, reluctant to leave him because he was the father of her child is what would happen.

Dara shook her head firmly. No! She could not allow that to happen. And what's more, she would not allow that to happen.

As much as it grieved her to do so, she knew there was but one course to follow if she wished for her sanity to remain intact. She had to leave her husband. Now. Tonight. This moment. Before they fell any further in love with each other than they already were.

Dara's teeth sank into her bottom lip as she considered the layout of the housing quarters. The most direct path to the forest lay opposite her parents-in-law's longhouse, Erik and Joran's dwelling being connected to Ragnar's via a short corridor.

She would have to chance it. She would have to find an escape route from Erik and Joran's.

She would take nothing with her besides the betrothal ring on her hand — the one item she refused to give up. After all, Dara thought, her heart breaking, she would want to have something to remember her husband by when she was back in the future, alone and missing him.

She shook her head, castigating herself. She would not, Dara told herself firmly, dwell on how miserable she already felt. If she did so, she'd never go.

Swiping away a renegade tear, Dara lifted her chin up a notch and took a steadying breath. She would do this. She could do no other. It was time to find the magical River Thund and go home.

Chapter 12

Dara quietly crept through the corridor that led from Ragnar's longhouse and adjoined his parents'. If she was going to escape, the time was upon her. It was now or never.

As she rounded the corner, Dara heard voices looming close. Frightened of being found out, she scurried into the nearest chamber and closed the door quietly behind her.

The voices drew nearer.

She glanced desperately around the room, looking for a place to hide when it became obvious that the voices planned to enter the very chamber she was currently inhabiting. Terrified, she breathed a sigh of relief when she espied bed curtains she could easily hide behind. She ran into them, gaining her hidden position the instant the door came crashing open.

Leif Boerge made his way into the bedchamber, two giggling female thralls in tow, including the auspicious Karil. Leif had a heavily muscled arm planted around both of them, squeezing their breasts and grinning as they giggled.

Dara sucked in her breath. As the handsome man drew nearer, a man she guessed to be no more than forty-years-old, she prayed to the heavens that he wouldn't find her out. But she needn't have worried. He was too busy concentrating on the now naked slaves who were disrobing his well-muscled form.

Envious feelings ensued as Dara got a good look from behind the bed curtains at Karil, Ragnar's former blonde bedmate. She was, in a word, exquisite. Her breasts were high, yet so enticingly large—Karil probably would have taken a double D cup if bras existed in this time. Her buttocks were perfectly rounded, her tummy flat, her face every man's dream come true.

And she wasn't shy about her body at all. Just the opposite, she reveled in it. She giggled as Leif instructed her to lie upon the edge of the bed and splay her legs wide for his viewing pleasure.

Karil did as she'd been bade, opening her legs in a wide vee, then parting the lips of her vagina open with her fingers so he could get a better look. But then, how could he not? His face was scarce inches from her vagina.

Karil's swollen clit stood out as her vaginal lips were folded away, causing Leif to smile. He flicked the taut bud with his tongue, then instructed the other naked thrall to drop to her knees and suckle his cock while he probed at Karil's pliant body. The other slave, the beautiful red-headed thrall that had oiled down Dara's body in preparation for Ragnar on their wedding night, dropped to her knees before him and took him into her mouth. Apparently neither slave understood Norwegian, for Leif continued to give his sexual orders in Saxon.

"Mmm 'tis good Brenna. Take the whole of him into your mouth." Leif sucked in his breath as his impressively endowed cock elongated and thickened. "Ahh yes, just like that," he rasped out. "You've a sore talented mouth, sweet."

"Don't give her all of yer juice," Karil semi-teased, smiling as she continued to lay with her thighs spread open. "I wish to suckle of it too."

"'Tis plenty for both," Leif assured her. He shook a finger at her. "I will not abide your jealousies, Karil, for my nephew warned me of how greedy you were for his cock. Brenna is the longest of my bed thralls and I will continue to give her much of my cock to be assured."

Karil pouted for a brief moment, but apparently thinking better of it, relented with a small moue. Leif grinned down at her as he plucked her nipples between his fingers, inducing the slave to release a shuddered breath. "Fear not, my beauty, for I've been desirous of rutting in you for nigh unto a year."

Craning his neck, Leif flicked his tongue over Karil's aroused pussy. She cried out, begging him with the sound to continue. He lowered his head in response, then suckled vigorously on her swollen clit. She thrashed about on the bed, moaning and groaning until the pleasure stole over her and she burst. Moments later, Leif raised his head and shuddered as he emptied his ejaculation into Brenna's mouth.

Leif took to his feet, motioned for Brenna to stand, and pointed toward the bed. "Join Karil. I shall lie between you whilst the deuce of you work to bring my staff back up. 'Twill not be as easy this time," he said with a wink. Brenna giggled, then took one last suckle from his sated cock before alighting to her feet to comply.

Dara felt her body responding, both to Leif's words as well as to the scene unfolding before her. She'd never seen anything like this, at least not outside of what one might see on the Playboy channel.

Leif was lying on the massive bed, his eyes closed, his hands behind his head. The look on his face was intense as the two thralls shared of his body, one sucking on his erect penis while the other one licked and sucked at his scrotum. Every now and again Karil and Brenna would trade jobs, but they never removed their mouths from Leif's body. This warrior held all power over their lives and he didn't balk at putting such privilege to use. Not that the slaves seemed to mind.

"Mmm, 'tis a fetching mouth you have, Karil." Leif opened his eyes to rake her body with his gaze. "Now let us see if the rest of your body is as sweet. If you desire me to purchase you from my newly wedded nephew, you best give me good reason to do so."

Dara's eyes widened from where she watched behind the bed curtains. Ragnar was giving up Karil for her? Her jaw tightening, she forcefully told herself that such knowledge not only didn't change her mind, but that she was in the process of running away, albeit very badly.

A moment later, Karil impaled herself onto Leif's jutting erection and moved up and down atop him with practiced ease. He groaned in reaction, apparently pleased by the slave's efforts to satiate him. Brenna popped one of her translucent pink nipples into Leif's mouth as she ran her hands over his sleekly muscled chest and smiled down at him. It was obvious that she loved the man. And just as obvious that she didn't mind the fact that Karil was screwing his brains out. Amazing, Dara thought. She could never accustom herself to sharing Ragnar's body.

Dara stiffened at the mental concession, refusing to dwell on the fact that leaving her husband was already killing her inside...and technically she hadn't even left him yet, she thought morosely.

Time travel. The River Thund.

Dara forcibly removed her attentions from the ménage a trois unfolding before her and concentrated instead on how to ease herself from behind the bed curtains, out the door, and into the woods...and all of it while remaining undetected.

From this angle, the only one who'd be able to see her if she inadvertently made her presence known was Brenna. She decided to chance it, hoping against hope that the beautiful thrall was too busy seeing to her master's pleasure to notice her scurrying out from behind the bed curtains.

Tip-toeing out from her hiding place, Dara crept on light feet from the enclosure. She had almost made it all the way to the door when Brenna happened to glance up and met Dara's rounded eyes. The slave removed her nipple from her master's mouth and sat up slightly on her knees.

Dara gulped nervously. Would the slave make her presence known? Would she alert Leif, bringing down all kinds of trouble on her head in the process?

Much to Dara's amazement and relief, Brenna did neither of those things. Instead, she smiled slowly, conspiratorially, and winked at her, telling her without words to hurry along. Unfortunately, Leif picked that moment to turn his head, no longer having Brenna's nipple in his mouth to snag his attention. But Brenna saved the day once more, popping her other nipple into his mouth to both distract and placate him. Leif closed his eyes and groaned, contented again.

Dara exited the bedchamber to the sounds of Leif's hoarse cry of completion, apparently having emptied himself into Karil's body. He rumbled something or another about wanting both thralls to suckle his cock again, and then Dara heard no more, for she was making her way through another door and closer to freedom.

Her heart rate sped up when at last she located the tiny unguarded alcove that would take her to the woods. The woods would lead her to the River Thund. And the River Thund would take her home.

Chapter 13

Feeling forlorn, Dara sighed as she ambled about the dark forest having no idea where she was, no idea where she was going, and no idea how to go back to Ragnar. And perversely, or perhaps inevitably, she did want to go back to her husband.

She'd spent the last three hours doing a great deal of thinking and had made some decisions. First of all, she had to be in the year 820 for a reason. Fate, Freya, Loki, or whatever power had done this thing to her wouldn't have whisked her back through time *just because*. There was a reason behind it...there had to be. And she wanted to know what it was.

Dara's other conclusion was far less pragmatic and a thousand times less logical, but it existed nevertheless. She could try to sugar coat the truth, she could continue to play the coward and run from it, but facts were still facts. And the fact was that, for better or for worse, she was in love with her husband and she wanted to stay with him.

And was it so bad, being in love with Ragnar? she asked herself in a nostalgic moment. It was true that 820 was not exactly a prime vacation spot let alone a happening place to move to. But then again, she asked herself for the hundredth time, did staying in the past *have* to be such a bad fate either? Dara took a deep breath and expelled it on a groan. Who, in all honesty, could answer that question?

The year 820 was far from ideal. No TV, no books, no Chocolate Mousse Royale from Baskin & Robbins, no emancipation proclamations. But there was one thing that 820 possessed that 2003 didn't and that claim to fame was her husband. Ragnar was a great warrior, an honorable husband that deep down she knew she could trust with her heart, and better yet, he was also her very best friend. She enjoyed his company, anticipated his lovemaking, and, she thought dreamily, his smiles could light up the darkest of nights.

He would always care for her, he was fiercely attracted to her, and he would always love her. And, Dara admitted with a grin, she felt the exact same way. The man could do things to her emotions and libido that no man besides Ragnar could ever hope to lay claim to.

Dara smiled as she sought out the path that she hoped would lead her back to the longhouse, to her real home. If a month ago someone had told her she'd be running back to her Viking captor instead of away from him, she would have called them nuts. But that's just what she was doing. Now if only she could find her way back...

* * * * *

Leaving his mount a ways back, Ragnar crept quietly through the trees, careful to make not a sound. 'Twas a feat he was ever accomplished at, needing such a skill to be a capable hunter. He narrowed his predatory gaze when he caught his quarry within his sites. He was angry — angry that the game he was hunting today was none other than his very own bedamned wife.

Ragnar took a steadying breath, knowing 'twas necessary to calm himself before he forced Dara back to their longhouse. Leastways, his temper wasn't always pleasant on a good day. This was not a good day.

For two hours he had hunted for his wife, knowing she had fled from him and realizing she had a good hour's head start. It hadn't been overly difficult to track her down, knowing as he did that she would make haste for the River Thund.

What had been difficult was the chastisement he had thrashed himself with for having been the fool to think Dara held a care for him. She had feigned it well — pretending concern over the scratch Aran's sword had dealt him, clinging to him in her passion as they had made love, snuggling into his side and smiling up at him with the moon in her eyes — oh aye, she had feigned it well.

But, of course, the very moment Ragnar turned his back, his bride fled from their home and took to trekking the woods in the hopes of leaving him behind. 'Twas not the actions of a woman who loved her husband, but the actions of a woman who loved none but herself.

Did she not understand by now that the gods had decreed their union? Did she not realize that she could never go back to her future, that she was bound to him for all times?

And was that so bad a fate? Ragnar asked himself, nostrils flaring. He was, after all, heir to one of the most important jarldoms in Norway. And, he admitted in grim resignation, he was also besotted with his liar of a wife.

A tick in his cheek began to pulse as Ragnar watched Dara duck under branch after branch to make her way into the next clearing. The idiot wench was obviously unawares that she was almost upon a warring jarl's lands. He best take her now before the situation turned bloody.

Moving up behind her so quietly that not even a fallen leaf rustled in his wake, Ragnar clamped his hand over his wife's mouth to stave off her screams, swept her flailing body up into his arms, and carried her back to his steed. He sprawled her unceremoniously across the horse, that her legs hung from one side of the mount and her arms dangled about the other.

"Ragnar!" Dara cried, trying unsuccessfully to maneuver herself so she could better see his face. "I'm so glad you found me! I was lost—"

"Silence!" His hand shaking with anger, Ragnar hiked up the back of his wife's finely woven dress and swatted her arse soundly. He ignored her yelp of protest, jumped up on the mount, and commanded it to gallop away. "I will hear no more lies from your tongue this day," he snarled. His teeth gritting, he instructed her further. "Indeed, I desire not to hear your voice at all, leastways 'til I say 'tis permissible for you to speak once more."

Dara harrumphed. "Now wait a—*ouch!*" She flinched as the palm of her husband's hand met her bare bottom again. The sting was sharp enough to render her speechless for a moment or two, but only a moment or two. "Hey! Who do you think you — *ouch!* Damn it! That really hurts Ragn — *ouch!*"

Ragnar grunted. "Are you simple of the head or do you begin to see the way of it, wife? Each time you open up that liar's mouth, your arse gets spanked for disobeying your lord and master."

"Lord and master? I — *ouch!* Damn it! Stop — *ouch!* — spanking me — *ouch!* I'm not a child — *ouch!*"

Ragnar rubbed a roughened palm across her raised arse. He couldn't stop his betrayer of a cock from growing erect at the sight, but he refused to dwell on as much just now. "Hmm. 'Tis growing red down here, sweeting. Best bite your lying tongue before it prattles off more words that will serve to get you naught but a spanking from your lord husband. If you are a good wench, mayhap I will allow you to peak instead of feel the brunt of my hand."

Dara ignored that. "Why do you keep calling me a liar? I have never — *ouch!*"

"Aye, you are a liar," he gritted out as he gave her bottom another whack for good measure. "You pretended to have a care for my person even whilst you plotted ways to escape me." His nostrils flaring in remembered hurt and anger, he swatted her backside again.

"Ouch! Damn it! I didn't even speak that time, Ragnar! And I *did* care. I *do* care. I — *ouch!* You can smack me as many times as you please, but on this I am telling you the truth! I ran from you because I'm afraid, Ragnar, because I'm terrified of how much I love you and of what's happening to me. Can you understand that?"

He said nothing, but neither did he swat at her backside, so Dara continued on with her explanation, simultaneously praying that he would forgive her. "Can you even begin to imagine what it would feel like to fall asleep in one time and wake up twelve hundred years in the past?" she asked semi-hysterically. "Can you? Because if you can then you can understand why I am so incredibly scared. I didn't run from *you*,

Ragnar! I was afraid and I was merely running from everything!"

She closed her eyes and sighed. "Okay, maybe on some level I did run from you, because loving you means that I have to give up all hope of returning home and I just don't know that I'm ready to give up all hope yet."

Dara waited for him to respond, but he ruthlessly maintained his silence. She wished she could see his face, perhaps then she'd have some clue as to how he was feeling. Giving up, she sighed and closed her eyes. She was surprised when, a moment later, she was hoisted up into Ragnar's embrace and placed before him on the galloping mount, her back to his chest. He spoke not a word, but lifted the skirt of her dress up and began playing with her pussy, swirling massaging her there.

She blinked, not having expected him to switch gears so abruptly. Perhaps he was still angry, but she also recognized this was his way of trying to be close to her again.

Dara moaned as she arched her back and spread her legs wider atop the mount. He briskly rubbed her clit, the strokes unrelenting, over and over and over again. *"Oh God. Ragnar. Yes."* Crying out, she rocked back and forth, stimulating herself further, until she spiraled over the edge and into orgasmic oblivion. She groaned deeply, sagging against him a few moments later, limp in his arms.

The next thing Dara knew she was being forced onto her belly and impaled from behind with her husband's jutting cock. She sucked in her breath and expelled it on a low moan.

"'Tis mine," Ragnar said thickly, his own need sounding in the gruffness of his voice. "This sheath, this wench...'tis mine."

Dara was about to make a reply, but her husband picked that moment to order his steed to slow its pace from gallop to canter, the end result causing his cock to surge in and out of her in quick, fast, deep thrusts. *"Ohhhhhh God."*

Ragnar's fingers dug into the flesh of her hips as he groaned. "Take more," he ordered roughly. "Take all of me."

Dara gave herself up to the moment, just as she always did while in her husband's arms. Sitting up so that she sat with her back to his chest, she relaxed her legs, allowing them to go limp, providing deeper and better friction as the canter continued. Closing her eyes, she threw her head back against Ragnar's chest and moaned.

"Such a lusty piece," he murmured into the whorl of her ear. Lifting his hands further up her dress, he cupped a heavy breast in either palm and plucked at her nipples with his thumbs and forefingers. Her heightened moans caused his jaws to clench as he drew nearer to his own release. "Come for your lord and master," he ordered in low tones.

As if on cue, Dara cried out as her stomach muscles clenched and her insides erupted into climax. *"Oh yes. Oh God, Ragnar. Oh yes."*

Dara's vaginal tremors set off Ragnar's own release. With a hoarse shout, he possessively palmed her breasts and spurted his seed deep inside of her.

A nervous smile on her lips, Dara tried to turn around far enough to kiss Ragnar on the cheek, wanting to know all was well between them again. Her smile faltered when her husband refused the token of affection. Hurt and bewildered, she cocked her head as she glanced up at his face. The sight that met her eyes gave her the chills.

Ragnar's face could only be described as harsh, his features unrelenting. It was as if a mask of stone had been chiseled over her husband's face, letting her know that all was not yet forgiven.

Dara turned quickly toward the front. She couldn't bear to witness the wall that her thoughtless running away had erected between them. Ragnar's hands continued to roam the curves of her body, his fingers occasionally tweaked at a nipple, but his face showed no such desire for closeness with her.

Her heart sinking, she bit her lip as the canter erupted into a gallop. She had brought this on herself, she knew. All of this was her own doing.

Chapter 14

The minute they were within the confines of their private bedchamber, Dara braved a glance upward at her husband and offered him a shaky smile. Moonlight poured into the chamber, casting his features in grim light. "Can you give me another chance, Ragnar?" she asked quietly. "I'm sorry I ran from you. I never meant to hurt you."

The stony silence that greeted her question caused Dara to flinch. She splayed her hands at either side in a gesture of helplessness as she watched her husband take a dagger to one of his tunics and cut it into strips. She was too distracted with her own thoughts to give much consideration to his peculiar actions. "What can I do to make things better?" She sighed deeply. "I'm trying, Ragnar. I'm trying but you're not."

Ragnar turned to look at her then. He cocked a brow, but spoke not a word. He came toward her slowly, stealthily, reminding Dara of a predator honing in for a kill. Her eyes went wide and she gulped uncertainly. "Ragnar?" she said nervously. "Why won't you talk to m-me? Why are you l-looking at me like that? I'm—*oh!*" She gasped, watching in horror and confusion as her dress was cut from neck to waist with one long slash of her husband's dagger, exposing her breasts to his view. "What are you doing?" she asked, her voice hitching. "Wh—"

Whatever Dara had been about to say was cut off as a strip of cloth was fastened over her mouth, wound around the back of her head, and tied into a knot. Her tawny eyes widening, she shot a glance toward Ragnar's hands and surmised on the spot that the piece of cloth concealing her mouth wasn't the only strip of fabric her husband was carrying.

Ragnar's unrelenting blue gaze bore into hers. His face was expressionless, his tone of voice low and methodic. But his eyes were on fire, like heated ice. "I am your lord and master. Now. Yestereve. Always." His eyes raked over her exposed breasts possessively, eventually settling once more on her face. "'Twill be a lesson not soon forgotten after this night."

Reaching toward her, he gripped the tattered ends of her dress and pulled them apart with one rip. The frayed remains of a once finely made Viking dress were thrown to the ground, exposing her total body to his view. The gold circlet about her head was next discarded, her long tawny hair spilling down around her body as a result. Running the fingers of one callused hand through the golden pelt between her thighs, his jaw tightened. "'Tis mine by decree of the gods. 'Tis all mine."

Dara closed her eyes briefly, steadying herself as desire coursed through her entire being. His words were undeniably provocative, his visible desire for her like an aphrodisiac.

When she once more opened her eyes, it was to watch as Ragnar plucked her up off of the ground. He then carried her across the bedchamber, deposited her into a thatch of animal hides scattered about their bed, and methodically went about the task of tying up all of her limbs to various places on the bed. By the time he was finished, her arms were secured high above her head, thrusting her breasts up and out. Her legs were pinioned spread-eagle, causing her swollen labia and clit to come prominently into view.

Ragnar ran his fingers over her exposed pussy, first rimming the folds of her labia then flicking back and forth at the taut little bud nested in its center. Dara closed her eyes and groaned, unable to speak of her desire because of the cloth tied over her mouth. Ragnar then placed two fingers at the entrance of her vagina and thrust them inside of her. When he pulled them out a few seconds later, they were drenched.

"Who has fucked this lusty little body but me?" he asked arrogantly. The blue ice of his eyes broached no argument, the grim slash of his mouth took no prisoners. He wasn't in the mood for making love gently and sweetly. He wanted to claim and conquer, brand and possess.

Dara swallowed nervously, realizing as she did so that her husband would accept nothing less than her total surrender. He meant to dominate her will and he was demonstrating as much by dominating her body. He didn't want her to leave him. He would never let her leave him. She could see it in the set of his jaw, read it in the icy fire of his eyes. She was his possession. Now. Forever. There was no going back.

Dara knew that Ragnar didn't expect her to answer his question, for her mouth was bound and she couldn't had she tried to. But she also realized he understood that she had taken his point. He grunted with the learned arrogance of a warrior long accustomed to having his way, then stood up to divest himself of his clothing.

Ragnar's eyes scanned over Dara's vulnerable form, lingering at the better parts. He walked toward her lying position in a few long strides, took to the bed, and sat up on his knees between her splayed legs.

Dara's eyes involuntarily widened. He didn't have the appearance of the man she'd married, the one who'd loved her so gently on their wedding night. He was all warrior now, all predator. His heavily muscled body was tensed, the battle scars upon it prominently displayed. One side of his hair had been braided back at the temples—oddly she'd just now noticed that—letting her know that he had taken his job seriously when he'd set out to hunt her down this afternoon. She swallowed nervously.

Without saying a word, Ragnar lifted a breast into either hand and kneaded them possessively. Plucking at the nipples, he massaged them from root to tip, back and forth, over and over, until Dara's hips flared up as far off of the bed as they could manage. She moaned behind the cloth that covered her mouth, clearly needing release. He offered her none.

"'Tis my vessal, your body, given to me that I might avail myself of it at mere whim." His gaze flicked up to meet hers. "I've the whim." His hands and fingers still working her nipples into a fever pitch, Ragnar took to his stomach and buried his face between her legs. The first touch of tongue to clit caused Dara to whimper and buck up as far as the bindings would allow. From there it only got worse.

His tongue, lips, and teeth roamed everywhere, toying with her like a cat with an injured mouse. He sucked at her clit, licked and kissed her labia, made her convulse in orgasm more times than she'd thought humanly possible. But it wasn't enough, and her husband knew it. She wanted — no needed — him inside of her. She needed the thrusting, the deep invasion, the silken steel grinding into her.

Arching her hips up off the bed with a show of force that made the bindings give way a bit but not nearly enough, Dara moaned behind the cloth, begging him with both movement and sound to mate with her. She felt like a caged animal, his body there and visibly wanting her, yet she was unable to impale herself upon him and reach the ultimate pleasure. Worse yet, her mouth was bound, so she couldn't even vindicate herself by cursing him aloud.

Ragnar's lesson in obedience went from nearly unbearable to completely intolerable when, a moment later, he raised his head from between her legs and rubbed the head of his thick erection against her slickened clit. Psychologically, the experience felt like she'd been denied candy that had been dangled in front of her. Her eyes narrowed into gold slits.

Ragnar raised one arrogant eyebrow. "What vexes you, my love? Mayhap I have spoiled you too greatly, so now you think you have the right of it to command my cock at will?" He shook his head slowly. "Nay," he murmured, flicking a nipple back and forth with his index finger. "'Tis I who commands your body and not the reverse. Aye, little one?" He met her gaze dead-on. "Nod your head aye and I will allow you to peak." He said the last as if he knew who would emerge victor in this contest of the wills.

Stubbornly, Dara refused to meet his demands. Glaring at her husband murderously, she muttered something from behind the cloth that sounded rather crude and threatening. Ragnar merely smiled, infuriating her further. Swirling the head of his erection around her clit, he waited for her to whimper before asking her again. "'Tis I who commands your body and not the reverse," he said firmly. "Nod your head in agreement like a good girl and I will allow you to peak."

Dara whimpered. She was beyond the point of caring who won. She remained silent a suspended moment, but in the end, she relented with a nod. Immediately she was rewarded as Ragnar thrust his large cock deep inside of her. She moaned, her eyes rolling to the back of her head as she instantly climaxed.

"Mmm," he purred, his thrusts long and lingering, "'tis my favorite possession, this sheath." Burying his face in her chest, he resurfaced moments later with a nipple securely in his mouth. Tugging at it with his lips and tongue, he sucked at the crest while he continued to bore into her with slow, leisurely strokes. "Mmmm."

The effect was to drive Dara crazy. The lingering lovemaking was forcing her to become incredibly wet and needful, yet without faster thrusts she would never reach a hard climax. Half delirious, she ground her hips upward, her eyes flaring as she moaned like a mortally wounded animal.

He released her nipple, a popping sound echoing throughout the bedchamber as he did so. "How greedy you are for a pummeling." Rotating his hips, Ragnar ground his erection deep inside of her, but didn't quicken his movements.

Dara moaned and groaned, begging without words for completion. She was startled when, a moment later, the cloth was ripped unceremoniously from her mouth and her husband's possessive gaze was boring into hers. "Say it," he gritted out, his emotional needs as great as his physical ones. "Say you will never attempt to leave me again. Vow it this moment."

Dara licked at her lips, which had grown parched from the strip of tunic. Breathing heavily, she studied her husband's features and knew she could not nor would not do or say another thing to hurt him. Her actions earlier in the day had felt like a betrayal to the closeness that had developed between them over the past month of their marriage, obviously hitting him hard.

"I love you, Ragnar," she whispered, desire no longer the only motivator to give him what he needed to hear. "I love you and I will never, ever leave you again...so long as you are always faithful," she added feelingly.

Ragnar smiled so fully that a dimple she'd never noticed before popped out, giving his hardened warrior visage the look of a mischievous boy. "I love you, too. And never will I be with another. On this you have my solemn vow."

And then he was thrusting deeply into her, grabbing her by the flesh of her hips and pounding into her depths. With her arms tied above her head and her legs pinioned spread-eagle, the resulting feeling was that of submissive pleasure. She was completely at his mercy, totally within his power, and what's more, she was reveling in it. He loved her and would never hurt her, of this she was certain. Dara threw her head back and moaned, her breasts jiggling with each rapid thrust.

"I wouldst have come to the future to find you, Dara," he rasped out while thrusting. "I wouldst have brought you back and bound you to me."

Dara gave a half laugh and a half groan. "I wouldn't have complained."

Moments later Dara was climaxing, her vaginal muscles pulsing around his steel hard shaft. "Aye, wife," he said hoarsely. "Give me everything." Ragnar thrust into her once, twice, three times more, then threw his head back as his seed gushed into her womb.

A little while later as the couple lay snuggling together, Dara thought back on that night in 2003 when she'd dreamt of the fire god. "*You will not wed with Paul,*" he had said. "*You will be given to a real man, to a warrior some might say can rival even me.*"

Dara grinned. Loki had gotten that part right. Ragnar Valkraad was a god of fire if ever there was one.

Chapter 15

Nine months later

Aran, Selik, and Sven dusted the snow off their animal pelt coats before accepting the invitation of Ragnar's thrall turned adopted daughter Milla to enter into the longhouse. Milla, brought from Saxony as slave at thirteen years, had carried that status for all of a day before Ragnar and Dara had freed and adopted her. The men had never heard tell of a wife asking for a slave to be freed as her bride gift—the gift rendered to a wife in exchange for her maidenhead—yet this was precisely what the bride of the future jarl had requested and received.

Sven Haardrad slapped a hammy hand over his heart. "I daresay you get prettier each time I see you, Milla. You are fourteen now, aye? Fourteen and marriageable, I daresay. I—ouch!" Sven rubbed the spot where he'd just been thumped over the head by Ragnar, then glowered at him. "I did not see you here."

"'Tis obvious, dunce." He wrapped a hand around Milla's shoulder. "And I shan't be wedding my eldest to a warrior three wives deep."

"That's right," Selik said, grinning from ear to ear. "He'll be wanting to wed her with me instead."

"Nay, lack wit," Aran boasted. "'Twill be to my longhouse Milla becomes mistress."

Milla blushed and looked away. Ragnar harrumphed. "'Tis doubtful. Leastways, fourteen or no, my wife will hear no talk of marriage until Milla reaches eighteen summers."

"Oh?" Aran cajoled. "And she rules you so easily?"

Ragnar grinned. "Aye."

The warriors laughed. Sven winked at Ragnar, then motioned for him to get out of his way. "Shoo, boy. I've babes to meet."

Ragnar smiled as the warriors filed past him, all of them making beelines to the great chamber with the warmest hearth. Here Dara sat on a carved chair next to his parents, a newly born babe in Erik's muscled arms and another resting in Joran's smaller ones. Dara looked up as she heard the bevy of men approach. Smiling, she stood up to greet them. "Come on in, Sven. Aran, Selik, there's meade right over there."

"We came not for meade," Aran grinned, "but to see the fruit of Ragnar's fertile loins. Isn't that right, Selik?"

"Aye." Selik lifted an eyebrow as he regarded Milla. "That and other things."

Milla returned his pointedly amorous look with a haughty one. That accomplished, she sauntered toward her grandfather's chair, stopping only briefly to kiss her mother on the cheek en route.

Erik's laughter boomed throughout the chamber as he pulled Milla down onto his lap. "'Tis sorely apparent, boy, you'll have need of better lines do you hope to gain my granddaughter's affection."

Joran winked at Milla as the others in the room broke into laughter. Even Selik laughed as he accepted a tankard of meade from Myra. "Aye, 'tis apparent, my lord."

"Do not be greedy," Sven said to his longtime friend as he swaggered up to Erik's side. "Let me hold a babe. Think you I walked this distance in the snow to look upon bald heads and no more? I've an arm in sore need of a babe."

"And a head in sore need of a thought," Erik teased good-naturedly. "Aye, dunce, hold my grandson a moment, but only a moment, as Joran and I just arrived."

"I'll take my time, I'll have you know," Sven bragged as he hoisted the bundled babe up into his arms. Rubbing the tuft of golden hair atop the infant's head, he chuckled. "'Tis definitely a Valkraad, this one. Balder already possesses your overly large ears, Erik."

"You know what they say about the size of a man's ears..." Erik let the sentence trail off as the other warriors laughed uproariously.

Dara thumped Sven on the arm. "My son does not have big ears!" she laughed. "He's perfect!"

Ragnar came up behind Dara and circled her into his arms. "Perfect, aye, just like his papa." Dara rolled her eyes as she met her husband's gaze, but she didn't disagree. Grinning, Ragnar leaned down to kiss the tip of her nose.

"I've big ears," Selik announced as his eyes settled on a blushing Milla.

Erik chuckled. "As I said, boy, you're sorely in need of better lines." He glanced past Selik and grinned. "Ah, here comes my brother-within-the-law now. Leif the Wench Wooer will mayhap give you some tips."

Leif frowned as the room dissolved into laughter. 'Twas well known throughout the village that his thralls Karil and Brenna were wearing him out on a daily and nightly basis. Those two could not get enough of his manhood. Greedy wenches, the both of them. "Give me a babe," he growled, effectively ignoring his brother-within-the-law's jest.

Joran stood up to greet her youngest brother, pecking him on the cheek as she did so. Lifting the babe she was holding up to him, she boasted over her granddaughter. "She's a beauty, is she not?"

Leif accepted the infant's bundled form from his sister and cradled it in the valley of his arm. He grinned. "Aye. She's the look of our mother." Leif glanced over to where Ragnar and Dara were standing. "What name did you give her, Ragnar?"

Ragnar realized that the question had been directed at him for 'twas custom amongst Norsemen for the father to name his babes. Yet at his wife and mother's prodding, Ragnar had agreed to hear their suggestion and in the end had decided 'twas his favored name as well. "Freya."

Leif nodded. "'Tis a good name. The goddess will be well pleased."

Dara bit her lip. She glanced over at Joran and shared a secret smile with her. "A very good name," Dara murmured.

* * * * *

She had taken the explanation surrounding her arrival into Valkraad lands much better than he had expected. They had even shared a jest about it between them, as Ragnar had recounted for his wife his disgruntlement at being disallowed to take her by force. 'Twas all that had kept her from being mounted at the river, he had teased. Dara had grinned back, but also admitted she was glad she'd been given time to accustom herself to him before they became intimate.

She had been granted a day of reprieve from his lusty ways. Only a day she had laughed, but still a day. (Ragnar claimed 'twas wicked torture being kept from his prize a full rising.)

And so it was that Dara Valkraad now knew the full truth of why she had been brought to 820, and of why she had been given to Ragnar as wife. No more secrets existed between them and no more ever would.

Ragnar groaned as his wife's mouth worked up and down the length of his shaft. Reaching for the nape of her neck, he sucked in his breath as he watched his erection emerge from between her lips, then disappear once more into the depths of her throat. "Mmm, sweeting. Aye. Just like that."

Dara teased him with slow strokes, moving up and down his cock at a leisurely pace. Ragnar placed his hands behind his head and enjoyed every moment of it. Awhile later, Dara picked up the pace of her sucking, taking him into her mouth greedily as she used her hands to massage his scrotum.

Ragnar opened his desire-heavy lids to regard her. "Mmm. Aye. Love me with your mouth," he said thickly.

Dara did just that, her head working up and down rapidly, her fingers massaging his tightly drawn sac just the way he liked. A moment later, her husband's hoarse shout of completion echoed throughout their bedchamber as his body shuddered and his climax spurted into her mouth.

Raising her head, she grinned up at him. "I told you having to wait a few weeks before we make love wouldn't be so bad."

He chuckled, swiping at his perspired brow with the back of his arm. "And your lord husband appreciates the demonstration." Finding a burst of energy, he jumped up and reversed their positions, Dara now on her back, her thighs spread wide. She smiled.

Craning her neck a bit, her expression turned serious. "Are you happy, Ragnar? Do the children and I make you happy?"

Ragnar stilled, surprised as he was by the question. The look on his face broached no argument. "Never in my life had I thought to be so happy. I love you, Dara."

"And I love you, Ragnar."

"Good. Now hush your tongue, wench, and let a man enjoy himself." And with those sage words, his face disappeared between her thighs.

Dara sighed contentedly, stretching out her muscles and throwing her arms over her head. Grinning up to the ceiling, she said a quick thank you to Freya, then got down to the rather important business of enjoying her husband's ministrations.

Oh yeah. Long live the Vikings.

Chapter 16

Valhalla (The Hall of the Slain)
Somewhere in Time

Frigg pinched her lips together in a gesture of disapproval. She threw her arm toward the image unfolding in the Valkraad's bedchamber as she glowered at Freya. "Well at least *you* have gained something from this bedamned experience! A beautiful golden girl-child dedicated in your name!" She harrumphed. "And here I thought 'twas Loki gifted at mischief-making and bedevilry."

Freya raised an eyebrow. "Like you, mayhap?"

Frigg's mouth puckered into a frown. "I've half a mind to rip that bedamned feather coat of yours into shreds," she sniffed. "You tricked Loki into choosing Dara," the queen goddess accused, wagging her finger at Freya. "I had my eye on a hideous mortician sporting an obscenely large mole with hairs protruding from it, but Loki assured me that Dara wouldst be perfect for the role!"

The goddess of sex and fertility smiled slowly. She looked from the image of the two mortals making love then back to Frigg. "I think we both won this go around, old friend."

Frigg harrumphed. "Oh? And how so?"

Freya placed a gentle arm around Frigg's shoulders, then gestured toward the mortals' image. "A beautiful boy-child named out of deference to your beloved son Balder."

Frigg's chin went up a notch. Unwillingly, the heat around her temper gave way a bit. "He is rather winsome," she conceded. "Even looks a bit like Balder," she admitted, the heat lessening more and more.

Freya grinned. "Besides, old friend, 'twas your desire to keep Ragnar the Feared from Valhalla for many moon-risings yet to come." She licked her lips as she studied the mortals' image once more. "Tis safe to say 'tis done. You have bested Odin on this matter. Think no more of it."

Frigg giggled, a sound that made her age seem more like a couple of decades old rather than that of several millenniums. "Aye, I have, have I not?" She glanced toward the image one final time, a wicked grin smothering her lips. "Ragnar the Feared is mayhap Thor's favored, but 'tis obvious he was borne of the wily one."

Freya raised an eyebrow.

Frigg waggled hers. "Dara Valkraad has the right of it. He's a god of fire, that one."

Epilogue

Cuyahoga Falls, Ohio, 2003

"Dara? Dara?" Paul D'Abois frowned as he walked into the empty cottage. He had come here today to call an end to their engagement. He liked Dara well enough, and he supposed she liked him well enough too, but he knew deep down inside that marrying her wasn't the right thing for either of them. She would be much happier with a man closer to her own age. He'd be much happier with *several* women closer to his own age. Fidelity was simply not in his genes. He owed it to her to be honest about that.

"Dara?" Paul absently scratched his neatly clipped beard. She was nowhere to be found. At first he grew a little worried, but something inexplicable inside told him she was happy and would be all right.

He sighed. Something also told him he'd never see her again.

Paul's smile was accepting, peaceful, as he walked towards the television that had been left on, preparing to switch it off before he left. A show about an ancient Viking queen was playing on the History Channel.

...An interesting fact about the Jarl's wife, the show's host pontificated in his sophisticated English monotone, *was the legend surrounding her arrival into Valkraad lands. The widely believed consensus at the time was that she had been sent by the gods themselves and was the key to the survival of not only their people, but later their mystics would believe, to all people. How and why is not known by historians as records dating that far back are scarce.*

What is interesting to note, however, is that she encouraged her husband to build and live below the ground following a Celt raid some ten years after her marriage...a very early example of bunkers and safe houses military historians find intriguing. The elders of the clan believed the Viking queen, Dara, to be a time traveler...

Paul's eyes widened as a painting of the golden-haired, golden-eyed queen flashed on the TV. "Oh my God," he murmured. Chills raced up and down his spine. "Oh my God."

Author's Note:

I used a little artistic liberty — okay a lot of artistic liberty! — when writing parts of this story. First of all, regardless to the fact modern day English is linguistically related to medieval Saxon, the two languages are not nearly close enough to where Dara & Ragnar would have understood each other. Secondly, there is the issue of the wedding night consummation scene. Although it was common for ancient Viking brides to have their bodies oiled down by other women in the village prior to consummating their marriages, it is unlikely that such a task was carried out by slaves, but rather by women within their or their husband's family. It was also unlikely that anything sexual ever occurred between the women, but then again, you never know...

Nevertheless, I hope you enjoyed *God of Fire* as much as I enjoyed writing it. *GOF* was one of the first stories I ever wrote so it will always be special to me even if it lacks the explicitness my later works are known for *smiles*.

I'd like to take a moment to thank Ragnar Grimstad for his Norwegian translations. I'd also like to thank my incredibly loyal and wonderful fans for making me feel special on a daily basis. Your cards, letters, gifts, and the good vibes you send me in general mean more than you'll ever know. As long as you'll keep reading my books, I'll keep writing them!

About the authors:

Julia Templeton has written both contemporary and historical romances for magazines and book publishers and, most recently, erotic romances for Ellora's Cave Publishing. She also pens novels under the pseudonym Anastasia Black with writing partner and fellow Ellora's Cave author Tracy Cooper-Posey. Aside from her passion for writing, Julia also enjoys reading, listening to music, collecting research books, traveling, and spending time with her family.

Critically acclaimed and highly prolific, Jaid Black is the best-selling author of numerous erotic romance tales. Her first title, *The Empress' New Clothes*, was recognized as a readers' favorite in women's erotica by Romantic Times magazine. A full-time writer, Jaid lives in a cozy little village in the northeastern United States with her two children. In her spare time, she enjoys traveling, horseback riding, and furthering her collection of African and Egyptian art.

Julia and Jaid welcomes mail from readers. You can write to them c/o Ellora's Cave Publishing at P.O. Box 787, Hudson, Ohio 44236-0787.

Also by Julia Templeton:

- Dangerous Desires
- Forbidden (as Anastasia Black)

Also by Jaid Black:

- The Possession
- Death Row serial
  - Death Row: The Fugitive
  - Death Row: The Hunter
  - Death Row: The Avenger
  - Death Row: The Mastering (in *Enchained*)
- Trek Mi Q'an series
  - The Empress' New Clothes
  - Seized
  - No Mercy
  - Enslaved
  - No Escape
  - Naughty Nancy (in *Things That Go Bump In The Night*)
  - No Fear
  - Dementia (in *Taken*)
- Warlord (in *The Portal*)
- Tremors (in *Dark Dreams*)

Why an electronic book?

We live in the Information Age—an exciting time in the history of human civilization in which technology rules supreme and continues to progress in leaps and bounds every minute of every hour of every day. For a multitude of reasons, more and more avid literary fans are opting to purchase e-books instead of paperbacks. The question to those not yet initiated to the world of electronic reading is simply: *why?*

1. *Price.* An electronic title at Ellora's Cave Publishing runs anywhere from 40-75% less than the cover price of the <u>exact same title</u> in paperback format. Why? Cold mathematics. It is less expensive to publish an e-book than it is to publish a paperback, so the savings are passed along to the consumer.

2. *Space.* Running out of room to house your paperback books? That is one worry you will never have with electronic novels. For a low one-time cost, you can purchase a handheld computer designed specifically for e-reading purposes. Many e-readers are larger than the average handheld, giving you plenty of screen room. Better yet, hundreds of titles can be stored within your new library—a single microchip. (Please note that Ellora's Cave does not endorse any specific brands. You can check our website at *www.ellorascave.com* for customer recommendations we make available to new consumers.)

3. *Mobility.* Because your new library now consists of only a microchip, your entire cache of books can be taken with you wherever you go.

4. *Personal preferences are accounted for.* Are the words you are currently reading too small? Too large? Too...**ANNOYING**? Paperback books cannot be modified according to personal preferences, but e-books can.
5. *Innovation.* The *way* you read a book is not the only advancement the Information Age has gifted the literary community with. There is also the factor of *what* you can read. Ellora's Cave Publishing will be introducing a new line of interactive titles that are available in e-book format only.
6. *Instant gratification.* Is it the middle of the night and all the bookstores are closed? Are you tired of waiting days—sometimes weeks—for online and offline bookstores to ship the novels you bought? Ellora's Cave Publishing sells instantaneous downloads 24 hours a day, 7 days a week, 365 days a year. Our e-book delivery system is 100% automated, meaning your order is filled as soon as you pay for it.

Those are a few of the top reasons why electronic novels are displacing paperbacks for many an avid reader. As always, Ellora's Cave Publishing welcomes your questions and comments. We invite you to email us at service@ellorascave.com or write to us directly at: P.O. Box 787, Hudson, Ohio 44236-0787.

Printed in the United States
29848LVS00004B/64-459